A KILLING IN REAL ESTATE

— a mystery by —

Michael Castleman

—Also by Michael Castleman—

FICTION:

Death Caps

The Lost Gold of San Francisco

A KILLING IN REAL ESTATE

— a mystery by —

Michael Castleman

MacAdam/Cage
155 Sansome Street, Suite 550
San Francisco, CA 94104
www.MacAdamCage.com

Library of Congress Cataloging-in-Publication Data

Castleman, Michael.
A killing in real estate : a novel / Michael Castleman.
p. cm.
ISBN 978-1-59692-358-4
1. San Francisco (Calif.)—Fiction. I. Title.

PS3603.A884K55 2009
813'.6—dc22

2009027007

Paperback edition: June, 2010
978-1-59692365-2

Manufactured in the United States of America

10 9 8 7 6 5 4 3 2 1

Book and jacket design by Dorothy Carico Smith

To my parents,

Mim and Louis Castleman

—1—

Ed Rosenberg closed the front door and tried to admire his old Victorian's new four-color paint job—though that was impossible. The smell of smoke was too intense. It stung his eyes and constricted his chest. The previous night, only three blocks away, a half-finished condo behemoth had gone up like newsprint dipped in gasoline.

A snake of fear slithered up Ed's back. The fires were now too close for comfort. The loft building wasn't occupied, but his house was. For a moment, he plunged into a vision of hell, flames shooting out his windows, ten-year-old Sonya and infant Jake screaming. He exhaled deeply, forcing the nightmare away.

Until last night, all the buildings torched in the Mission's rash of arson fires had been located a dozen blocks east of Ed's quiet street, sufficiently distant to keep him from feeling personally threatened. Last night's fire changed that. It was practically around the corner, a twenty-four-unit development whose wooden bones went up like kindling. Even now, with every breath, lingering smoke stung Ed's nostrils.

He loved his house. He'd just completed nine long years of paying an army of contractors several body parts to transform a nineteenth-century workingman's cottage into a twenty-first-century family home. He'd lived in the neighborhood for years and thought he'd made his peace with its rough edges. Now he wasn't so sure. He had a family to consider.

Ed had spotted the flames on their way home from the movie, orange tongues licking the night. He and Julie held their breath before realizing the huge blaze was a few blocks from them. Returning from taking the sitter home, Ed felt like a moth drawn to a candle. But he couldn't get close. The area was cordoned off, red and blue lights flashing everywhere. The street was mobbed. The neighborhood had turned out to watch.

Julie shut their fancy new windows, but acrid smoke still seeped in. Neither of them slept well. She woke him at 2:30. "We have to talk."

Ed knew what was coming: another position paper in favor of moving. When it was just the two of them and Sonya, the house felt fine. But when Jake arrived, Julie announced that they needed more space. She had other gripes as well. The Mission was too funky for kids. A transit village might be built at the BART station, putting them in the shadow of monster high-rises. And now arsonists were at their doorstep. The house finally showed well. They should sell it and look for a bigger place in a better neighborhood.

"It's the middle of the night," Ed groaned. "Can't it wait till morning?"

Now it was a new, smoky day. Ed felt wrung out by years of steady work on the house. He wanted to kick back awhile, enjoy what they'd accomplished, and stop bleeding money. But he found it increasingly difficult to argue against Julie's position, especially after the night before.

Ed gave the paint job a last loving glance, then descended the stairs, trying to look on the bright side. The fire was out. The sun was shining.

He cherished their home, but he wasn't about to risk his kids' safety or his wife's sanity for a lousy piece of real estate. Still, moving felt drastic. They'd lived in the Mission a dozen years. Was it always this scary? Or was he just older now, with a mortgage, kids, and a worried wife?

Ed's watch said he had time to walk to Duffy's. He wanted to walk. He needed to experience the neighborhood through the soles of his shoes. He hoped his legs could persuade him that the Mission wasn't as risky as his head now feared. He inhaled deeply, hoping to discern the fragrance of jasmine from the vine encircling his neighbor's garage door, but the only discernible aroma was charred wood.

No doubt Duffy would have a great deal to say about the fire. Ryan Duffy was the *San Francisco Foghorn*'s urban-design critic. He covered real estate development and city planning, including, as Ed recalled, the plan to redevelop the site of last night's blaze, the old Morrissey Mattress factory, a fixture of the Irish Mission for more than a century. Morrissey's had closed in the early eighties. A dozen development plans had fallen through, and the abandoned building had become an eyesore. The city needed housing. Morrissey's was close to BART, meaning easy access to downtown. The developer's design blended well with the neighborhood. Duffy wrote a piece strongly endorsing condo conversion, calling it a slam dunk.

Duffy's article had led to an outpouring of community opinion. While a few letters to the editor agreed with him, most argued that the Mission needed housing that teachers and cops could afford, not high-end condos with granite countertops. After the approval of the Morrissey project, a neighborhood group opposing the development picketed the paper, calling Duffy a whore for greedy developers. Now Morrissey's was a charred ruin.

Real estate was part of the Business section, so Ed and Duffy worked on different floors of the *Foghorn* building. During Ed's early years at the paper, they shared a nodding acquaintance on the elevator and at Christmas parties. Then Duffy joined First Wednesday, the Sports editor's monthly poker game. Ed was a regular and quickly came to appreciate Duffy's wit and the Irishisms that had survived generations in America—lad for guy, malarkey for nonsense, footpath for sidewalk, taytoes for potato chips.

Poker progressed to lunches, Giants games, and speculation about who would be laid off next as the paper tried to survive in the twenty-first century. As Ed and Duffy became friendlier, the two couples—Ed and Julie, and Duffy and his wife, Sheila—shared occasional dinners, movies, and afternoons with the kids at various playgrounds.

Then Duffy and Sheila had their second child, and Ed and Julie fell into the bottomless pit of home renovation. When Duffy's mother was diagnosed with Alzheimer's, he stopped playing poker. Ed heard that Duffy's marriage had hit the skids. He called and e-mailed, but his buddy's replies felt preoccupied and distant. Finally, they had lunch, and a surprisingly upbeat Duffy announced that he was getting divorced, had a new girlfriend, and had bought his parents' place. He had his boys on weekends. When the dust settled, he hoped to play poker again.

Then no contact for months until one morning Duffy e-mailed Ed inviting him to brunch. Even more unexpected was Duffy's new address, a mere eight blocks from Ed. This made them brothers in the small fraternity of *Foghorn* reporters who actually lived in the city—and probably the only two over age thirty who resided in the Mission.

"Hey there, Ed." The voice evoked Arkansas, and came from within the open garage next door. "Smoky enough for y'all?"

It was Keith Andrews, half of his favorite neighbor couple, an affable bear of a man with a barrel chest, bushy hair, and a full beard the color of honey. But this morning Keith looked as blue as his flannel shirt. He uncoiled a hose and watered the jasmine. He and his partner, Calvin Liu, were training it up the trellis that arched over their garage door.

"You and Cal must have been at work," Ed said. Their crepe café in South Beach stayed open late.

"We were. A customer told us. We closed up early and got back here fast as we could."

"Fires have gotten too close for comfort," Ed said.

"Looks like somebody around here don' like gentrification," Keith said, "and that means they don' like *us*." He shook his head. "How many fires now? Feels like a hundred."

"Twelve confirmed arsons in the past four months," Ed said, quoting what he'd just read in the paper.

Keith gazed at his feet. "Calvin thinks maybe we should sell."

Ed sighed. "Julie, too. Only no 'maybe' about it. What do you think?"

"I don' know. You?"

"Same."

"Maybe we could buy two fixers close by somewhere."

Ed smiled. The two couples had bought their homes around the same time and had commiserated through each other's renovations. In the process, they'd become friends.

"You know what I don't get?" Keith observed. "If the fires are being set by poor people who've gotten pushed out by the likes of us, why burn Morrissey's? It's been closed for ages. Nobody got evicted." He shook his head and hissed, "Animals. You see they used pineapple lamps?"

Ed nodded. The *Foghorn* had mentioned that detail. Pineapple lamps were glass jars, shaped like the fruit, filled with flammable syrup and fitted with twine wicks. They were marketed as patio lamps—long-lasting, sweet-scented, and bug-repellent. But when lit and thrown, they became Molotov cocktails. The criminals had used pineapple lamps in all the recent fires.

Keith turned the hose on the hydrangea. "Fucking gangs."

Ed thought Keith's grumble could probably be traced to the *Foghorn*, which had quoted police who blamed the rash of arsons on Latino street gangs displeased about affluent whites moving into their turf.

"I miss the old days," Keith said, "when the gangs just shot each other and left the rest of us alone. These fires are killin' our values."

"Right," Ed said. "So it's not a good time to sell. That's what I keep telling Julie."

"I want to stay," Keith said. "But I don' know." He shook his head. "I just don' know."

"Me either," Ed said. "But this city was built on the ashes of arson fires." Ed wrote the *Foghorn*'s local history column.

Keith shot him a look. "Maybe so, Mr. Historian, but that was then and this is now and I got me a bad case of the shitty jitters."

"Hey, I want them to fry," Ed retorted. Then he realized he'd never devoted a column to San Francisco's arson-filled past. "So, big guy, what got you up so early?" With the restaurant closing late, Keith and Calvin often slept until noon.

"Couldn't sleep. Dreaming about fires. You?"

"Same. And brunch with a friend."

Ed checked his watch again. If he walked now, he'd be late. But he still wanted to walk. He needed to. He called Duffy. Voicemail. He was probably scrambling eggs and mixing Bloody Marys. Ed bid Keith farewell.

San Francisco was Fog City, but the low clouds that blew in from the ocean were channeled by its many hills. In some neighborhoods, especially in summer, you needed headlights by mid-afternoon, while in others the sky remained a Mediterranean blue all day. The Mission was among the sunniest neighborhoods—when it wasn't filled with smoke. That was a major reason Ed and Julie had chosen the district way back when.

Another was BART. Trains from the nearby station whisked them from Twenty-fourth Street to two blocks from the paper in just ten minutes. Julie was the *Foghorn*'s PR director. When they'd moved in, the neighborhood had a dicey reputation that kept housing costs low—of course, in San Francisco, "low" could choke a horse. But they wound up with a sweet deal on rent, which allowed them to save for a down payment on a mortgage. They looked for a year, fretted and stretched, and finally lucked into a dilapidated Italianate Victorian on Fair Oaks, a narrow byway that hugged the hillside leading up to Noe Valley. Julie immediately fell in love with the house—its ramshackle charm and proximity to BART drew her in, but the house's greatest selling point was the fact that Fair Oaks felt removed from the Mission's grittiness. Ed agreed. His interest in the house merged with his passion for history, and it didn't take him long in the City Archive to discover that the house had been constructed in 1889 for $2,800 for a blacksmith named Mulrooney, whose shop was once around the corner.

Initially, Ed and Julie bought into the romance of renovating old homes. But years of dry-rot repair, sheetrock dust, and tussling over cabinet knobs cured them. Now, finally, their painted lady was a reasonable facsimile of what they'd envisioned: three modest bedrooms, one-and-a-half small baths, golden oak floors, a skylight over the breakfast nook, and a little deck leading to a cozy yard. In addition, they had a sanctuary, an airy room behind the garage that accommodated Julie's sewing equipment, fabric, and yoga mat, and Ed's home office, library, files, and rowing machine. A house to love—only now Julie wanted to move. Even with all their renovations, Ed doubted they could sell for enough to afford anything larger in a better neighborhood.

A cool breeze softened the sting of smoke. Ed crossed Valencia Street, gentrification central, where second-hand stores had morphed into restaurants with white tablecloths and stemware. He strolled to Mission Street, the heart of the neighborhood, turned south, and felt the sun on his face. Overhead, palms swayed. He threaded his way through the Sunday throng: Latino families dressed for church, young mothers pushing strollers and pulling shopping carts, a pack of black-haired Latino kids on skateboards, a Mariachi band in jeans and cowboy hats, young whites in tattoos and T-shirts, and people of every age and race sipping coffee, lined up at ATMs, hefting laundry baskets, and considering cantaloupes. Most faces smiled. Ed caught snatches of English, Spanish, Chinese, and languages he didn't recognize. Mission Street smelled like pizza, espresso, croissants, carne asada, and chow mein—with faint hints of smoke and sewage. Looking at the faces, it was impossible to guess the existence of nefarious gangs lurking in the shadows lighting pineapple lamps.

Ed passed a *Foghorn* coin box and sighed. As a longtime newspaperman, he understood that journalism is to truth what law is to justice: an approximation of ideals seldom realized. He usually felt charitable about the daily distortions that passed for news, especially now, with newspapers in trouble and decimating their staffs. Mix the milk of deadlines with the rennet of the bottom line, and the cheese was bound to be peppered with holes. But there were also times when the *Horn* published articles that made Ed want to strangle someone—for example, that very morning's piece on the Morrissey fire.

Parts of it were informative: half-built loft condos, pineapple lamps, damage figures in the millions. But Ed had a hard time believing gangs protesting foie gras had set the blaze. Vandalism as class war? Sure, Mission housing prices had gotten ridiculous and a whiter, more affluent crowd was moving in. But even with all the upscale development, the neighborhood still had affordable apartments, battered pickups, and auto repair shops. Immigrants from south of the border still loitered on corners hoping for day labor. And in many doorways, the vacant eyes of the homeless still peered out from filthy sleeping bags. The Mission had been changing slowly for years. Why fires now?

Ed knew the reporter who'd written the fire story, a silly girl a few years out of J-School who lived in a distant suburb. She knew nothing about the Mission. He also went pretty far back with the editor who'd sent the piece to press, a once-promising talent until he became best friends with Jack Daniel's. Now he was a twig of deadwood who should have been pruned a few buyouts ago. The story was about fires at a housing site, but the reporter interviewed no one involved in housing or construction—just the SFPD Gang Task Force. Naturally, they blamed gangs.

Everyone knew there were rival Mexican and Central American gangs in the Mission. Every immigrant community spawned its own *Godfather*. After a dozen years in the neighborhood, though, Ed rolled his eyes when the reporter quoted a cop as saying the Mission was "ruled by gangs." That was like saying the opera was ruled by the ushers. Ed wished the reporter and her boozy editor were along for this stroll down Mission Street. They'd see a very different neighborhood.

Of course, Ed was all too familiar with the root of the problem—a serious disregard for history. *Horn* reporters had little understanding of San Francisco's transformations and how the city was still evolving, especially kaleidoscopic neighborhoods like the Mission. In his column, "San Francisco Unearthed," Ed did what he could to provide perspective, but daily mayhem had a way of overwhelming his weekly attempts at the long view.

In a previous life, Ed's history Ph.D. had landed him an assistant professorship at Cal State East Bay. But it didn't take long before he and his department chair agreed he was ill suited to academia. He drifted into journalism, wrote for the local alternative weekly, and wound up at the *Foghorn*. He started as a cop chaser, moved to general assignment, and finally a new executive editor bought his pitch to become the paper's resident historian.

The column became a modest hit. Periodically, the *Foghorn*'s book division published collections that sold well enough to finance the renovations that converted a rickety Mission shack into a sweet, if cramped, family home.

One of these days, he'd write a piece on the many forces reshaping the Mission. But bottom line, crime was down, including gang crime, and gentrification was proceeding at a canter, not a gallop—in part because the geniuses at a certain newspaper kept stoking the myth that the neighborhood was a war zone.

Still, if crime was down, who was setting the fires? Maybe Julie was right. Maybe it was time to move. Ed was eager to hear what Duffy thought. If he had bought his parents' place, he must have grown up in the Mission, which meant he'd seen it morph from Irish to Hispanic to young hipsters and arson fires. But Duffy hadn't invited him for omelets and home fries to discuss gentrification. He was interested in his grandfather.

Duffy's e-mail said he'd stumbled on a diary the old man kept during the dock strike of 1934, the biggest, bloodiest labor dispute in San Francisco history. But Grandpa Pat was no writer. Duffy couldn't understand what he was talking about, between his outdated language, striker's jargon, and his cramped, nearly illegible penmanship. He wanted to know if Ed was familiar enough with the strike to read the diary and help him decipher it.

Ed was quite familiar with the strike, a bitter dispute that caused several deaths. It culminated in the largest general strike in U.S. history—and the shipping industry's grudging recognition of the longshoremen's union. As he'd e-mailed in reply, he was happy to come for brunch and examine the diary.

Lengthening his step to avoid a deep pothole, Ed skirted the craftspeople whose wares—jewelry, ceramics, T-shirts, bongs—were arrayed on folding tables around the entrance to BART. One displayed a sign: TRANSIT VILLAGE EVICTING US! HUGE DISCOUNTS!

Ed smiled. The sign was years premature. But if the proposed developments were ever built, the spot where he stood would be the gateway to a huge apartment complex. The brick plaza and its artisans would disappear. And the Mission would become home to several thousand new upscale residents.

Naturally, neighborhood activists were up in arms. The *Defender*, the alternative weekly where Ed started in journalism, railed against "Manhattanization of the Mission." The Sierra Club was opposed on environmental grounds, and the Mission Coalition accused the Planning Department of threatening the neighborhood's Hispanic character.

Ed feared the Mission might be ruined if a forest of towers rose over the BART station. But unlike Julie, he wasn't ringing alarms. Approval was by no means assured. The Planning Commission still had to vote, and after them, the Board of Supervisors. If the plan passed, lawsuits were sure to hamstring the developers for years and force them to downsize their buildings. Ed figured his ten-year-old daughter would be in college before anything higher than four stories loomed over Twenty-fourth Street.

Ed turned onto Twenty-sixth, Duffy's block. It was a mix of weary Victorians, post-earthquake Edwardians, three-flat places from the 1920s, and storefronts that included a Mexican bakery and a boutique for the tattoo-and-piercing set called GarbAge. Duffy lived next to the bakery in a large single-family Edwardian in desperate need of a paint job. A dozen shingles had fallen off the façade and some trim boards were curling. Ed gave the building a long, appraising look. The urban design critic's parents had lived here? Apparently, they hadn't believed in home maintenance.

Ed ascended the creaky stairs and turned the antique key of the old bell built into the door. It echoed but there was no answer. Ed rang again, then knocked. Nothing. The door had a stained-glass window, dark maroon and blue. He peered in but couldn't see much. He pulled out his phone and called. Voicemail again. He tried the door. Locked. He rang again and knocked harder. Silence.

This made no sense. Duffy should be setting the table. Where the hell was he? Why hadn't he called?

Ed descended the stairs and gazed up at the house. It was considerably larger than his place, a lot of house for a divorced dad with kids only on weekends.

Could his friend have stood him up? Ed doubted it. Duffy always e-mailed if he couldn't make poker or lunch. Not to mention that Ed was doing him a favor reading his grandfather's scribblings.

Ed climbed back up and leaned close to the stained glass. Like an old photo in a chemical bath, an image slowly emerged. The foyer led down a hall to the kitchen—where Duffy should be cooking. But Ed discerned no movement. To the right, an arched entry led into the living and dining rooms. Nothing.

Ed was about to dismiss Duffy as a thoughtless jerk, when through the dark glass something on the living room floor caught his eye. A foot, perfectly still, heel on the floor, toes pointed to heaven.

Ed leaned over the porch rail and tried to peer through the living room window. Drapes blocked his view, though they weren't completely closed. Ed leaned way out and peered through the gap.

Duffy lay on his back, naked and spread-eagled, obviously dead. One eye stared up at the ceiling. The other was obscured by dried blood on the side of his head, where it had been bashed in. Nearby, a large statue of Jesus lay in two pieces. Once, it had been white. Now much of it was red. Whoever bludgeoned Duffy broke the statue doing it.

A bright red ball gag protruded from Duffy's mouth. His wrists were bound with thick rope tied to two legs of the sofa. Strewn around the room were paddles, floggers, and a riding crop.

Fighting nausea, Ed reeled himself back to the porch. As a police reporter, he'd seen corpses. But that was years ago. And none of them were friends with booming laughs who said *arra* for *all right*.

Duffy had been bound, gagged, and beaten to death. Ed felt

woozy as he stumbled into a seat on the crooked steps. He swallowed hard, pulled out his phone, and called 911. Then he dialed the paper.

—2—

"You found the body." It wasn't a question. Detective Sang Joon Park frowned as he looked Ed up and down on the front porch of the home of the late Ryan Duffy.

"That's right," Ed replied softly. "Saw him through the window."

Behind Park, police tape was strung across the front door. Two cruisers were parked out front. Their light bars bathed the street in a pulsating crimson glow. On the sidewalk, two uniforms interviewed shocked neighbors.

Ed tried to look Park in the eye, hoping to show the dour detective he had nothing to hide. Only after dialing 911 did he recall that the person who finds a body is always a suspect. But he found it impossible to lift his eyes from the scene beyond the tape, the bloody mess that had once been the side of his friend's head.

A medical examiner knelt beside the body. A photographer took pictures. Techs worked the living room carpet on hands and knees. They collected the kinky paraphernalia strewn around the room: a blindfold, a whip, and a magazine with a naked woman hogtied on the cover. *Bound for Love*.

Park wandered among them, chewing gum. His name was Korean, but his English, free of any accent, announced that he was either American-born or had arrived young. He looked about forty. His black hair matched the plastic frames of his glasses. His beige shirt matched his complexion. He was around Ed's height, but round-shouldered and thicker around the middle. His suit looked expensive. His tie was splotches of green and brown. Then Ed realized the splotches made an abstract pine tree.

"And you were looking in—why?"

Ed explained who he was. A brief flash of recognition crossed Park's face. He knew the column. Ed related that Duffy had asked him for a historian's perspective on his grandfather's diary.

"This diary, where is it?"

Ed shrugged. "He was supposed to give it to me—" It felt bizarre to have this conversation with Duffy still splayed out on the living room rug. Duffy wouldn't hurt a fly. How could he have been beaten to death?

"You got a diary?" Park called to no one in particular.

A black tech on hands and knees raised his tweezers from the rug and said, "No."

Ed realized that if there was no diary, he had a problem. "Maybe it's in the kitchen."

Park unfastened the tape, then reattached it behind him. "Wait here." He strode down the hall, passing a plastic basket containing new sports gear: a soccer ball, shin guards, and two baseball gloves. What were Duffy's boys' names?

The detective rooted around the kitchen. "I don't see it."

"What about the dining room?" Ed's armpits suddenly felt clammy. Brendan and Tommy. Brendan was the older one, finishing high school. Tommy was a few years younger. Now their father was—

From the porch, Ed saw only a corner of the massive old dining table. It was piled high with—Ed couldn't see what. Park rummaged and found a large manila envelope. "Says: 'For Ed R.'" He stepped over Duffy's leg and returned to the porch. When Park opened the envelope, three old-fashioned composition books slid out. He opened the top volume. The penmanship was ragged, but legible: June 2, 1934.

"That's it," Ed said. "May I?"

Ed flipped pages, noticing the dates, all summer of 1934. A wave of grief washed over him like incoming tide. He and Duffy would never get to discuss the diary.

Park slipped the notebooks back into the envelope, which he tucked under his arm. His jaw worked the gum. The day was getting warmer. He loosened his tie and undid his top button.

"'Scuse me, Detective." It was an older man, one of the living room crew. His jacket said Medical Examiner. His expression said he resented getting called out on a Sunday.

"George."

Ed recalled the drill from his cop-chasing days. They'd know more when the lab results came back, but impressions at the scene were important.

"Preliminary CoD…" Cause of death. "Multiple blunt-instrument trauma. The statue crushed his skull. I figure five or six whacks."

"ToD?" Time of death.

"Nine to midnight." A three-hour window was typical, Ed remembered.

"Confidence?"

"High. Everything agrees: temperature, rigor mortis, blood flaking, and retinal exam."

Ed exhaled. If Park still harbored any suspicions after finding the diary, he had an airtight alibi for that time last night.

"What about the BDSM?" Park asked.

"Standard kink. You can find that kind of ball gag at any sex shop. The rope is cotton-nylon, the kind kinksters like. But no welts or bruises. The bloodflow shows that right after he got bound, he got it. The perp skipped the flogging and went right for the statue."

"Semen?"

"None on the rug or furniture. I swabbed his mouth and anus, but I'm guessing probably not."

"DNA?"

"We bagged the statue and beer glasses and picked up some hair and fibers. We might get lucky. But God knows if we'll get approved for a full analysis." With the city's budget woes, the crime lab had taken a hit, like every government vehicle.

"Drugs?"

"A couple beers."

"Weed? Coke? Meth? Poppers?"

"We'll have to wait for the blood work, but no signs, no paraphernalia."

"Prints?"

"Not many. Looks like our perp wiped the place down pretty good. Maybe wore gloves. The lab'll recheck the gag, statue, and glasses."

Park nodded. "Anything else?"

"I've never seen anyone tied to furniture like this. And the knots are dipshit."

"Meaning?"

"Not sure."

"Conclusion?"

"Our boy had a party and things got out of hand."

Park scanned the living room, fastening on the two halves of Jesus. "Wouldn't the perp have to be pretty strong to bust that statue?"

"You mean, was the killer a big strong man?"

"Yes."

"Hard to say. The statue looks pretty old. Over time, plaster develops micro-cracks. It might have been ready to break."

"So it could have been a woman."

"Maybe. But no lipstick on the glasses."

If the killer was a man, then Duffy was bisexual?

"All right. When?"

Ed knew the question meant: When would Park get the lab results?

The medical examiner frowned. "Who knows? If we're lucky, end of the week. But lately, I haven't been lucky."

Park returned to Ed, and asked how well he knew the deceased. Ed described their poker games, lunches, family outings, and Duffy's divorce.

Park raised an eyebrow. "How bitter?"

"I'm not sure. When things got bad with Sheila—that's his wife, his ex—he stopped paying cards. I didn't see him much the past year."

"Enemies?"

"None that I know of. He was a great guy. Everyone loved him."

Park shot him a sour look. "Did you know he was into *this*?" He nodded toward the clear plastic evidence bags containing floggers and whips.

"No."

Park gave Ed a card, and said to call if he remembered anything else.

"What about the diary?" Ed asked.

"What about it?"

"Can I have it? It was meant for me. I feel like I owe it to Duffy—to his family—to read it."

"Call me in a few days."

Ed descended the stairs. On one side of the house was an old plank door. It had been closed when Ed arrived, but the police had opened it. Now it was open. The reporter in him had to have a look.

At the end of a long breezeway, Ed's jaw dropped. Duffy's back yard was nothing like Ed's postage stamp. It was an estate. There was no house behind his. The yard extended all the way across the block to a high fence at Twenty-seventh Street. Ed was amazed that no house had ever been erected. But there it was, a vacant lot in the middle of a prime residential block, the San Francisco equivalent of wide open spaces.

A brick patio extended back from the house. It bristled with weeds, ending at a barbecue pit and a statue of the Virgin. Beyond the patio were the remnants of a once-elaborate garden, dead fuchsias and withered roses. Only the crabgrass was green.

Ed could understand Duffy's attachment to his childhood home. But it needed tons of work, which meant mountains of money and years of headaches. But looking at the lot, Ed could see why his friend was up for the project. He could divide the property, sell the lot to finance renovations, and probably do quite nicely.

Ed skirted two new skateboards and climbed rickety stairs to a rotting deck that should have been replaced years ago. Draped over the railing were sweatshirts that said SI—Saint Ignatius, one of the city's Catholic high schools. Ed recalled that Duffy's older boy went there.

There was no tape across the back door, no officer to keep out the riff-raff. Ed crossed the mud room and stepped into the kitchen.

It smelled of mustard and bleach. The floor was a checkerboard of black-and-white linoleum tiles. Many were cracked or missing their corners. The white ones were yellowed. The cabinets looked like they'd been installed during the Kennedy Administration. The counters were stained. In one corner, the plastic countertop was coming unglued and curling. Dirty dishes filled the sink. A half-eaten bag of microwave popcorn sat on the stove. Pizza crusts moldered in a grease-stained box. Duffy didn't win any prizes for homemaking.

Ed stepped into the dining room. The table was piled high with old magazines, battered board games, and assorted junk, including a manual typewriter. Stacks of yellowed magazines—*Life* and *National Geographic*—were piled by the kitchen door. The furniture reminded him of his grandparents' home.

"Hey!" a cop called from the living room, his voice sharp as a razor. "Out!"

Ed emerged from the breezeway as two young Hispanic men carried a collapsed gurney up the stairs. A big milk-skinned blonde followed them. She could have passed for the woman on the St. Pauli Girl label. Ed had known her for years: Catherine Wheelwright, the *Foghorn*'s senior police reporter.

Many journalists, Ed among them, cut their teeth on the police beat then moved on. Wheelwright had been chasing cops for a good decade, and was shaping up to be a lifer. She seemed to revel in the grim business of crime. But she was a sweetheart whose hobby was taking close-up photographs of flowers in bloom. Every autumn, she selected a dozen and used them to decorate a calendar she distributed at Christmas. It was the one Ed and Julie hung in their kitchen.

"Sang." She smiled at the detective, extending the "a" in his name—Saahng.

"Cathy." Park nodded back with a tight smile. "Didn't expect to see you on a Sunday."

"Yeah, well, you know." She shrugged. "When Metro heard who it was—and how he was found—they didn't want to send a rookie."

"Cathy," Ed called ascending the stairs.

"Ed. I hear you found him."

"We were supposed to have brunch."

"You knew him?" Park asked Wheelwright.

"A little. But I had no idea he—"

"Me either," Ed said.

Wheelwright pulled out her pad and interviewed Park, who said it looked like kinky sex gone bad. She was a big woman, but carried herself gracefully. Her wardrobe exuded what Julie called personal style: bright colors, big earrings, and elaborate necklaces, with sensible shoes.

"Suspects?" she asked.

"Not yet."

She turned to Ed. "I didn't know you and Duffy were friends."

Ed explained again about poker, lunches, and the diary, the words already feeling hollow.

The crime scene crew packed their gear. The medical examiner's aides zipped the body bag and hefted it onto the gurney, then wrestled it down the stairs. Ed, Park, and Wheelwright followed.

It was warm now, but pleasantly breezy. The bakery gave off a wonderful aroma. Wheelwright asked about the lab report. Park told her to call at the end of the week. Then he turned toward an unmarked police car.

Ed and Wheelwright crossed the street to her hybrid in silence. A Conservatory of Flowers decal graced the rear window.

"You see many like this?" Ed asked. He couldn't remember the paper covering anything similar.

"Every now and then. It *is* San Francisco, after all."

It was no secret that the City by the Bay was a mecca for kink. Ed recalled the paper's coverage of the Health Department's class on bondage safety. And the annual Folsom Street Fair, a celebration of the South-of-Market leather bars and sex clubs, included a Flogging Festival. Ed knew there was no predicting who might be kinky. But Duffy? It was hard to fathom.

Wheelwright called Metro and reported that it was all true. She was starting the engine when Ed asked, "How are you going to play it?"

"Straight. How else?" She smiled but sounded annoyed. Ed knew his question was out of line. Of course she'd describe the scene—ropes, whips, gag, and all.

"I'm just thinking about his boys—and the shit they're going to take over this."

"Yeah, well, I can't help that. Anybody else, we'd report the kink. I can't make an exception just because it's Duffy. Not to mention that the Desk already knows."

Ed sighed. Brendan and Tommy were in for a rough ride. Sheila, too. Duffy's murder was bad enough. Ed wished he could do something to soften the blow, but he couldn't.

"You have a car?" Wheelwright asked.

"I walked. I live nearby."

"Want a ride?"

Ed considered it. "Thanks, but no. I want to walk. Clear my head."

As Wheelwright drove off, Ed wondered if he'd ever wipe his mind clean of Duffy splayed, bound, and disfigured.

Then he flashed on Julie. She'd have to release a statement with obligatory quotes from the publisher and executive editor mourning a respected colleague. He pulled out his phone. He hoped that her shock and grief would spare him another lecture on the horrors of living in the Mission. But he doubted it.

—3—

JULIE DIDN'T SAY A WORD ABOUT MOVING. WHEN ED GOT HOME, SHE fell into his arms and sobbed. The commotion attracted Sonya, who had never seen her mother cry. Ed explained that a friend had died, the father of Brendan and Tommy. That set off Sonya's tears. Julie stifled her own grief to deal with her daughter's. From her stash of greeting cards, Julie produced several that said Sympathy. Sonya selected the one to send.

Then it was Sunday afternoon. They took the kids to Dolores Park playground, ate picnic sandwiches and watermelon, and rigged a blanket over the backpack as a sunshade for Jake's nap. On the climbing structure, kids cavorted and parents said, "Be careful." Above them, on the hillside known as Dolores Beach, hundreds of gay guys sunbathed wearing next to nothing. Toward Mission High, the rolling lawn was a patchwork of blankets, Frisbees, kites, and musicians. A beautiful afternoon—except for all the ugliness in the world.

The next morning, reading the paper on BART, Ed couldn't believe his eyes. Wheelwright's piece didn't say a word about BDSM. Ed felt as relieved as surprised. At least Sheila and the boys wouldn't have to deal with that. He pulled out his phone to call the police reporter, then stopped—no cell service underground, he remembered. In his office, he dialed the phone, then looked at his watch and hung up. Wheelwright would have to wait. He was on deadline.

Ed stacked books and files by his keyboard. He should have tackled this subject ages ago. But he needed a hook and hadn't had one until now.

ARSON BY THE BAY:
THEN AND NOW, PART I

Huge fires illuminating the San Francisco night. New construction in flames. Buildings reduced to ashes. Millions in damage. Gangs blamed.

That might describe the Mission district these past few months—12 arson fires destroying half-built condominium buildings. But those blazes, appalling as they've been, don't compare with the devastating conflagrations during the city's explosive infancy. During the 19 months from December 1849 to June 1851, a series of disastrous fires destroyed San Francisco *six times*. The fact is, San Francisco was built—and rebuilt—on the ashes of arson fires.

Gold was discovered in the Sierra foothills in January 1848. Months later, when news reached the tiny hamlet of San Francisco, the town emptied as everyone literally headed for the hills. Their spontaneous rush for gold became the Gold Rush.

As news spread, toward the end of 1848, the first outsiders arrived, young men from Oregon, Mexico, Chile, and Hawaii: sailors, shipping clerks, and ranch hands, most of them honest souls who hoped to strike it rich quickly, then return home.

In early 1849, a second wave of gold-seekers arrived, a large contingent from Australia. But these were men of a different sort. In *The Barbary Coast*, a history of San Francisco's underworld, Herbert Asbury claims the Australian Forty-niners were "100 percent criminal," escaped convicts from the British penal colonies around Sydney. Actually, some honest Australians also contracted gold fever. But so many Aussie immigrants were "villains" that Asbury wasn't too far off the mark.

A large number of these hooligans settled on the eastern slope of Telegraph Hill near the present-day corner of Broadway and Battery. For more than 10 years, the Australians' collection of rude shacks was known as Sydney Town. Its marshy shore attracted waterfowl, and the loose confederation of criminals from Down Under became known as the Sydney Ducks. After heinous crimes, early San Franciscans said, "The Sydney Ducks are cackling in the pond."

The Ducks engaged in burglary, robbery, murder, and pimping Mexican, Chilean, and Native American women. But they also had men numbering in the hundreds, and that allowed a new level of organization for more lucrative plundering. Eighty years later, it would be dubbed organized crime. They ran a protection racket, threatening to burn out merchants who did not pay handsomely. Some paid. Others did not.

On Christmas Eve 1849, the Ducks set a fire that destroyed most of San Francisco. The blaze didn't require much expertise. The town's few hundred "buildings" were canvas tents or wooden shacks. But the Ducks made one smart move. They picked a day when the wind blew from the northeast, *away* from Sydney Town, the only neighborhood to survive intact. During the fire, the Ducks looted anything they could lay their hands on.

As San Francisco exploded into a city of 20,000, the Sydney Ducks set fires in May, June and September of 1850 and in May and June of 1851. All five followed the same pattern: extortion, then arson and pillaging.

By the spring of 1851, San Francisco had a rudimentary government, but only a 12-man police force, no match for the Ducks. However, after the May fire, which destroyed 2,000 buildings, the merchant community had had enough. Prominent businessmen organized the first Vigilance Committee and warned the Ducks that miscreants would wind up at the end of a rope.

On June 10, a notorious Duck, John Jenkins, was caught stealing a safe from a business on the Long Wharf (later Commercial Street). Jenkins was promptly hanged—or, depending upon one's perspective, lynched. The execution was cheered by the several hundred Vigilance Committee members, but denounced by city officials, and rightly so. The Committee was little more than a bloodthirsty mob. But it included most prominent businessmen and was supported by much of the arson-weary population.

The Ducks retaliated on June 22, another day with winds from the northeast, setting their sixth and final fire. It caused considerable damage. By this time the Vigilance Committee had 400 well-armed members. They marched on Sydney Town, seized several Ducks and strung them up. According to Asbury, this "caused a veritable panic. Sydney Town's rascally inhabitants left San Francisco in droves."

Today, the seal of San Francisco depicts a phoenix rising from its ashes. Most people think this recalls the great firestorm of 1906. Actually, it was adopted in 1855 and pays homage to the fires from 1849 to 1851.

Today's arson fires in the Mission are appalling. I pray the police quickly catch those responsible. But as shocking as they are, today's fires pale next to the blazes during the Gold Rush. Of course, those fires have been largely forgotten, because of an even greater fire that reduced a much larger San Francisco to ashes 56 years later. More on that next time.

Ed hit the SEND key and another column was on its way to lining birdcages. He reshelved books, slipped files back into his cabinet, and answered e-mail. Then he called Wheelwright, but got voicemail. He glanced at his watch. No sense trying the honchos. They were in their daily meeting deciding tomorrow's front page. He reread Wheelwright's story. She must have reported the kink. So who cut it?

Ed felt restless. Duffy's closest friend on the paper was an occasional poker player, Tom Ferguson, who covered the politics of real estate development. Maybe he'd know something. Without quite realizing it, Ed found himself taking the stairs two at a time to the third floor.

Ferguson was in his cubicle typing with the phone between his shoulder and ear. He was older than Ed, a cherubic man with silver hair, a salt-and-pepper beard, and a shy smile. He raised an index finger, motioning for Ed to pull a chair from the conference table into his cube. As Ed sat, Ferguson hung up.

"Ed! I was going to call you. I hear you found Duffy."

"But you might not have heard *how* I found him."

"Actually, I did. Roy told us." Roy Evans was the deputy Business editor.

"Listen, Tom, can I buy you a beer?"

—4—

THEY WALKED DOWN THE NARROW ALLEY BEHIND THE PAPER. Between a grimy apartment building and a motorcycle shop, they pushed open Old West swinging doors and entered The Poets, the oldest bar in the area. Ed had once written a column about the place. Under various monikers, the squat building had housed an Irish pub since 1858. Long, narrow, windowless, and dark, the walls of its current incarnation were painted with quotes from Yeats and Joyce. These days, the street outside was a mix of small businesses, immigrant Filipinos, and new lofts that heralded gentrification. But The Poets endured, a faint echo of nineteenth-century San Francisco's Irishtown.

Ed brought two Guinnesses and a basket of popcorn back to a booth whose table was gouged with initials and what Sonya called "bad words." Ed asked what Roy had said. Ferguson had most of the details, but Ed filled in the rest.

Ferguson swallowed a big gulp of beer. Then he choked up and clamped his eyes shut. When he opened them, they glistened. "Hard to believe he's gone."

"I couldn't get hold of Wheelwright. Did Roy say why the kink got cut?"

"No. Just that Walt did it and Cathy's pissed." Walt was Walter French, the paper's executive editor, the top dog. Ed might have known. Walt had a habit of monkeying with copy at the last minute.

"Did Duffy mention his grandfather's diary?"

"Just that he found it in the attic and asked you to take a look."

"It's funny," Ed said. "We were friends. But when his marriage went bad, he disappeared."

"We got closer. We were both getting divorced."

"I thought you were friends all along."

"Oh, we were. I've been in Real Estate fourteen years. I knew him from day one. We collaborated on stories, joked around the office, played at First Wednesday, had lunch. But when our marriages tanked, we were like an AA group. My wife went to a high school reunion. Left me for the old boyfriend. Duffy was having an affair. His wife kicked him out. We wound up with the same lawyer."

"So you talked about your divorces."

"Ranted is more like it. Divorce is a bitch."

"Sorry. You ever see his house in the Mission?"

"A couple times. A real pit."

"I know. You figure a guy as deep into real estate as Duffy would—"

"Oh, he tried, believe me." Ferguson swallowed a handful of popcorn. "It was his grandparents' originally. They passed it to his parents. Duffy grew up there. His father died, oh, eight, ten years ago. His mother stayed on. She loved the garden and did okay, until her mind started going. Eventually, he moved in with her. You have any idea what it's like caring for someone with Alzheimer's?"

"No, but I imagine it's not easy."

"Black hole. Sucks everything out of you. And more."

"With the divorce and his boys and work and the girlfriend, I'm surprised he did it."

"I was, too. But moving back home killed three birds with one stone. The house was big enough for him and his boys. He could supervise the aides who looked after his mother. And being so involved in her care took his mind off the divorce."

"What happened to his mother?"

"Nursing home. A few months after he moved in, it became clear she needed round-the-clock care."

"So it was his mother's house? I thought he owned it."

"He did."

"Bought it from her?"

"No, no. He and his brothers and sisters bought it from her after their father died. She got money to live on. They got tax deductions."

"You'd think Duffy would have maintained it better."

Ferguson grunted. "Oh, he tried. But after his father died, his mother turned strange. Didn't want anyone touching anything. Any changes around the house, she'd scream bloody murder. Drove Duffy crazy. Eventually, they realized that it was the first stage of her dementia. After she went into the home, he started cleaning things out."

"So Duffy bought the house from some family partnership?"

Ferguson nodded. "The original idea was to sell the place to support their mother in the home. Then Duffy decided to buy it. His sibs were thrilled. They liked the house staying in the family."

Ed bought another round and returned with another basket of popcorn. "Awfully big house for one person," Ed said. "And it needs a ton of work."

"He knew what he was getting into," Ferguson explained. "After the divorce, he needed a project. He'd renovated other places. And he was very sentimental about that house."

Ed flashed on the vast expanse of withered rose bushes behind the house. "You know anything about the back lot?"

"Just that it's been in the family forever."

"I'm surprised nothing was ever built on it."

Ferguson shrugged.

"Is it all one property? Or two?"

"Two. Duffy just bought the house. He wanted to buy the lot, but couldn't afford it."

"Really? I'm thinking that half of three big flats in the Marina buys a lot of property in the Mission." Duffy and Sheila had owned a three-flat building near the Palace of Fine Arts; they lived in one and rented the others.

"True, but his ex couldn't afford to buy him out entirely. He wound up hanging onto—I forget—something like twenty percent of the Marina building, so he couldn't swing both properties."

Now things about the house were starting to make sense. Before he was killed, Duffy had been clearing out three generations of accumulated junk. That was why the dining room was piled high with detritus and why he'd been poking around the attic. His grandfather's diary must have gathered cobwebs up there for seventy years.

"You ever meet Sheila?"

"A few times. Seemed nice enough—until things fell apart."

"And then?"

"Ball buster. She was furious about the other woman, and wanted all the money. To hear Duffy tell it, even after they signed the papers, she kept screaming for more."

"Doesn't sound like the Sheila I know. Not that I know her all that well. But Julie and I socialized with them a bit. She was sweet."

"Yeah. Until her husband started banging someone else."

"You ever meet the girlfriend?"

"No. All I know is she's got a big corporate job."

Ed couldn't argue with the medical examiner. Duffy's death certainly looked like kinky sex gone wrong. But if the first suspect is the person who finds the body, the second is the spouse, especially a bitter ex with a greedy streak.

"Tom," Ed asked, "have you talked to the police?"

"No." Ferguson toyed with his beard.

"I think you should."

Ferguson's brow furrowed. "Sheila?"

"You said she was on him for money. With Duffy gone, doesn't she get more?"

"But tying him up? Bashing his head in? She's not the type."

"I wouldn't think so either, but who is?"

—5—

ED PUSHED OPEN THE HEAVY GLASS DOOR AND LEANED INTO THE office of Metro Editor Tim Huang. "Lunch?"

Huang checked his watch. "I'm up to my eyeballs."

"You always are. What's with Walt? Why'd he cut the kink?"

Tim rolled his eyes. "All right. A quick sandwich at the FP."

Ed and Tim went back twenty years to Ed's days in grad school, when Tim was still in high school. They had met at the dojo run by Tim's late uncle. Tim made black belt. Ed never got past green. Then they lost touch. Years later, Ed had noticed Tim's byline in the *Defender*, and the two old sparring partners reconnected—with Tim all grown up. Neither could believe the other had landed in journalism. Eventually, Ed helped his friend move to the *Horn*. Tim clawed his way up to Metro editor on his own, but made only a fraction of what his wife, Kim Nakagawa, earned as the morning anchor on Channel 5 News.

The two men descended to the ground floor and stepped into the uproar of the Front Page, the deli that occupied a corner of the *Foghorn* building. All the sandwiches had newspaper names, and a *Horn* ID got you a discount. They slid plastic trays down aluminum rails. Tim ordered a Headline—ham and Swiss. Ed opted for an Editorial—grilled chicken breast.

The FP was crowded, but they found a two-top by the window that looked across Mission Street to the Old Mint.

"So? Cathy's piece?" Ed pressed.

"Walt's losing it." Lately, whenever the *Foghorn*'s executive editor emerged from his office, Tim reached for antacids.

During the innocent era before the Internet, Walt had been popular with the paper's department heads because he was open to having his mind changed. But now that Craigslist was publishing classified ads for free, the *Horn*'s classified section had dropped from twelve pages to two—slicing revenue $30 million a year. The *Horn* was losing money and Walt was under enormous pressure to turn things around. A long cold bath in red ink changes a man.

Tim swallowed. "Cathy played it by the book. Mentioned the gag and restraints, but in the style of a professional description of a crime scene—solid reporting, nothing lurid. Everyone was fine with it. Then Walt killed it."

"Why?"

Tim looked like he'd sucked a lemon. "And I quote: 'To spare Duffy's family any embarrassment.'"

"What's wrong with—?"

"It was total bullshit, that's what. You think Walt gives a rat's ass about Duffy's family? It was to spare him. You know where he's going next week? NANE."

The National Association of Newspaper Editors. French was prominent in the organization.

"Walt wants sympathy over the loss of a good writer, not teasing about how weird everyone is out here." Tim frowned. "We don't report the news. We filter it."

"But what about TV and radio?" Ed asked. "Weren't they all over the kink?"

"As a matter of fact, they didn't say a word. Walt called in a few favors."

"What about the *Defender*?"

"The predictable rant on their Web site. The self-serving *Horn* suppressing embarrassing news. But no traction there."

Ed wasn't surprised. The mainstream media used the alternative weeklies as farm teams, but made a point of ignoring their coverage.

"What about the investigation?" Ed asked. "Wouldn't the cops want the details out there? Maybe shake a peach from the tree?"

Tim sighed. "Welcome to my life. At the meeting, several of us raised that very point. Walt got defensive, called Wheelwright on speakerphone, asked if cutting the details would compromise the investigation. She wasn't happy, but she's a pro. Said no, it wouldn't. The cops had already been to the sex clubs. Word's out."

San Francisco had two BDSM clubs. One was upscale and decorated like a nineteenth-century bordello. The other had the tawdry look of a motel bypassed by the Interstate. The clubs operated a block apart in what was left of the industrial South of Market area, not far from the paper, where Mission Street swung south into the Mission neighborhood. It wasn't clear how long they would last. Lofts were going up everywhere. The area's risqué elements, the sex clubs and several gay leather bars, were being pushed out by rising rents.

"But suppose the killer's a tourist," Ed mused, "someone Duffy picked up and took home."

"We raised that. But no dice. Walt was adamant."

They ate for a while, nodding at *Horn* folk who took tables nearby.

"I sympathize with your frustration," Ed said, "but personally, I'm kind of glad Walt did it. Keeps the boys from being taunted."

"I hear you. But it's dishonest. Anybody else, and the whips and chains would have been up top."

"You're right. But Brendan and Tommy are fourteen and eleven. I'm not defending Walt. I'm just saying—"

"You know what I can't believe—that Duffy was into that shit."

"Well, you know what's next to Phan Lam."

Phan Lam was the Vietnamese hole-in-the-wall where Ed and Tim often had lunch. It served a perfect lemon chicken salad—if you didn't mind an occasional roach on the wall. Next door was the elegant kink club, Roissy, named for the chateau setting of *The Story of O*. The sign called it "a safe play space for adventurous adults." Its well-undressed patrons called it a dungeon.

"So?"

"So you and I aren't into it, but plenty of people are. And judging by a piece I read recently in a certain newspaper, the folks who go there are a cross-section of middle America."

Tim knew. He'd assigned the story.

"May I?" It was Cathy Wheelwright holding a tray, her blonde hair looking straight out of a conditioner commercial.

"Cathy!" Ed exclaimed. "I've been calling you. Where've you been?"

"Sorry," she said, pulling a chair from another table, "I've been buried under the coke bust." The owner of the biggest auto dealership in town had been caught with five pounds of snow.

"So?" Ed asked.

"Doesn't look good. Preliminary tests show no prints on the statue. No prints around the house, except Duffy and his kids. DNA, but no matches so far. Duffy's girlfriend is kinky, but she was in Seattle all weekend and can prove it. Her ex has a bombproof alibi, too."

"What about Duffy's ex?"

"Fifty people saw her and her boyfriend dancing at the Plough and Stars." It was an Irish bar in the Richmond district. "Duffy got it between nine and midnight. No forced entry. He let the guy in. Two beer glasses. No traces of lipstick. And the fracture pattern shows hard hits. So Park's pretty sure the bad guy's a man."

"So Duffy *was* bi?"

"Looks like."

"Enemies?"

"Half our readers," Tim interjected. In San Francisco, real estate development was a blood sport. Duffy's articles elicited more hate mail than anything else in the paper.

"But no serious threats," Wheelwright said, "no assaults. No enemies the cops know of, so…."

She didn't have to spell it out for a former police reporter. Ed knew that in homicides, if the police didn't arrest someone quickly, they rarely did. The SFPD solved less than one-third of the city's murders. Ed flashed on Duffy on the living room floor. His stomach turned. He no longer wanted his sandwich. He pushed it away, just as he heard a tinny rendition of *Bye Bye, Birdie*.

Wheelright pulled out her phone. "Yes?...When?...Damn!" She hung up, wrapped her sandwich, and stood. "They moved up Farmer's arraignment. Got to go." Preston Farmer was the car dealer with the trunk full of coke.

Tim noticed that Ed looked queasy. "You okay?"

"I've been better. I keep seeing him. I'm not sleeping well."

"Is that just because of Duffy? What about the baby? How are you guys holding up? We haven't seen you since he was born."

"I know. I'm sorry." Ed willed himself out of Duffy's house and back to the FP. "We're good. Better than I expected. Jake's five months. Started daycare. Julie's back to full time. He's been sleeping most of the night. Everyone told us: Two is more than twice as hard as one. But so far, no. Jake's mellower than Sonya was."

"You're lucky. All three of ours were a trip."

"I remember. But get this: Julie's itching to move. With the Morrissey fire, she flipped."

"I don't blame her. It was awfully close to you."

"Tell me about it. Three blocks."

"So you *don't* want to move?"

Ed sighed. "I don't know. Julie makes a strong case. I can't really argue against it. But we just finished renovating. Room by room. Year after fucking year. You know what we went through."

"I do."

"The damn paint's hardly dry. I don't want to jump into another huge renovation project—especially with an infant. We did that with Sonya. Never again."

"You don't have to buy a fixer."

Ed looked at the friend whose TV-anchor wife made more than the two of them combined. "That's all we can afford—unless we move halfway to Sacramento, and who wants a big commute?"

"I remember when you guys moved into the Mission," Tim said. "Julie loved it—the sun, the easy commute, the burritos."

"I know. I miss the old Julie."

"It's called motherhood."

"Yeah."

"So what are you going to do?"

"What we always do. Talk it to death."

"I hear you, bro." Tim and his wife had had serious problems—and years of therapy. Now they were okay.

Ed reconsidered his sandwich and took a small bite. "I'm nervous about the fires. But none have hit single-family homes. I don't want huge towers at BART. But even if they fast-track a transit village, it's years away. The neighborhood will fight it every step. Meanwhile, Julie talks like they're breaking ground for Rockefeller Center on Friday."

"Well, maybe you'll get lucky. Maybe the fires and Duffy's murder will scare off developers for a while."

"You know, I hate to feel good about that—but I do. Only it's cold comfort. Duffy gets his head bashed in, and the cops are ready to drop it. Pisses me off."

—6—

ARSON BY THE BAY: THEN AND NOW, PART II

AFTER THE SYDNEY DUCKS WERE RUN OUT OF TOWN, SAN Francisco suffered no noteworthy arson fires until the great conflagration of 1906. It lasted four days, April 18 to 21, destroying 500 blocks, 28,000 buildings. Arson was not the primary cause of that fire. The earthquake shattered gas lines and water mains, and the leaking gas ignited fires all over town. Meanwhile, water drained from the ruptured mains, crippling firefighting efforts. But human hands played a major supporting role in the disaster.

Much of downtown was on fire by mid-morning on the 18th. Several businessmen whose stores, warehouses or factories burned that morning decided that misery should have company—namely, their competitors. Rather than having to rebuild from scratch while the competition quickly recovered and reopened for business, they struck a few matches and tossed them where they would level the post-quake playing field.

Some evidence also suggests that the chaos of April 18 allowed people with grudges to settle personal scores.

Meanwhile, shortly after the shaking stopped, a Hayes Valley woman, who lived near today's Davies Symphony

Hall, made breakfast for her family. She had no idea the earthquake had damaged her chimney. Sparks from the fire in her stove escaped the chimney and set her house ablaze. The Ham and Eggs Fire burned 100 blocks.

In addition, starting on the afternoon of the 18th, the U.S. Army began dynamiting buildings, hoping to create fire breaks to stop the blaze. But in the hands of soldiers who didn't know what they were doing, the dynamite simply created more fuel for the voracious flames.

Finally, there was the strange fire that destroyed Claus Spreckels' mansion on Van Ness Avenue and several blocks around it. Spreckels (1828-1908), a German immigrant, arrived in San Francisco in 1856, opened a brewery and made a fortune. He invested in land in Hawaii, planted sugar cane and made a second fortune from his California and Hawaii Sugar Company (eventually C&H Sugar). In 1906, burning cinders supposedly landed on the stable behind his 40-room palace and no one noticed until it was too late.

That explanation doesn't square with the observations of James Stetson, an official with one of San Francisco's private streetcar lines before they were merged into San Francisco Municipal Transportation Agency. Stetson watched the Spreckels mansion burn. He also kept a diary made public years later, in which he noted that the stable burned not first, but *last*, catching fire from the house. This might have happened if the earthquake had damaged the chimney, as in the Ham and Eggs blaze. But Stetson reported a healthy stream of smoke issuing from the chimney, strongly suggesting that it had remained intact. What started the Spreckels fire?

No one knows. But at the time of the earthquake, a federal prosecutor was gathering evidence of wholesale corruption throughout the San Francisco city government. A major target was lawyer Abe Ruef, who funneled enormous amounts of graft money to the mayor and more city officials than anyone imagined possible. As a result, the investigation required more money than the federal government was willing to spend. So a group of prominent San Franciscans chipped in. One was Spreckels' son, Rudolph, who contributed $100,000 (the equivalent of several million dollars today). Rudolph also provided a secure room to store sensitive documents—in his home, a Van Ness Street mansion a few blocks from his father's.

Shortly after the quake, city officials, including Ruef and his staff, gathered at City Hall (before it burned) and attempted to deal with the unfolding disaster. But on day two of the fire, Ruef's aides were oddly absent from the command center. Then word reached officials that Claus Spreckels' home had burned. The usually even-tempered Ruef was uncharacteristically upset at the news.

Putting the pieces together, some have speculated that Ruef ordered his henchmen to torch Rudolph's home to destroy the documents that later sent him to San Quentin. But evidently, the arsonists burned *the wrong mansion*, the father's instead of the son's.

Police contend that the Mission arson fires have been set by Latino gangs outraged by gentrification. Perhaps. But the Mission has been going upscale—slowly—for more than 30 years, since BART began operation in 1972 with two stops in the neighborhood. Yet, until recently, the Mission hasn't faced any widespread threat from arson.

If today's fires are a reaction against loft condos and BMWs, they would be the city's first experience with arson triggered by anything other than greed. Ever since the Sydney Ducks burned down early San Francisco six times in 18 months, every major arson fire seems to have been set for either financial gain or to destroy evidence of ill-gotten gains.

Who's setting the Mission fires? We won't know until the police catch the arsonist(s). But when they do, history suggests the motive will not be Latino rage at an influx of white professionals, but rather cold hard cash.

—7—

ED PULLED OUT OF THE PAPER'S PARKING LOT AND HEADED FOR A church seven blocks from the crime. Julie sat in the passenger seat. Tim and Kim sat in back.

As usual, Ed felt underdressed. Julie was wearing all black: dress, shawl, shoes, hose, and purse. Kim was similarly attired. Tim wore a charcoal-gray suit and black knit tie. The closest Ed could come to funeral fashion was the navy blue suit he'd worn to his wedding—he was delighted it still fit—and a tie in a black-and-white soccer-ball pattern, his gift for coaching Sonya's team.

"I hate funerals," Kim sighed.

"Especially when it's someone our age," Ed said.

"Especially when they go *that way*," Julie said. "Oh, if anyone's allergic to flowers, we shouldn't sit down front. The paper donated three huge bouquets."

"Your doing?" Kim asked the PR director.

"Seemed like the right thing."

"Meanwhile," Ed said, "the investigation is nowhere. Park's got nothing. I feel so sorry for Brendan and Tommy. Sheila, too, but mostly the kids. Their father's murdered—and now they grow up never knowing who did it or why."

"The cops haven't given up yet," Tim said.

"I think they have."

They traversed the South of Market and crossed into the Mission. The sky was sunny and bright, Mediterranean. To the west, a fogbank nestled against Twin Peaks. It reminded Ed of their bedroom, the fluffy white comforter over two piles of pillows.

"It's warm," Tim said, cracking his window.

"It's the Mission," Ed replied with a realtor's flourish. "San Francisco's Riviera."

"If you don't mind the fires and murders," Julie murmured.

The car window framed her profile. Even when she was upset, Ed felt moved by her exotic beauty, the product of a black father and Jewish mother. He reached over, took her hand, and squeezed. She squeezed back and tried to smile, but didn't quite.

Ed took a side street up the hill to the southern end of Noe Valley and parked a block from St. Paul's, the setting for the Whoopi Goldberg movie *Sister Act*. A throng of people shuffled into the huge church.

"Big crowd," Julie observed.

"Who knew Duffy was so popular," Ed said.

Somber mourners filed by, several dabbing their eyes. Aside from the *Foghorn* contingent, Ed didn't know a soul.

They shuffled inside and sat toward the rear. St. Paul's was modeled on the churches of Renaissance Italy; its six-story interior was supported by huge wooden beams. Stained glass bathed the sanctuary in celestial light.

Kim asked Julie about Jake's childcare, and their conversation was off and running. Ed saw Tom Ferguson and waved him over. "You have any idea who all these people are?"

"Some are in real estate, but I imagine most are family and parish people. Duffy had deep roots here. His great-grandfather helped build this place."

A murmur ran through the crowd as a woman in black shuffled by, her face veiled down to a tear-stained chin. Sheila was propped up by a beefy man with thinning blond hair in a dark suit. Brendan and Tommy followed behind, awkward, grim, and red-eyed. They sat in a pew down front.

"Her boyfriend?" Ed asked Ferguson.

"Must be."

"You know anything about him?"

"Just that Duffy knew him. The three of them went to high school together."

"Did Duffy know they were—?"

"Yeah. He was happy about it. His affair ended the marriage. He felt relieved that Sheila was involved with someone, someone he liked."

Mourners shuffled past and filled the pews. The boyfriend stood over a sobbing Sheila, shaking hands with the parade of people offering condolences.

Ferguson pointed at a man in his forties who pushed a wheelchair down the aisle. In it sat a frail ancient woman with sparse white hair. "Eric McCain," Ferguson said, indicating the man. "Big developer."

"I've heard of him," Ed said, "but I forget how."

"Probably the Civic Center transit village. His baby."

"Ah, yes."

"It hasn't been approved yet," Ferguson explained. "But it will be. McCain and Duffy grew up together. When Duffy came out in favor, the *Defender* howled that he was bending over for his childhood buddy."

"Was he?"

"Duffy insisted he wasn't, that it was a good project. That area isn't residential. There hasn't been much opposition—for San Francisco."

"Who's the old lady?"

"No idea."

McCain pushed the wheelchair down to Sheila's pew. When she saw him, she rose and fell into his arms sobbing. He held her for quite a while. When they let go, McCain wiped his eyes. Then he hugged the boyfriend while Sheila bent to embrace the old woman.

"I don't believe it!" Ferguson exclaimed. "See the gray-haired guy behind McCain?"

As the developer pushed the wheelchair away, an elderly man stepped up and took Sheila's hands in his.

"Mitch Callahan."

"The developer?"

"Yes. He and Duffy *hated* each other."

Ed recalled their feud over the Armory. For thirty years, the huge landmark on Mission Street had sat vacant. Callahan wanted to transform it into a Tuscan hilltop village—five stories of office space in the existing structure with apartments and townhouses ringing an open plaza on the roof. Ed loved the idea. The artist's concept in the *Horn* envisioned a magical enclave, in the city but above it, with million-dollar views of downtown and Twin Peaks.

But Duffy wanted the Armory torn down and replaced by the reincarnation of the site's original occupant, Woodward's Gardens, San Francisco's first amusement park. As a historian, Ed felt some pull to recreate the famous Gardens. But the city desperately needed housing and Duffy always banged that drum. It was out of character for him to oppose a housing plan, especially one so charming.

Mitch Callahan and the boyfriend wrapped their arms around each other. Then Callahan kissed Sheila's cheek.

"Duffy's turning over in his coffin," Ferguson said.

Sheila's boyfriend looked like a fullback. Maybe the cops were right, Ed mused. Maybe it was kinky sex gone bad. But maybe the boyfriend had wanted to make sure the Duffys would never reconcile. Anyone could have tied him up. Sheila and her guy had a bombproof alibi. But with an upper body like that, it wouldn't take much to break a statue of Jesus.

Ferguson pointed across the sanctuary. Mitch Callahan clamped a hand on the shoulder of a beach ball of a man whose trim gray beard could not conceal a receding chin. "Fred DeCampo, president of APOD."

APOD was the Association of Property Owners and Developers, the lobby for the city's landlords and builders—and a political powerhouse. DeCampo was a local kingmaker and arm-twister. He and APOD turned up in the *Horn* as frequently as the mayor and governor.

"He looks well fed," Ed observed.

"Oh yeah," Ferguson replied, "on the blood of widows and orphans. DeCampo's a prize ass. Couple weeks ago, I did a piece on the twentieth anniversary of rent control—"

"I liked it."

"Thanks. He hated it. Wrote a letter calling me a left-wing lunatic."

"Why?"

"Because I treated rent control as a fact, not an outrage."

"But it *is* a fact."

"Not to him, it isn't. DeCampo thinks 'rent control' should be one of the things you can't say on TV. When I interviewed him, he said—off-the-record, of course, but I quote—'Rent control is a Communist plot.'"

Ed's eyes widened. "Has he noticed that Russia and China have gone capitalist?"

"With DeCampo, everything's calculated. Every word is carefully planned. It's his *job* to talk crazy. That way, no matter what the big developers demand, by comparison, they sound reasonable."

Callahan sat down near DeCampo.

"The people around DeCampo, they're all APOD, all here to pay their respects to the late lamented urban design critic." Ferguson snorted. "What a joke."

"What do you mean?"

"They hated Duffy. Cursed the ground he walked on."

"Why? He supported big condo projects. All the new buildings in South Beach. The Civic Center transit village."

"True. But he also supported *rent control.* Which put him on APOD's shit list—forever. And there's more. Duffy not only supported rent control, he was a *landlord.* That really galled APOD. He wasn't just the enemy. He was a *traitor.*"

Rent control was the third rail of San Francisco politics. Starting in the 1970s, Baby Boomers became enchanted by the city's siren song. Rents soared and landlords converted thousands of units to condos, selling them out from under renters for big bucks. Embittered renters formed Tenants United for Fairness. TUF couldn't match APOD in fund-raising, but two-thirds of the city's housing units were rentals, and TUF got legions of renters to the polls. TUF-backed candidates won a majority on the Board of Supervisors. The Board enacted rent control, eviction controls, and a condominium conversion limit of just two hundred units a year, one-tenth of 1 percent of the city's housing stock. APOD had been trying to untie that knot for thirty years, so far unsuccessfully.

Ferguson nodded toward a crowd of well-dressed middle-aged men behind the APOD staff. "Developers. Biggest in town. The guy next to Callahan is Roger Claussen. You ever hear of Bridge Haven?"

"The big building going up near the Bay Bridge?"

"Try *three* buildings. Forty-five stories each. They'll dwarf everything around them. The short guy next to him is Seth Levine. Performing Arts Plaza." It was a monster mixed-use development near the Opera House.

Ferguson pointed out a half-dozen others and ran down their claims to high-rise fame. Then Eric McCain, minus the ancient woman in the wheelchair, approached the group and shook hands all around.

"He's not happy," Ferguson said, "and not just because he lost his childhood friend."

"Do tell."

"He's spent millions acquiring options on property around the Civic Center BART station. But despite the boost he got from Duffy's endorsement, the Planning Department is still iffy. So he's been shoveling money at APOD. Their people have been all over the Commissioners like five coats of paint. McCain's sweating. But my money's on approval. Oh, look." He gestured a dozen rows back from the APOD group. "The other side."

The other side was younger and less elegantly dressed. "The guy with the ponytail is David Heckendorf, president of TUF, another prize asshole. My piece on the anniversary of rent control? He hated it. Why? Because I didn't call for running APOD out of town. He's totally convinced that APOD owns the Rent Board."

"What? Didn't they just limit this year's increase to one percent?"

"Less. Eight-tenths. But Heckendorf thinks all rent increases are criminal, and that no rental property should ever be allowed to convert."

"But if nothing converts, how is anyone supposed to buy anything?"

"They're not. Heckendorf thinks everyone should rent forever—and throw money at TUF to protect them from evil landlords."

"So they must have loved Duffy for supporting rent control."

"But they despised him for supporting condo conversions. When he came out in favor of McCain's transit village, they were ready to kill him."

Their eyes met.

"Poor choice of words," Ferguson said.

"Seems like Duffy had quite a few enemies. You think any of them could have—?"

"God knows. APOD accused TUF of setting the Mission fires. I wouldn't be surprised if they think Heckendorff did Duffy."

Ed made a mental note to ask Cathy if Park had looked at TUF and APOD. Still, it seemed far-fetched. Duffy had been infuriating both sides for years. Why kill him now?

"I don't understand why TUF opposes transit villages," Ed said. "I thought the deal was that every displaced renter is guaranteed an apartment—at their previous rent."

"True. But it takes years to build those buildings. How many displaced tenants are going to show up down the road and claim their units?"

"Good point."

"And politically, it's all about numbers. The transit villages will be mostly condos. As they fill up, the city's ratio of renters to owners shifts toward owners. TUF can't stand that."

Organ music filled the air, and for Ed, the ceremony became a blur. The casket was closed. The mourners wept. The priest choked up reminiscing about playing on a basketball team with Duffy in sixth grade. Duffy's brother said all the heartfelt, forgettable things people say in eulogies. Then it was over and everyone filed out. Ed and Julie waited in line to have a moment with Sheila and the boys.

Afterwards, atop Twin Peaks, the fog bank looked like cotton candy. A stiffening breeze blew wisps off the top that tumbled across the sky toward the Bay.

Three old men walked gingerly past Ed, clutching the rail as they descended the steps.

"Mooney's?" Ed overheard one say. It was the Irish bar across the street.

"By all means," another replied.

Then in unison all three said, "You don't just *bury* an Irishman. You *drown* him."

"Check *her* out," Julie said, nudging Ed and nodding toward a tall, voluptuous woman whose jet-black hair sported a white streak that started at a widow's peak and swept back behind an ear. Her black dress was a little too short for a funeral, her ankle-strap heels a little too high. "Either she's making a fetish fashion statement, or she was one of Duffy's playmates." Could the woman be Duffy's girlfriend? If so, Ed had some questions. He took a step in her direction, but a big group of *Horn* people exited the church, blocking his way. By the time he sidestepped them, she was gone.

A Business writer asked Ferguson if he was covering the transit village hearing.

"Yeah, but if you want it, you can have it."

"What hearing?" Julie asked. "I thought transit villages were a done deal."

Her question floated away on the afternoon breeze as the APOD group descended the stairs to one side of them with the TUF people on the other. DeCampo caught Heckendorf's eye. With a mischievous grin, he flashed the fingers of both hands twice. Twenty. Heckendorf scowled and flipped his middle finger, then raised five more. Six.

"There's your answer," Ferguson said to Julie, pointing to the finger play. "The Board passed the *concept* of transit villages. But the Planning Commission has to thrash out the details. Our friends were presenting their positions. APOD wants twenty-story buildings. TUF wants six."

"What's the limit now?" Julie asked.

"Three straight up. Four if the top floor is set back."

"So why is TUF saying six?"

"Because if they argue for any less, they won't be taken seriously," Ferguson explained. "They're calling for three stories straight up to blend in with the neighborhoods, then a big set-back and just three more."

"Doesn't sound too bad," Ed ventured.

"But there's no way Planning's going for it. Looks like the staff is ready to recommend ten stories. The real battle is over the set-backs. APOD doesn't want them because they cut way down on the number of units—and developer profits. The staff is on the fence. But I think they'll go for major set-backs."

"If we have to have these monstrosities near us," Julie said, "*I* want set-backs."

"If you feel strongly," Ferguson replied, "testify at the hearing."

"You know I can't." The paper had strict rules prohibiting staff from doing anything publicly that might appear partisan. "But I think I know someone who can. When is it?"

Ed shot her a quizzical look.

"Next Thursday afternoon."

"He'll be there," Julie said.

"Who?" Ed asked.

Instead of answering, Julie replied, "If they allow twenty stories with no set-backs, we're moving."

Wait a minute. Don't I have a say? Ed was about to raise the issue, but held his tongue. This was neither the time nor the place.

—8—

ED DIDN'T MEAN TO CALL TOM FERGUSON. HE HAD A COLUMN TO research: the fiftieth anniversary of Lawrence Ferlinghetti's acquittal on obscenity charges for publishing Allen Ginsburg's *Howl.* Ed's fingers just seemed to dial the Real Estate writer on their own. He got voicemail.

Ed loved the story of the *Howl* trial. In 1957, a San Francisco judge ruled that its use of a word that rhymes with truck was not obscene because the poem had "redeeming social importance." The ruling established a legal test that allowed dozens of banned books to be published in the United States, including *Lady Chatterley's Lover.*

But Ed couldn't concentrate. He kept thinking about Ferguson's remark that there was bad blood between Duffy and the old developer, Mitch Callahan. The question was, how bad?

He clicked into the *Foghorn* archive and began to search. Up came an article by P.J. Alvarez detailing Callahan's Armory development plan—offices in the existing building, and on the roof, a park-like plaza surrounded by housing. The Armory's walls were two feet thick. The corners could easily support four five-story buildings containing a hundred apartments. Between them, Callahan proposed townhouses. The engineering worked as long as the center of the roof didn't bear much extra weight. Hence the plaza, a private park for residents high above the street. Callahan had the financing. All he needed was a height variance.

Local architects hailed the proposal as innovative and exciting. Real estate people predicted Callahan would have no problem filling the development. Even the Mission's notoriously prickly community groups climbed on board after Callahan pledged to hire neighborhood people for the build-out and rent one quarter of the apartments to Mission families at below-market rent.

Ed fantasized about moving his family into what Callahan was calling Armory Heights. The views would be incredible, and he could see Sonya and Jake cavorting in the park. Then he woke up. He wasn't poor enough to qualify for a below-market unit, nor rich enough to afford anything else. Still, the plan seemed like a good way to deal with the derelict Armory. Why was Duffy opposed?

Ed typed in a new search, and found Duffy's rejoinder. According to the late critic, the Armory was already too big and bulky for its low-rise neighborhood. It made no sense to build it five stories higher. Callahan's promise of jobs amounted to a few dozen laborer positions for two years. His promise of affordable housing applied to only twenty-five units, which hardly scratched the surface of the city's housing shortage. Meanwhile, Callahan would sell the rest of the apartments and the townhouses for tens of millions altogether. The Armory's neighborhood was becoming increasingly residential, but was devoid of greenery. Ironically, during the nineteenth century, it had been the site of the city's first large park. Why not knock it down and rebuild Woodward's Gardens?

Ed scrolled down the list of articles: Hearings before the Planning Commission. The decision to deny the height variance. Callahan's appeal. The Board of Supervisors throwing it back to Planning. And Planning's decision to kill the hilltop village for good. The byline on all of them was P.J. Alvarez, a young reporter Ed didn't know well.

Ed leaned back in his chair and clasped his hands behind his neck. Duffy's park idea was intriguing, but very out of character. He'd made a career of championing housing. Yet here he was blowing off one hundred and fifty cool new homes, including affordable units, on the Mission Street bus line and only two blocks from BART. Very unlike him.

The phone rang. Ed figured it was Ferguson returning his call.

"Tom?"

"No," a woman replied. It was Marilyn Bishop, the new features editor, a hotshot from the *Boston Globe* who'd been at the *Foghorn* a month. She was thirty-five and looked dangerously thin. At her welcome-aboard lunch, Ed thought she'd seemed bright and affable. She'd complimented his column. Since then, word was that she was smart and hard-working, but that her way was the only way. "Stop by my office?"

"Sure. When?"

"How about now?"

"Be right there."

Officially, Bishop was Ed's boss. Compared with the rest of the gnomes in their cubicles, though, he was less firmly under her thumb. As the man behind "San Francisco Unearthed," he had his own bailiwick, plus an office with a door—not to mention that Macy's paid dearly for ad placement next to his column. But the editorial niceties still had to be observed, especially when newspapers were floundering and no one's job was safe. Her predecessor was now deputy editor. He'd assured Ed that Bishop wouldn't rattle his cage. Ed figured she wanted to get acquainted and chat him up about finding Duffy's body.

As it turned out, sympathy over stumbling on a colleague's corpse came and went in one breath. Bishop had asked him in because she had *concerns* about his column. So much for not messing with him.

"I've just finished reading your last year of columns," she said, sipping tea from a Wellesley College cup.

Fifty-two columns. Indeed, a hard worker.

"I like them. I like them a lot. And I know the focus groups rate them high. But you have a tendency to use history to comment on current events."

"History provides perspective."

"Of course. But so much of what we publish is bad news. I'm hoping that features can, whenever appropriate, leave readers smiling."

"Happy talk?" Ed held his breath. Happy talk was a buzzword for reporting only good news. Publishers pushed it when they feared that bad news was scaring off advertisers.

"No, not at all," Bishop retorted. "But I think one of the attractions of your column is that, for a few welcome moments, it transports people from the problems of today to a more innocent time."

"The good old days."

Bishop smiled.

Ed sighed. "The thing is, when you take a hard look at the good old days, you find they never were."

"Of course. Every era is messy. You do a fine job of pointing that out. But here's my problem: When everyone is on edge about arson fires, I don't think it's prudent—or appropriate—to dismiss them by saying the city was founded on arson."

"I *never* dismissed them. And it was."

Her chin jutted his way. She'd been hoping for a different response.

"I live three blocks from the most recent fire," Ed continued. "If anyone is on edge, I am. I just tried to provide some historical context—"

"—that made a mockery of the paper's coverage. I have a problem with you ridiculing Metro reporting."

So that was it.

"I didn't *ridicule* anything. I just pointed out that history argues for greed, not gangs."

"Maybe so. In either case, your piece ran long. I cut the stuff about the recent fires and wrapped it up after the Spreckels business."

Ed couldn't believe his ears. He forced himself to smile and breathe. She was young, full of herself, and prickly as a cactus. A younger Ed might have blown up. But experience had taught him the path of Elvis Costello: "I used to be disgusted. Now I try to be amused." Bishop had the authority to edit his piece any way she pleased. End of story—for now. But down the road, when this column became a chapter in his next book, he would play it *his* way. Books lasted longer than newsprint. "You're the editor."

Bishop looked relieved. "I'm glad you're a team player." Meaning: You know who's boss.

Ed's lips curled into a tight little smile. *Let me out of here.*

"I look forward to a long and cordial relationship," she said.

"Me, too." He stood to go.

"One more thing," Bishop said. "Not that every piece has to leave 'em smiling, but do you have any ideas that would?"

"Uh..." Ed thought about his list. Certainly not the *Howl* trial. Then he had a thought. "Have you ever heard of Woodward's Gardens?"

"No."

"San Francisco's first amusement park. Opened in the 1870s, near where the freeway crosses Mission Street. It was very popular for twenty-five years—rides, a lake, an eccentric museum. Very cool place. In its day, a must-see."

"Sounds great." Bishop smiled and licked her thin lips, a lioness after the kill. "Let's work it into the mix."

Ed muttered all the way back to his office. As he pushed the chrome bar across the heavy glass door, his phone rang.

"You called?" Ferguson asked.

"You know P.J. Alvarez?"

"Pedro? Sure. Sits two cubes from me. Nice guy. Why?"

"He covered Callahan's plan for the Armory."

"He's still on it."

"What? I thought Planning killed it."

"Oh, they did. But Callahan's lobbying them to reconsider."

"They do that?"

"Not often, but it happens—if the developer is...*persuasive*."

"What? Bribes?"

"Not cash. Too risky. It's usually sweetheart deals. The developer's got a project somewhere and sells a condo to a Commission member for a few hundred thousand less than it's worth—through third parties, of course, so it can't be traced. I've caught whiffs over the years."

"Great story."

"It would be—if I could find someone willing to talk on the record."

"You think Callahan will get approval?"

"No idea. But he's very persistent, not to mention rich and connected. He might get lucky."

Speaking of luck, Ed realized, Callahan had just found a four-leaf clover. The most vocal critic of his Armory project wouldn't be writing any more diatribes.

—9—

YERBA BUENA PARK WAS AN ACRE OF LUSH LAWN, SHADE TREES, AND A waterfall two blocks from the paper. But to Ed, it was an open-air haunted house.

For a century, the area had been residential, working class, and heavily Irish. Then, in the 1960s, San Francisco's leaders decided to bulldoze the tenements to give tourists museums and Moscone Convention Center. The residents, many getting on in years, screamed bloody murder, but lost. Thousands were displaced. Their bitterness poisoned the city's political well. It took twenty-five years for the park to be built. By the time it opened—to glowing reviews—the former residents were long gone, most to their graves.

Ed and Pedro Alvarez sat in shirtsleeves on the grass and drank coffee near the waterfall. Near them, a young man on a stool played classical guitar, his case open for tips. On the lawn around them, people of every description soaked up the last rays of afternoon sun as the first wisps of fog floated by. In an hour, coats would be necessary.

"Duffy and Mitch Callahan," Ed asked. "How bad was the blood?"

"Pretty bad." Alvarez was in his mid-twenties, stocky and prematurely jowly. He grew up in the Mission, went from Catholic schools to the University of San Francisco, wrote for the college paper, interned at the *Horn*, and wound up getting hired, a strangely direct route to journalism compared with Ed's own experience.

"The reason I'm asking is—and please don't take this wrong—it doesn't come through in your stories."

Alvarez smiled. "Right. Marty's orders." Marty DeVeer was the business editor, a crusty journalist who'd spent eighteen years at the *New York Post*. He liked screaming headlines and stories that hit the high points, with insight optional. "At one point, Callahan came *this close* to popping Duffy." He mimed a punch with a lot of shoulder behind it.

"What?"

"I reported the scuffle. Marty cut it."

"What happened? When was this?"

"Couple years ago, at the final hearing when Planning nixed Armory Heights."

"I read your piece."

"So you know they bought Duffy's critique—too tall for the neighborhood."

"Yes," Ed replied. "But personally, I liked the concept. The idea was a *hilltop* village. I thought it was cool."

"Me, too," Alvarez said. "But there was more to Duffy's opposition than just the development's height. This is pretty close to a quote: 'Callahan's an asshole from a long line of assholes.' Their families had some kind of feud."

Ed's eyebrows arched.

"After he got turned down, Callahan was furious. Duffy and I were in back. Callahan stomps toward the door. Sees Duffy. Marches up to us. Jabs a finger in his face. Says, 'This isn't about a variance and you know it. It's about my father and your grandfather.' Then he pulls back ready to slug Duffy, but his people grab him, pull him out of the room. I'm stunned. Duffy says the two families were on opposite sides of some strike."

"The dock strike of 1934."

"I wrote it up: Fists Almost Fly at City Hall. But Marty cut it."

Ed's heart played a drum roll in his chest. "Have you told the police?"

"No."

Ed frowned.

"It happened years ago—and nothing really happened. Planning hearings can get pretty wild."

"I'm encouraging you to tell the police."

"What are you saying? That Callahan—?"

"I'm not saying anything. Just that the police should hear about this feud."

"It's not like Callahan's the only developer Duffy ever trashed. He was a critic. He criticized. And pissed off lots of people."

"But how many tried to assault him?"

Alvarez combed the grass with his fingers.

"Isn't Callahan trying to get the Planning Commission to reconsider?"

"Yes."

"So we have to ask: who benefits? With Duffy gone, he's got a better shot at approval, doesn't he? And if he gets it, he makes millions."

"But Duffy was all done up for weird sex. You think Callahan—?"

"I don't know what to think. But the cops should hear."

Alvarez watched an elderly couple toss some bills into the guitarist's case. Then he looked at Ed. "Okay."

Ed gave him Park's contact information. "And do me a favor, would you? Use my name. Tell him I urged you to contact him."

"Why?'

"He has something I want. A diary."

Alvarez opened his mouth to ask a question, but Ed beat him to it.

"Written by Duffy's grandfather. About that strike."

—10—

Ed thought he had the column nailed, but that Friday, riding home on a packed BART train, he realized it needed tweaking. After dinner, he dropped off Sonya at a friend's for a sleepover, then descended to his basement lair and clicked into the paper's system.

SAN FRANCISCO'S FIRST FAVORITE PARK:
WOODWARD'S GARDENS

To San Franciscans, "the park" is Golden Gate Park. But from shortly after the Civil War until the end of the nineteenth century, the phrase conjured a different oasis: Woodward's Gardens, in the inner Mission between today's Armory and the freeway. An 1876 account called it "a spot of beauty without compare on the Pacific Coast...[whose] attractions rival the celebrated parks in other cities whose age in decades outnumbers San Francisco's in years."

Woodward's Gardens was the brainchild of Robert Woodward, who arrived from Rhode Island early in the Gold Rush but never panned for gold. Instead, he opened a grocery store on the waterfront. As Woodward chatted with his customers, young men from around the world, he realized they missed the comforts of home. In 1852, he opened the What Cheer Hotel near Portsmouth Square. It offered rat-free rooms with clean sheets and decent meals at reasonable rates. The What Cheer was an instant success, despite being the only hostel in town that did not serve liquor. Woodward soon owned a hotel empire of 1,000 rooms, and became one of the boomtown's richest men.

But early San Francisco was wild and violent, and Woodward feared for his wife and daughters. In 1857, he bought four acres of wooded hills near Mission Dolores an hour's carriage ride out muddy, rutted Mission Road (now Mission Street). Atop a hill overlooking Mission Creek, he built a white mansion with domes and spires reminiscent of the Taj Mahal.

Woodward loved to travel. In 1861, he took his family to Europe for 18 months. He bought hundreds of paintings and sculptures, plus exotic plants and a menagerie of wild animals. Some of the art adorned his hotels, but most graced the walls of his hilltop home, whose size he doubled to accommodate his acquisitions. He returned from other trips with additional art and wonders, and added more rooms to his house. For his children, he built an arboretum and a zoo.

Woodward enjoyed showing friends his treasures. Word spread, and on Sundays, crowds gathered outside his gate hoping for an invitation to tour the grounds.

In 1866, Woodward moved his family to an estate in Napa Valley. He spent two years renovating his Mission estate, then opened it to the public. Woodward's Gardens was San Francisco's first amusement park. Admission was ten cents (equal to about $10 today). It quickly became a landmark.

Woodward's former home became the Museum of Natural Wonders, displaying thousands of items he'd acquired overseas. For the exotic plants, he built a conservatory. He added fountains to the grounds and redirected Mission Creek to flow into lakes stocked with fish, ducks, and swans, with rowboats for rent. A skiff ride splashed down a fast-moving flume. For children, there were rides on camels and miniature carriages pulled by goats. Woodward's zoo included tigers, kangaroos, buffalo and grizzly bears. Tame deer and ostriches wandered the grounds. He built an octagonal pavilion seating 1,000 and offered plays, dances, and roller skating. In 1873, Woodward built the first salt-water aquarium in the United States, sixteen enormous tanks stocked with Pacific fish, crabs, abalone, and octopus.

"I enjoyed circuses," recalled socialite Astrid Knotts in a reminiscence published in 1929. "I enjoyed the theater and opera. But I *loved* Woodward's Gardens. My family spent many a happy Sunday there. The ostriches were my favorites. When the birds shed, the attendants gave the big feathers to children. I had quite a collection."

For almost 30 years, locals flocked to Woodward's Gardens, and for visitors from around the world, it was a must-see attraction. Its conservatory, lake, zoo, and pavilion inspired William Hammond Hall to include similar features in Golden Gate Park, built after Woodward died in 1879. Ironically, Golden Gate Park slowly drove Woodward's Gardens out of business. It closed in 1894.

Soon after, its lakes were drained. Mission Creek was buried in a culvert. The buildings, including Woodward's huge white mansion, were razed. And the hill that dominated the property was leveled.

The original plan was to build housing on the grounds, but with World War I looming, civic and military leaders decided that San Francisco needed a new Armory to replace the one destroyed in 1906. They settled on the former park's site. A 200,000-square-foot brick fortress was erected, with walls two feet thick. It stored munitions for the California National Guard and served as the barracks for Guard troops ordered to San Francisco when the dock strike of 1934 turned into the largest general strike in U.S. history. During World War II, the Armory stored supplies headed to the South Pacific. But since 1970, the enormous building has remained vacant.

Today, all that remains of Woodward's Gardens is Woodward Street, a one-block alley, and a restaurant by the freeway called Woodward's Gardens. Stand at Mission and Fourteenth, and it's hard to imagine that such a grimy corner was once the gateway to the city's most verdant playground.

So far so good. The hang-up was what followed, three grafs on Callahan's development proposal and Duffy's fantasy of resurrecting the park. It was contemporary and Bishop wanted to cage him in the past. It was controversial and Bishop wanted him to leave 'em smiling. Perhaps he should kill those grafs, and lay low until Bishop calmed down.

But history wasn't comic relief. It was a lamp. It should illuminate. Ed reread his last three grafs. He deleted one and left two. If she didn't like them, she could cut them.

Ed was wrapping up when he heard the stairs creak. Julie appeared cradling a squirmy, whimpering Jake in her arms. His big eyes were red with tears. Ed reached up for him and sat the baby on his lap.

"Still teething, I see."

"I put him to bed an hour ago. He woke up."

"Tylenol?"

"Half-hour ago. He's still unhappy."

"Poor guy."

Ed bounced Jake on his knee, which had been eliciting his latest feat, giggling. But not this time. He just frowned with sad wet eyes and a trembling lower lip.

"What now?" Ed asked.

"It's really warm. Let's take him for a walk. Might knock him out."

"Can we go past the Armory? I'm writing about it."

—11—

EVERY SO OFTEN, ED'S FAVORITE ROCK STATION POLLED LISTENERS and assembled a set called Hits from Hell, horrid songs that sent the stairway to heaven straight to the devil. High on Ed's all-time list was Eric Burdon's ode to "warm San Francisco nights." Who was he kidding? Nights in San Francisco ranged from cold to colder, with gusting winds that made you wish your coat had thicker lining. Perhaps the singer had never actually visited. Or maybe he'd gotten lucky. Maybe he'd shown up on one of the few nights each year that was magically warm, when all you needed after dark was a T-shirt.

Ed donned the backpack. Julie strapped Jake in. The baby rocked back and forth as if to say, "Giddyap." They stepped into a warm San Francisco night.

They weren't the only ones. The sidewalks were jammed. The cafés were jumping. The ice cream parlor was mobbed. At a sidewalk table, a church was selling frozen bananas. Tricked-out lowriders rolled by, windows open, monster sound systems blaring. The air was fragrant with grilled meat, cold beer, and marijuana.

Jake stopped crying and turned this way and that, wide-eyed, taking everything in.

"Want to split a *churro*?" Ed asked as they approached the Mexican bakery. *Churros* were Mexican donuts, except they were long fluted sticks.

"No," Julie said. "I shouldn't. But you go ahead."

"Nah, I don't need it."

Julie was still on her new-mom mission to get her body back. For the second time, she'd developed a bad case of post-partum self-loathing. She was fat. Her boobs were too big. Her stomach was too flabby. Her butt could qualify for its own zip code. The walk wasn't just for Jake.

After Sonya's birth, as Julie binged on aerobics and yoga, Ed tried to console her: Give yourself a break. You're nursing. You look fine. He meant it, but in his wife's eyes, his opinions marked him as either blind or stupid or both. This time around, he held his tongue and focused on being affectionate. It was her body. He loved it. But she had to make peace with it.

Still, it pained Ed to see her distressed about anything, especially her appearance. Julie had always been so self-critical. As far as he was concerned, she was a fox: caramel skin, big, dark, expressive eyes, and thick wavy hair that fell to her shoulders in bronze ringlets. She had gotten her body back last time, she'd do it again. Why beat herself up? But he knew why. Because she was Julie.

She set a brisk pace, but Ed slowed as they passed the neon-bordered windows of San Francisco Billiard Supply. Beautiful pool tables called out to him: Buy me! Ed grew up with a table in his basement. He had played in college and placed in a few tournaments. Then life intruded and it was hard to find the time. These days, he played—poorly—at the Inner Mission Youth Center where the director, his old buddy, Jerry, regularly cleaned his clock. When they bought the house, Ed had regarded its proximity to the pool store as a Commandment received on Sinai: Thou shalt buy a table. Of course, they had no room. Desperate, Ed had measured the garage. If he used a short cue and parked on the street, they could almost squeeze in a seven-footer. Julie wouldn't consider it. So Ed yearned, mostly in silence—but not always. "I *really* want a table."

Julie laced her fingers into his and kissed him on the cheek. "I know."

"I want to teach the kids. Play with them. See the look on their faces when they sink a bank shot."

"Don't you want to play with me?" Julie's hand squeezed his.

She walked the fingers of her free hand lightly from the front of his thigh toward the inside, then withdrew it.

He kissed her. "I love playing with you. I'd also love to shoot pool with you. All we need is a table."

"All we need is a bigger house."

"And a mountain of money to buy it."

"Come on, Fast Eddie, let's walk."

They passed a taqueria, a thrift store, RadioShack, and a new restaurant the *Horn*'s critic liked. Across the street, salsa music blared from Ritmo Latino, and a knot of teens danced on the sidewalk. Jake smiled and seemed to sway to the music.

"Speaking of housing," Julie began tentatively, "the Planning Commission meeting is Thursday afternoon. Calvin's testifying." Calvin Liu was half of Keith and Calvin next door.

"So you recruited him."

"I did. And I'll be there to cheer him on. What about you?"

Ed saw the yearning in her eyes. "If you want, I'll be there."

She shot him a look. "But you don't really care, do you?" Her tone fell somewhere between disappointment and disdain. "Ten thousand new people in the neighborhood and you don't give a shit."

Ed was surprised by her irritation. *What set this off?* "Whoa. I care. I care a great deal. But let's be realistic. There's no way any Twenty-fourth Street village is going to house ten thousand people. Planning won't approve twenty stories—"

"How do you know? APOD's going to roll out an army of developers, realtors, and construction unions." Her tone was plaintive.

"And TUF will bring just as many community groups arguing for six stories with big set-backs. Ferguson says they've already pretty much decided on ten stories with seven set back pretty deep."

"Maybe. But as a certain husband often says: assume nothing. If the community doesn't turn out, around the corner we could have—"

Ed finished it for her. "Rockefeller Center. I've heard."

Jake's eyelids started to droop. Then a half-dozen motorcycles rumbled by and grabbed his attention. He gurgled. For a moment, Ed thought he said, "Yamaha."

A mariachi band played on the corner, the guitar case filling up with coins and bills. Two girls who looked Filipina ogled the gowns in a bridal shop. A skateboarder zipped by, a scorpion tattoo on his arm. Outside the Walgreen's, a weather-beaten couple of indeterminate age, homeless and missing teeth, held out plastic cups.

"I'm confused," Ed said. "On the one hand, you say the house is too small, that we should move. But we can't move because even with the renovations, we can't pull enough out to buy anything bigger. But if a transit village goes in, property near the BART station should get a bump and we're probably close enough to ride the coattails. But here you are about to testify against the very thing that could give us the boost we need to move. I don't get it."

"I *hope* we can move—before Jacob starts kindergarten. But I'm *afraid* we won't be able to—which is why I'm testifying. I want a livable neighborhood."

"Me, too."

They crossed Fifteenth Street and the massive Armory rose before them, a medieval castle with turrets like chessboard rooks. But its glory days were long past. Now the old fortress was a dirty eyesore marred by graffiti and trash. Around its perimeter, homeless people guarded shopping carts heaped high with belongings.

"Suppose we *could* move..." Julie ventured.

"Honey..." Ed replied, trying hard not to sound exasperated.

"I know, I know. But bear with me. Just *suppose* we could. Where would you want to live?"

"No more than a fifteen-minute drive from school."

Sonya attended a public magnet school near the Mission in the Excelsior, a modest little neighborhood far from tourist San Francisco that was becoming popular because homes there were still almost affordable. They liked the school. They could live anywhere in the city and still send her, with Jake automatically admitted thanks to sibling preference.

"I agree," Julie said. "Fifteen minutes from school. That puts us in the Excelsior, Bernal, Glen Park, the Mission, or Noe Valley."

"Homes in the Excelsior, Bernal, and Glen Park are no bigger than ours."

"We could add on."

Ed snorted. "Who gritted her teeth through years of renovations? And God knows if we'd be able to."

They couldn't add on now. Under the building code, their lot was too small to build back, and the cost made it impossible to build up.

"All right. So that leaves the Mission and Noe Valley."

"Forget Noe Valley," Ed sighed. It was considerably pricier than the Mission. "They should call it *No Way* Valley."

"Which leaves the Mission." Julie's tone combined resignation and disappointment.

"I like the Mission," Ed countered.

"I do too—except—"

"It's too funky and scary."

"I'm worried about the kids."

"Hey, you grew up in the Bronx and you're proud of it." She was wearing a Yankees T-shirt. "What if your mother had moved to some soulless suburb?"

"She couldn't afford it."

"Neither can we."

"We haven't looked," Julie insisted.

"Every Sunday, we scan the Real Estate section."

"That's not looking. That's glancing."

"You want to put the time into looking? Remember what we went through? Finding the house was practically a full-time job."

Jake was asleep now. Julie adjusted him in the backpack. She sighed. "Where's gentrification when you need it?"

"Let's count our blessings," Ed said. "The house works, for a while. We're done fixing it up—finally. The kids are healthy. Our jobs are tolerable. And—" he wrapped an arm around her shoulder, "my wife's a hottie."

Julie smiled. "Thanks, but—I'd love a place in Noe Valley."

"Buy some Lotto tickets. We might get lucky."

"We *are* lucky," Julie said. "Just not lucky enough."

They skirted Mission Dolores and Dolores Park, then climbed the big hill to Liberty Heights and descended the other side back to their cute little home on their quaint little street.

Jake was out cold. Julie nestled him into his crib and kissed his forehead. She found Ed in the kitchen peeling an orange. He slipped a fat section into her mouth. "You really want to look?"

She remained silent, but her eyes said yes.

"Okay. Call Ravi."

Ravi Singh was the agent who had helped them buy Fair Oaks.

Julie's expression changed. Her eyes asked a question that remained unspoken.

"I'm sick of busting our asses to support contractors," Ed said. "I'm tired of floor coverings, light fixtures, and fifty kinds of toilets. But if you really want to look, and if you deal with the agent, I'll go to open houses. "

"I'm tired, too." She kissed him. "But not of you."

Ed whispered in her ear. "Just one thing—and it's non-negotiable. There has to be room for a pool table."

—12—

IN A TERSE E-MAIL, MARILYN BISHOP SAID SHE LIKED THE WOODWARD'S Gardens column, but "cut the last two grafs for space—sorry." Ed sighed. If she was sorry, he was Mark Twain.

Still no word from Detective Park. Ed had requested the diary in three polite voicemails, but so far, nothing.

Ed called Alvarez. "Did you call the detective?"

"I did."

"What'd he say?"

"That the almost-fight was quote-unquote 'interesting.' Then he told me what I told you. Duffy pissed off a lot of developers."

"Did you mention that I gave you his number?"

"I did."

"Any reaction?"

"No."

Ed wanted the diary. He had to have it. Now it was more than just a last favor to a murdered friend. Duffy's grandfather and Callahan's father had a beef over the dock strike that somehow still echoed after seventy years. Presumably, the diary contained details. It was a sweet, juicy plum hanging just out of reach. Park had *no right* to keep it from him.

That evening, Ed was on kid patrol. He paid bills, put Jake to sleep, and straightened up the kitchen after Sonya and her friend, Rosario, made popcorn. *How could microwaving one little bag make such a mess?* Then he flashed on Park with a large envelope under his arm.

Ed's feet carried him to the basement. He'd written about the dock strike, but not recently. He was fuzzy on the details. When he finally laid hands on the diary, he wanted to be up to speed. He opened his file cabinet.

The firestorm of 1906 was a disaster, but ironically, it proved a godsend for San Francisco labor organizing. Rebuilding the ravaged city took millions of tons of material, and almost all of it arrived by ship. This gave dockworkers—affectionately, wharf rats—unprecedented leverage. They formed the International Longshoremen's Association (ILA) and rode it to higher wages and the West Coast's first waterfront job safety rules. The ILA quickly spread to every port from Seattle to San Diego.

But the Russian Revolution triggered an anti-labor backlash. Terrified of Bolshevism, San Francisco employers organized the Industrial Association (IA) to battle Communism—meaning anything that resembled a union.

A 1919 strike closed every port on the West Coast. As usual, strikebreakers clubbed union men, but in this case, the strike held. Then the shipping companies got creative. They encouraged the strikebreakers to join the union en masse and declare their faction the "real" union. The companies recognized the strikebreakers' group, and imposed a contract that slashed wages, gutted safety rules, and declared that dockworkers would be hired daily at morning "shape-ups" that took place at company-run hiring halls. To work, longshoremen had to present passport-size Blue Books and bribe crew bosses with money and whiskey. Members of the worker-led ILA were denied Blue Books—blacklisted.

The Depression pushed dockworkers' low wages lower. By 1933, 50 percent of Blue-Book-carrying longshoremen were on welfare. That year, Roosevelt's National Industrial Recovery Act established workers' right to independent unions. After it passed, 95 percent of dockworkers deserted the Blue Book ILA and rejoined the worker-led union.

The newly reconstituted ILA was headed by Harry Bridges, an Irish-Australian hell raiser. Folksy and fiery, he demanded higher wages, abolition of Blue Books, and hiring through union-run halls. The shipping companies branded him a "Communist" and refused to negotiate.

On May 6th, 1934, the ILA went on strike, blocking the docks with picket lines. For two months, no cargo moved into or out of San Francisco. A month into the strike, more ships lay at anchor in San Francisco Bay than at any time since the Gold Rush, when thousands of vessels were abandoned by sailors who deserted for the diggings. The wharf rats were suddenly dukes of the docks and Harry Bridges was their king.

The companies waited, figuring they could starve the longshoremen back to work. But with no end in sight, they hired strikebreakers.

It turned out they didn't have to. In 1934, San Francisco's city government was staunchly Republican and fiercely conservative, totally opposed to Bridges and the ILA. One morning, pickets along the Embarcadero found themselves facing off not against strikebreakers but police. Mayor Angelo Rossi had put the police force at the disposal of the Industrial Association. Violence flared up almost daily.

Many longshoremen were Irish. So were most of the police. Neighbors stopped talking. In playgrounds all over town, strikers' children scuffled with cops' kids.

Eight weeks into the strike, on July 3rd, the shipping companies announced plans to reopen the docks. Trucks filled with cargo would roll—with police protection. Picketing longshoremen erected barricades, threw bricks at windshields, beat up drivers, and dumped cargo into the streets and burned it. The police, on horseback and motorcycles, fought them with clubs and the nation's first domestic use of a weapon introduced during World War I—tear gas.

Two days later, on July 5th, longshoremen and police clashed near the western anchorage of the Bay Bridge, then under construction. During the Battle of Rincon Hill, the police shot and killed two men, striking dockworker Howard Sperry and Nick Bordoise, of the cooks union. Thirty people were treated for gunshot wounds and forty-three were hospitalized with other injuries. Police were also injured, but most casualties were strikers and their supporters. In San Francisco, July 5th became known as Bloody Thursday.

San Franciscans were appalled at the carnage—particularly, at police clubbings of observers uninvolved in the strike. Public sympathy, formerly divided, swung decisively toward the longshoremen. Four days later, fifteen thousand strikers and sympathizers marched up Market Street in silence behind the coffins of the two slain men.

The governor, a conservative, called out the National Guard, ostensibly to protect state property. In fact, the Guard reinforced the police. Along the waterfront, Guardsmen set up machine-gun nests behind sandbag ramparts. Two thousand patrolled the Embarcadero carrying rifles with fixed bayonets. It looked like the show of force would break the strike.

Bridges knew he was outnumbered and outgunned. He appealed to the public, and the city responded. More than 120,000 San Franciscans, half the city's workforce, walked off their jobs. Stores closed and many businessmen and professionals announced support for what quickly became a general strike, only the second in U.S. history and by far the largest. For four days, San Francisco completely shut down, with the National Guard patrolling eerily empty streets.

Roosevelt cajoled both sides into arbitration. Federal arbitrators granted the longshoremen's demands: a wage hike, time-and-a-half for overtime, and an end to Blue Books, with all hiring through union-run halls.

Now Ed coveted the diary even more. Duffy's grandfather was a striker. Was Callahan's father a cop? Where were they on Bloody Thursday?

Fingers itching, Ed pulled out a book and reshelved it. Everything he knew about the strike had been written by journalists or historians. He knew of no participant accounts—except the Duffy diary. There had to be others.

His Google search turned up three hundred thousand hits. He scanned the first hundred. Six participant accounts, all brief, none substantial.

On a hunch, he hit a few keys and landed on the home page of Dissertation Abstracts, the compendium of PhD theses. Most dissertations were utterly forgettable, including his own on the demise of whaling out of Sausalito. But every now and then…

Ed typed in a few keywords. Two hundred listings. Forty minutes later, he was starting to go blind when he stumbled on a dissertation concerning the role of the city's newspapers during the strike. He'd researched nineteenth-century San Francisco journalism: Mark Twain, Jack London, Bret Harte, and Ambrose Bierce. But nothing more recent. He pulled out his credit card. A half-hour later, a pile of paper sat on his printer tray.

The *Foghorn* and three of the four other dailies had opposed the strike and condemned the strikers. Editorials called Bridges an anarchist and a Communist on Moscow's payroll. A *Chronicle* editorial asked, "Are the sane, sober working men of San Francisco to permit these communists to use them for the purpose of wrecking this country?"

But the dissertation focused on the strike's impact *inside* the newspapers. The publishers vehemently opposed it, but reporters and editors sympathized, many vocally. During the Depression, layoffs had decimated newsrooms, and survivors' wages had fallen to a pittance. Journalists had no union and anyone who so much as mentioned the nascent Newspaper Guild was fired.

The publishers insisted that coverage praise the police and flail the strikers. But every day, their papers published stories sympathetic to the strike. They couldn't fire everyone. So they turned to the typesetters. The publishers gave them a hefty raise. In exchange, the typesetters reworked copy downstream from editorial to make it more palatable to their benefactors. Reporters and editors went ballistic and joined the Newspaper Guild in droves. Within a few years, the Guild represented editorial employees at most Bay Area papers.

Great story, Ed mused. Conniving publishers, duplicitous typesetters, outrage in the newsroom. Ed felt a surge of freshly oxygenated blood. Labor Day was approaching. The typesetters were long gone, their jobs eliminated by computerization. But maybe he could find a geezer who'd been around then, or some reporters who recalled the early days of the Guild.

But would Bishop go for it?

Why not? The strike was ancient history. That publisher was long gone; his family had sold the paper ages ago. The *Horn* had published a *mea culpa* for supporting Japanese internment. This story was like that one. It was also in line with her marching orders. Solidly in the past. No current events. Ed dashed off a memo and hit Send.

Then he left another message for Detective Park.

—13—

"DADDY!" SONYA CALLED. "LOOK WHAT WE GOT!"

Ed glanced up from pruning the passionflower to see her bound across the deck and down the stairs. She was carrying a white box in shrink-wrap.

"What, honey?" Ed lay down his shears, removed his gloves, and wiped his brow.

Sonya thrust the box toward him. "Monopoly!"

Ed hadn't played in twenty years, but the box looked just the same.

"I couldn't resist," Julie said, at the deck rail, Jake happily straddling her hip. "It was on sale. And I'm so sick of Chutes and Ladders."

"Isn't Monopoly a bit old for Sonya?"

"No, Daddy, no. I *like* it!"

"She wanted it."

"Can we play?" Sonya jumped up and down. "Can we? Can we?"

"Sure, honey. But after lunch, okay? I still have some gardening left to do."

"And you, young lady," Julie added, "have to make your bed."

"Oh, Mommy." Sonya rolled her big eyes.

"Don't 'oh, Mommy' me. Go."

After lunch, with Jake napping, they unwrapped the game on the dining room table. First, they told Sonya in no uncertain terms that the dice, player pieces, houses, and hotels *absolutely* had to be kept away from her brother because he might choke. Sonya nodded solemnly.

Julie, the dressmaker, selected the thimble. Ed went for the sports car. Sonya couldn't decide between the horse or the dog. In the end, she opted for the pooch.

Julie doled out the money. Sonya's eyes widened at her big wad. She played with her piece, barking as Ed attempted to explain the rules.

"I don't want to buy property," Sonya announced, clutching the multi-colored bills. "I want to keep my money."

"If you want to keep your money, and make more," Ed advised, "you have to spend some on property. That's the whole point. You should buy as much as possible."

"Why?"

"Because you can charge rent. When Mom or I land on anything you own, we have to pay you."

"Why?"

"Because that's the way it is. You can charge even more when you get a monopoly and put up houses or a hotel."

"Why?"

"Because—" Ed took a breath. "Let's play. You'll get the hang of it."

They went around the board a few times buying property, landing on Community Chest, going to Jail and getting out, sometimes for free. Ed scored the first monopoly, the greens—Pacific, North Carolina, and Pennsylvania. Shortly after, Sonya landed on Pacific and he demanded double rent.

"But I *don't want to* pay double," Sonya whined. "Why do I have to pay more just because you got a monopoly?"

"Because monopolies can control pricing," Ed explained. "It's basic economics."

Sonya slumped in her chair, folded her arms, and thrust her lower lip.

"Read the bottom of your cards, honey," Julie explained, then read it for her. "'If a player owns all the lots of any color group, the rent is doubled on unimproved lots in that group.'"

"But I'll run out of money." Sonya whined.

"No, you won't. You get more every time you pass Go. And if you get a monopoly, you can charge double rent."

"But how can I get one? There's no more cards."

"We can trade," Julie said. "See? You have two reds, Illinois and Kentucky, and one orange, St. James. I have the red you need for a monopoly, and you have the orange I need. So we can trade, and both get monopolies."

"Okay."

"But wait," Ed interjected. "Red properties are worth more than orange, so you should pay Mom some money to make things even."

"But that's *no fair*," Sonya protested.

"Ed," Julie admonished, "forget it."

"I don't like this game." Sonya scowled.

"You'll like it more when you get some houses. Then you can charge even more."

"But houses cost too much," Sonya complained.

Ed's eyes found Julie's. "Tell me about it."

—14—

"WAY TO GO, CATHY," ED SAID, STEPPING INTO WHEELWRIGHT'S cubicle. "Great work!"

She held up a CD. "Our consolation prize for no arrest."

"Let's have a look."

She slipped it into the slot. It was a copy of Park's file on Duffy. Ordinarily, cops didn't give homicide files to reporters. But Cathy and the detective went way back. He owed her a favor. And Park understood the value of cordial relations with the *Horn*. With the case going cold, he felt just embarrassed enough to make her a copy, which was how Ed had it figured when he cajoled Cathy into asking him for the file.

"I still don't understand why you want it," she said. "It's not like you're going to pull a rabbit out of the hat."

"I knew him pretty well, and Tom knew him better. Maybe something Park didn't notice will ring a bell for one of us."

"Okay, Sherlock."

Wheelwright clicked and a list of documents appeared. Ed leaned into her screen. She clicked to a file called "Scene," transcripts of the interviews at the house. They read the five screens in silence.

"No cars in the driveway," Ed said. "No sounds of a fight. No one seen going in or out. Nobody saw anything. Jeez, whatever happened to nosy neighbors?"

Wheelwright clicked the lab report. No prints, except those of

Duffy and his sons. Not much DNA, and what little could be analyzed wasn't in any database. The restraints and other gear were all standard issue, and all Duffy's. No forced entry. No semen. And no lipstick on the glasses. The killer was almost certainly a man Duffy knew, and from the angle of the blows, he was right-handed.

A file called "Personal" showed no red flags in Duffy's e-mail or voicemail. No hostility. No threats. He paid his bills, owed nothing on his credit cards, and had no recent large cash withdrawals.

"So he wasn't being blackmailed."

A file called "Girlfriend" had her name blacked out and a notation by Park that she'd asked for anonymity. She was a VP at B of A and didn't want the boss to know she was kinky. On the weekend in question, she was in Seattle for her father's ninetieth birthday. There were copies of her round-trip ticket, and a photo from the party. She had no idea who might want to harm Duffy. According to the file, they'd been an item for a little more than a year. They met at Roissy. She was a sub and he was a dom. They played a little and then fell in love. She left her boyfriend and he left his wife. And as far as she knew, he never played with men, and was always the dom, never the sub.

"Well, he was as sub as they come when I found him."

"And no lipstick," Wheelwright said. "Even lip gloss leaves residue. It was Saturday night. No woman goes out without wearing something. The killer had to be a man."

"Either Duffy was bi in secret, or she didn't know her boyfriend very well."

A file called "Frayne" was an interview with Christopher Frayne, the man who'd lost his lover to Duffy and might have been filled with jealous rage. He had been in Reno playing blackjack and had the receipts to prove it.

"What's this mean?" Ed asked, pointing to a notation after Frayne's statement: "OK'd swab. Not performed."

"DNA," Wheelwright explained. "They asked him for a cheek swab. He said okay, but they didn't do it."

"Why not?"

"Didn't have to."

"I don't understand."

"Out in Televisionland, people think DNA is infallible. So the fact that he was happy to give the swab means he had nothing to hide. Ergo, they didn't have to do the test. But if Duffy didn't play with men—"

"He must have picked up the wrong woman."

"But no lipstick," Wheelwright said. "Maybe he asked her not to use anything. Or maybe she was butch."

"Or maybe the girlfriend didn't know everything about her man. Maybe he was a dom with women, but a sub with men."

A file called "Trust" documented the trust Duffy had set up for his boys as part of the divorce. One section was underlined. In the event of his death, everything passed to the trust, except some photos that went to his sister, Beth. The trustee was his brother.

"Sheila can't touch the money, so she has no financial motive."

"Here's her file." Wheelwright clicked.

This was the big interview. About half the time in murder cases, the spouse or ex is the killer. Park had conducted the interview with another detective, Curtis Fluker, and a psychologist, Mary Ann Charles, PhD.

Sheila said her ex had no enemies she knew of, but that since he'd moved out, they'd had very little contact, just arrangements about the boys. She and Duffy were basically happy for sixteen years. Then he got interested in BDSM. She hated it. That's what broke them up. Early on, he asked her to join him. She refused and begged him to stop. When he began hanging out at Roissy, she insisted he talk to their priest. When that didn't turn him around, she insisted on couples counseling. And when that didn't work, she threw him out.

For the millionth time, Ed marveled at the fragility of marriage, how Dr. Jekyll could become Mr. Hyde.

But on the night in question, Sheila had a rock-solid alibi. The file included names and contact information for a dozen people who'd seen her and her boyfriend, Billy Jameson, at the Plough and

Stars. Jameson's driver's license photo showed he was the big guy who'd propped her up at the funeral.

Sheila told the cops that Billy was an old friend. They had dated in high school, but she picked Duffy. Billy married someone else and eventually divorced. Six months ago, he heard his old flame was available, and they got back together. He was a contractor. No priors.

A file titled "Alvarez" documented Pedro's call to the detective and his report of the Planning hearing where Duffy and Mitchell Callahan almost came to blows.

"Who's Mitchell Callahan?" Wheelwright asked.

"Big developer. Locked horns with Duffy over the Armory. Had to be restrained from socking him."

Park had interviewed Callahan, who could prove that he was at a Sacred Heart fundraiser until nine, and at his daughter's house till eleven.

"But Duffy got it between nine and *midnight*," Ed said, "so Callahan still had an hour."

Park had asked Callahan for a cheek swab, but he refused. Park asked the DA for a court order, but got denied. The DA said Callahan was seventy-five years old, had no priors, and was well-known in the business community. People seventy-five and older committed less than 3 percent of all murders. There was no evidence that Callahan was kinky. And who goes from church to his daughter's and then kills a guy?

"I don't know," Ed said. "He had the means, the motive, and an hour of opportunity."

Two pages documented police contact with the sex clubs, including the flyer Park posted. But no one came forward with anything.

"So..." Ed said.

"So either Sang gets lucky real quick," Wheelwright said, "or this one's on ice. Looks like Park had it right at the scene. Kinky sex gone bad."

"I'm surprised Park didn't lean harder on Callahan."

"He's got seventeen open cases."

"I'd like Tom to have a look."

Wheelwright hit a button and the disk ejected. Ed held it by the edges. "I almost forgot. Did Park mention the diary?"

"No."

"Damn. He's still got it, and I still want it."

"Call him."

"I have. Four times."

"Doesn't look like it has any relevance. You'll get it. Eventually."

When Ed returned from leaving the CD with Ferguson, the light on his phone was blinking. The message was from Park. "You can pick up the envelope any time. Good luck with that diary. It's incoherent."

—15—

I'm writin this because Susie dared me. I'm writin this because she's fed up hearin me bellyache about Mike. I'm writin this because she shoved this notebook under me nose at dinner. Here ye go, ye spiteful man, she says, pour yer blessed heart out. I'm no writer, I says, I havent written a damn thing since ninth grade and ye know it. Well, she says, your one helluva talker. Ye been talkin my ear off about Mike for weeks. Write it down, why don you? I cant, woman, I says. Yes ye can. Heres yer first line: I'm writin this because—No fuckin way, I says. Susie flinches and the kids go quiet around the table. Susie opens the notebook and pulls a pen from the drawer. Here, Mr. Foul Mouth, she says, I dare ye. She crosses her arms like to stop a truck. Ye dare me, do ye? Well, I says, Patrick Duffy never shrinks from a dare.

I'm writin this because Father Gallagher says it will help me forgive Mike, understand him. What does that drunk old gasbag know? Forgive Mike? Understand? Never. Mike, me brother, how could ye? How could ye crack good Irish heads?

I understan Sean doin it, that son of a bitch. Clubbin the lads. Callin us Communists. Knowin us his whole life don count for nothin with that bastard. Years of him and his boys gettin cut in on the swag don count for nothin neither. If the brass calls us Bolsheviks, then by Jesus thats what we are. But Mike, yer not that way. Leastways, I never thought you was. Mike, what have ye done, lad? What have ye done?

I'm writin this because if I don do somethin besides drinkin I'll surely drown. With the strike, McCarthy dropped his prices. Thats been good for me and the boys. And he's a good man, Davey McCarthy is, extendin credit. Course Susie don like it one bit. I'll not have ye drink yerself to death, she says, I'll jes not have it. Well, I says, what else is a man to do when his best friend—but hes no friend o mine. Never again.

I'm writin this so I don march over there and break every bone in Mike's body. Itd serve Susie right if I did. Shes the one stopped me from rebuildin the fence. No fence is comin between Liza and me, she says. I'll jes not have it. But I left the post holes so he'd know. Oh Mike, me heart's a dry twig snapped in two.

I'm writin this because tomorrow mornin I'll be out there in me padded coat, helmet and boots, with me bat. And they'll be out there, the long blue line with their clubs and horses. We'll mix it up and good lads will fall. And if I get my hands on certain ones o them—Hear me Sean? Hear me Mike?—if I get a good swing, yell go down and never get up. No, good Lord, I don mean that. Not Mike anyways. Or maybe I do. I have no fuckin idea. Me brother. No! Brother no more.

I'm writin this because I don understan. We was best friends forever. Then it goes to hell. I'm writin this because me eyes have cried an ocean. I'm writin this because I don know what else to do.

The diary's opening entry was dated June 1, 1934, three weeks into the strike and a week after the police and strikers began skirmishing along the Embarcadero. Susie had to be Pat's wife. Mike and Sean were clearly cops—"the long blue line with their clubs"—and cops Pat knew well. Mike was also a close friend—"me brother"—or had been until he started battling the strikers. Mike had lived nearby. Pat wrote about "marching over there," and not even a fence between them, until the strike, when Pat dug post holes for a new one. Then Susie stopped him. Had Mike's house once stood on the vacant lot?

There was more to the entry. Pat wrote about "Harry"—presumably Harry Bridges. He alluded to breaking the windows of a police car he and some friends spotted parked off the Embarcadero, and afterwards celebrating over beers.

But as the entry continued, its pages became marred by circular amber stains and smudged ink. Pat's penmanship, poor to begin with, became illegible. By the end of the entry, the few recognizable words made little sense. Ed flipped pages. Park was right. Most of it was incomprehensible. No wonder Duffy had asked for help.

Ed sighed. He'd seen similar stains on other primary sources. The circles marked the bottoms of tumblers overflowing with liquor. Pat wrote while drinking, while drunk. Most of the entries were like the opener. They began coherently enough, but after a few pages, circular stains appeared, followed by spills and smudged ink, and the words became unintelligible.

Throughout June 1934, Pat wrote about clashes on the docks. He got clubbed on the shoulder and had to stop picketing for a few days. He and Susie argued about him returning.

Yer in no shape, she says. I says I have me duty. I have to stand with Harry and the lads. Yer a stubborn man, she says. When will ye think of yer family? I am thinking of me family, woman. Who do ye think I'm takin billy blows for? For us. So we can eat.

Pat also observed that he never saw Mike on the docks. *He must know the piers I'm picketin. He makes sure hes nowhere near. Its a good thing, too, for his sake—and Liza and the kids.*

Liza had to be Mike's wife.

In addition to his rage at Mike, Pat was none too pleased with his wife. Susie and Liza were close. Despite their husbands' falling out, they continued to visit daily, which infuriated Pat.

Which side are ye on, woman? Ye know full well, Patrick, yours and the union. But ye keep carryin on with the other side. It aint right. Feud with Mike if you like, but I'll not have ye interferin with Liza and me. Were Keenans. Blood goes deeper. So does a friendship yeve had yer whole life. Leastways it should. Not this time, I says, not when the cops do the scabbin. Susie shakes her head and gives me her ice look. She turns her back and marches over and climbs the stairs. I want to cry. I want things back like they was. But thats all over now. Mike's no friend of mine. No more. Never again.

Entries for the rest of June chronicled the seesaw on the docks. The police had clubs, horses, motorcycles, fire hoses, and tear gas—

plus guns, though they didn't use them. The strikers had baseball bats, ax handles, bricks, slingshots, and cobblestones. Every day there was blood in the streets.

On June 19th, Pat and Mike had their first contact since the police began fighting the strikers. A cop Pat knew, Jimmy O'Hara, came at him with his club raised. Pat raised his bat and screamed at Jimmy to back off. He did. That evening, Pat sat in his backyard drinking and hurling invectives at Mike.

Jimmy's a coward, I says, and so are ye, Michael Kincaid, ye son of a whore. Mike was in the house. I seen him in the window. I kept up. Fuckin this. Fuckin that. Susie come out and says, Mind yer tongue. Ye got children. Ye got neighbors. And ye got a wife whos sore embarrassed. Embarrassed? About yer man defendin his livelihood? Then who come out his back door? The son of a whore himself. I've had enough of yer cussin, he says, ye know why I'm doing it. No I don, I says, I got no fuckin idea. He says, ye know I got a gun to me head. Malarkey, I says. Ye can quit. Ye can walk away. Mike looks down at his shoes. He steps down the stair. Hear me out, he says. Theres things ye don know. Turn yerself around, I says. If ye dare set foot on my property, ye better come armed—because I am. And I shows him me hook.

Pat's hook had to be a cargo hook. It certainly appeared that Mike lived in a house that once stood on the vacant lot.

Mike stopped dead in his tracks, jes like Jimmy. He turned aroun and went back inside. Fuckin coward.

On July 3rd, the shipping companies announced their plan to reopen the docks by force. The strikers dug in.

Theyll not get a single truck through our lines. We got sand bags. We're buildin barricades. We got slingshots. Bolts through their windshields. We got ice picks lashed to poles for popping tires. We got strong hands itching to turn trucks over and set em ablaze. And if the boys in blue draw their guns, some of our lads have guns too.

There was no entry for July 5, Bloody Thursday, nor for the following day. Then, on July 7:

Im at me post by Pier 30 when we hear shoutin and see a dust-up at the foot of Rincon. Trucks pull up. Flaps open. A big lot o them jump out.

A long blue line is movin on our lads. And horses. Out of nowhere. Fuckin horses. Someone yells, Come on! We're all runnin over there quick like, maybe 30 of us. Another gang is runnin up from Pier 24. We're all lookin at the horses. Huge vicious beasts. Our lads fall back.

Just then, loud pops. Jesus, Mary, and Joseph. Gunshots! I drop down behind a parked car. Im in the gutter. More shots. I cant move. I cant think. Im like to piss myself. I peek around the bumper. I see two lads in a pool of blood, one still, the other floppin like a fish just landed. Then he stops movin. Someone rolls them over. It's Howie, he yells, Howie Sperry. Oh my Lord. Howie! I knowed him since third grade. Know his whole family. Sons o bitches. Those sons o bitches killed Howie!

I crawl back, see the horses bearin down. Cops are swingin clubs from their backs. Our boys turn and run. Then someone jumps to the roof of a car shoutin stand firm! Its Harry. The fleein lads come back and do like he did, jump on cars to gain height against the beasts. They start throwin things and taking aim with slings. A horse goes down. Then another. We circle round behind the police. We mix it up. Clubs flyin. I take a hit, but give better than I get. I'm swinging for Howie. But we're outnumbered, pushed back toward the main scuffle. Then someone shouts Harry! Run! Its boys in blue clubs raised makin right for him. And whos leadin it? Sean, that fuck, clubbin Harry. And behind him, club raised, eyes wild, I see—oh me poor hearts breakin.

That page was stained with amber circles and the entry became illegible.

Ed felt a moment of déjà vu. The scene Pat described—the cop clubbing Bridges—was among the most famous photos to come out of the strike. Pat must have been within spitting distance of the photographer.

July 9th marked the slain strikers' funeral. Pat, Susie, and their children were among the fifteen thousand who marched silently up Market Street behind their coffins. Afterwards, some buddies joined Pat in his back yard. They drank beer and hurled curses at the man of the house across the way.

Musta been midnight. I was in the livin room listenin to Benny Goodman while conversin with John Barleycorn. Susie come down sayin she smells smoke. Then we see flames. Susie screams Liza! The children! She runs over. Mike's house is goin up like Christmas wrap. I yell Susie stop! She gets to the stair. The heat pushes her back. I'm yellin Susie! For the love of God! You crazy? She runs back, flies past me like the Devils after her, sayin I got to get over there. She flings open the front door.

Theres Liza and the kids about to ring the bell. Wheres Mike? At the McCains. And thats where were goin. No, come in, come in here, Susie says. Ill not do that, Liza says. Well be at the McCains. Susie goes with them. I go to the back porch and watch Mikes house burn. Fire trucks pull up. Theyre sprayin water, but its no use. The house is too far gone.

Then circles appeared. Several unintelligible pages later, Pat ended the entry in a very unsteady hand:

Son of a bitch got what he deserved. Got less than he deserved.

After that entry, something changed. Pat seemed to lose interest in the diary. Entries became less frequent and shorter, almost telegraphic.

A day after the fire, Pat was arrested, evidently charged with arson. The diary did not elaborate. A union lawyer bailed him out. But he wrote very little about it. Or his time in jail. Or his role in the fire. All he wrote was:

I knowed theyd come for me. Knowed it like I know Mikes goin to hell.

On July 16, the General Strike began. It lasted four days. With National Guard machine guns in place along the Embarcadero and a dusk-to-dawn curfew, Pat wrote little notes about fixing cars and sweeping up at St. Paul's for Father Gallagher and someone named Molly. He didn't mention the arson charge.

Ed didn't know what to think. Pat was a staunch union man keeping a diary in the middle of the largest general strike in U.S. history, but he had next to nothing to say about it. That made no sense.

The last entry was dated July 24, two weeks after the fire. Pat's penmanship was shaky and the pages were stained:

Susie come down with the kids. Everyone dressed for church. Where you off to? St. Pauls, she says. Yer a terrible liar, I say. Where? It takes a while but finally she spills. A farewell party. She don have to say for who.

So theyre leavin. Yes. She tears up. I step in front of her. No wife o mine is goin to that. Not for the like of them. She give me a look could melt glass. No husband o mine can stop me. The kids eyes are like hubcaps. Im blockin the door, starin down at her. Let me pass, Patrick, she says all quiet like, the way she does when she wont be crossed. No fuckin way, I says. She bolts for the back. I chase her into the kitchen, grab her arm. Lemme go, she screams, flailin at me. I grab her other arm. The kids start cryin. Yer stayin right here. She starts screamin and carryin on. Youll not deny me a last embrace with Liza. Yer stayin right here. No party for the like of them. Next thing I know, she gets a hand free and grabs the big knife. Shes got it raised. Shes yellin in a voice Ive never heard and hope never to hear again. Shes screamin Stand aside, Patrick Duffy! Stand aside or yell know the wrath of God and the Keenans! It was a voice from hell. I let her pass. Then I sat down and cried.

The pages were smudged, but there were no brown circles. That could mean only one thing. Tears. Ed could barely read the diary's final words:

I cried for the strife in me marriage. I cried for the children seein it. I cried for me poor broken heart. I cried for the loss of me one true friend. Ill be cryin till the day I die. I imagine Mike will too.

As Ed closed the notebook, he noticed a square of paper stuck to its back cover by a spot of something purple. Grape jam? He peeled it off and saw a PG&E bill. Duffy must have placed the diary on top of it. When he slipped the notebooks into the envelope, the bill went with them.

In the bill's margins, Ed noticed phone numbers next to names in shorthand: Rod, Simon O'C, Eric McC., VT Ave. Partners, CT Ave. Devel., and MG Prop.

Eric McC had to be Eric McCain, the childhood friend who became the big developer. Rod and Simon O'C were probably other buddies. The other three looked like businesses. Real estate ventures?

Vermont and Connecticut were streets on Potrero Hill. Its north side had spectacular views of downtown and housing prices to match. Now the University of California was building a biotech campus at the base of the hill on a huge tract of derelict rail yards and warehouses. The development had sent Potrero Hill real estate into the stratosphere. Presumably Vermont Avenue Partners and the other ventures were players in that story. Duffy was probably covering it before his own story ended.

Ed crumpled the bill and was about to toss it. Then the historian in him decided otherwise. *Never discard a primary source.* It was just one slip of paper. It took up no space. He flattened it and stuffed it into the envelope.

—16—

THE *FOGHORN*'S ELECTRONIC ARCHIVE WENT BACK TO 1970. FOR everything earlier, the paper had microfilm and a morgue stretching back to Volume One, Number One, March 11, 1874. But with the *Horn* hemorrhaging money, the suits had laid off the librarian and donated the big bound volumes of yellowed newsprint to the Bancroft Library at Cal. The paper retained its microfilm, but with no librarian, the collection was a mess. Ed couldn't find the reel he needed, so he headed for the main branch of the public library.

Ed loved its periodicals room. It held microfilm of every paper of consequence ever published in San Francisco all the way back to the pre-Gold Rush *California Star*.

He started with the *Horn*. He found 1934, fished out July, and threaded the celluloid ribbon through the machine. Pages flew by in a blur. He slowed when he reached July 10, the day after Mike's house burned, the first day it could have gotten ink.

Ed turned the focus knob. Page One was devoted to the huge funeral march. No surprise. The rest of A-news dealt with the strike. Two thousand Guard troops patrolling the streets. Their commander saying he was determined to maintain order. The police chief, the mayor, and the governor all pleading for calm. The Industrial Association demanding that the strikers stop rioting and accept their generous offer. The union calling for a general strike. And Roosevelt appealing to both sides to bargain in good faith. There was nothing about a fire on Twenty-seventh Street.

The next day, July 11, Ed found a little headline: "Dock Worker Charged in Mission Fire." The story ran just one graf. Striking longshoreman Patrick Duffy of Twenty-sixth Street had been charged with arson in connection with a fire at the Twenty-seventh Street home of San Francisco police officer Michael Kincaid. Ed swiped his credit card and hit Print.

He searched through several months but found nothing more about the fire or arson charge.

He did the same with the other papers. The *Examiner* and the *Call-Bulletin* both mentioned the fire. The *News* and the *Chronicle* mentioned the arrest. None said any more.

The *Chronicle* was the final paper Ed checked. As he rewound the microfilm, he happened to pause on July 6, the day after Bloody Thursday. The screen filled with photos of the battle, including the famous one—the cop raising a club over a skinny man on the pavement in a fetal position. The caption read: "Sergeant Sean Callahan attempts to subdue Harry Bridges." *Subdue?* More like what happened to Duffy. Ed magnified the image then printed it.

The photo was grainy but powerful. You could see the hatred in Callahan's face. On the right, strikers were scuffling with police in an effort to rescue their leader. On the left, several cops had Callahan's back. The diary had said Mike was right behind Sean, club raised. And there he was, looking more appalled than vicious.

Back at the office, Ed called the Police Department and asked for PR. The woman spoke with a Russian accent.

"How long does the department keep records?"

"Depends. What kind?"

"Arrests. And case dispositions."

"Ten years here. Another fifty in the archive."

"Then what?"

"Bye bye."

"You throw them away?" As a historian, Ed felt offended.

"Yes."

Sixty years of retrievable records, and wouldn't you know, the fire was seventy-odd years ago.

Ed Googled the union. The home page had an East Bay phone number. Ever since cargo had become containerized, shipping had moved to the Port of Oakland. San Francisco's piers were turning into offices and restaurants.

The union's records went back to 1910, but included only members' vital statistics, dues, and offices held.

Ed was out of ideas. Had Pat torched Mike's house? Pat didn't write a word, which was odd. In diaries, people usually told their secrets. Of course, between the lines, there was certainly room to speculate that Pat lit the match. He'd been drinking most of the day. He'd been furious with Mike for weeks. Emotions around Bloody Thursday and the funeral could easily have turned his thoughts to kerosene. When he was arrested, he wrote, "I knew they'd come for me," and Mike "got *less* than he deserved." And after the house burned, Pat seemed to experience a catharsis. His business was concluded. He no longer needed the diary afterward, presumably, having come up with a more effective therapy.

But if Pat set the fire, why no follow-up to his arrest? Why no trial? Given the war on the docks, it seemed like arson at a cop's home by a striker would have become a *cause celebre*, with the cops screaming for Pat's head and the union embracing him as a martyr. But nothing like that had happened. After Pat's arrest, the story died. Not another word was published.

Back at the office, Ed had e-mail from Bishop. She was open to more coverage of the 1934 strike, but wasn't interested in the publishers paying off the typesetters to slant coverage. "Makes the paper look bad."

—17—

JULIE WANTED TO PAY A CONDOLENCE CALL. A DECENT INTERVAL HAD passed since the funeral, and maybe Sheila knew something about the fire. Ed called her.

They parked by the dreamy lagoon bordering the Greek temple. It was the last vestige of the 1915 Panama-Pacific International Exposition, the huge party San Francisco threw to celebrate its resurrection from 1906 and the opening of the Panama Canal. Now it housed the Exploratorium, the hands-on science museum Sonya loved.

It was a cool summer afternoon. The gusty breeze carried a salty tang, the harbinger of fog. The posh homes bordering the lagoon made Ed feel poor. Duffy always said he had "three flats," but that was like calling the White House a single-family home. On a newspaperman's salary, Duffy never could have afforded his building. But real estate was not just his beat; he also invested, started out with two ramshackle flats in Glen Park, and over sixteen years bought and sold two- and three-flat buildings, traded up, and eventually landed in the Marina.

A buzzer let them in. They climbed three long carpeted flights of stairs, strewn with sweatshirts and sports gear. The top landing offered a postcard view through beveled glass of the bay and the towers of Golden Gate Bridge.

Sheila had not dressed for their visit. She wore a shapeless warm-up suit with her strawberry-blonde hair pulled into a ponytail. Her cheeks were hollow, her eyes dark. They each embraced her, and she managed a weak smile.

Julie presented a plate of homemade brownies. Sheila accepted them on autopilot. The flat was about twice the size of their house, with ceilings a foot higher. Ed felt jealous. She ushered them into the living room, which looked across the Bay to Tiburon. For such a grand flat, the furnishings were decidedly funky, with tidiness fighting a losing battle against two teenagers.

"Thank you for calling," Sheila said. "You were on my list, but things have been…difficult. Especially for the boys."

"How are they doing?" Ed asked.

"As you'd expect. They adored their father."

Sheila nodded toward the sofa, then shuffled into the kitchen and returned carrying a tray with a teapot, three cups, the brownies, and a tin of butter cookies with a sticker: *Made in Cork, Ireland*. She set the tray on the coffee table, dropped into a chair, and poured tea, motioning toward the sweets as if to say help yourself.

"I hope you got our note," Julie said. "Terrible thing."

"I did. Thank you."

"Sorry it's taken a while to call," Julie continued, "but when we saw the crowd at the funeral, we figured you'd be inundated and maybe we should wait."

"Yes, thank you. It's been wall-to-wall people. And that's helped. But the house is a mess. I'm a mess. And the boys are having a hard time. Death is bad enough, but murder is worse. Especially when they don't know who did it." She sipped tea. "The one *good* thing has been Billy. Did you meet him? Billy Jameson?"

"Just briefly, at the funeral."

"He's been wonderful, especially with the boys. We all met in grade school—Billy, Ryan, and me. It's a comfort to the boys that Billy knew their dad so well. He's told them stories I didn't even know."

"And how are *you*, Sheila?"

She teared up. "I don't know. Shocked, confused, grieving. I'll always love Ryan. But it's been a while since I was *in love* with him.

What's it been? A few weeks? But to me, I lost him over a year ago—" She bit her lip. "Which is why you were on my list to call. I wanted to thank you both."

"For what?"

"For what the paper said—what it *didn't* say. Things have been hard enough. I'm grateful I haven't had to deal with *that*. The whole world knowing."

Ed and Julie exchanged a glance. "We really didn't have anything to do with it," Ed said. "It was Walt's call." *And it had nothing to do with you.*

"I know. But I think he knew that people at the paper wanted Ry remembered for who he *really* was, not...." She wiped her eyes and blew her nose. "I'm grateful I didn't have to explain it to the boys—because I *can't*. And I'm grateful they don't have to bear that cross the rest of their lives."

"We are, too."

"The thing is, I *predicted* it. I warned him. When he started playing—that's what he called it, *playing*—I told him, 'You could get hurt, maybe even killed.' But did he listen?" She stared out the window. "When the police showed up, my first thought was: Oh God, one of the boys! When they said no, Ryan, they didn't have to say another word. I knew. I knew immediately."

Sheila asked about Sonya, and they joked about her passion for *American Idol*. Then Sheila recalled that the last time she'd seen them, Julie was pregnant. They told her about Jake from birth to teething and day care.

"Since you go so far back with the Duffys," Ed ventured, "I'm wondering if you know anything about a fire that destroyed the house behind theirs."

"No. I didn't even know there *was* a house. When was this?"

"1934."

"And you're interested...why?"

"Because it looks like Ryan's grandfather set it. He kept a diary. Ryan found it, didn't understand it, and asked me to help. That's why I went over there that morning."

"Ry never mentioned any fire. Neither did his parents."

"Did you know his *grand*parents? Pat and Susie?"

"I met them. In high school, when we started dating. Grandma Susie had an oxygen tank and tubes in her nose. Grandpa Pat had a stroke. They just sat in the living room and watched TV."

"Did Ryan talk about them?"

"Not much. Just that Susie planted the garden and Pat had worked on the docks and at St. Paul's."

"I assume you knew Ryan's parents."

"Oh, sure. His father was quiet. Spent most of his time in the basement brewing beer. Catherine I liked. We were close. Such a shame what's happened to her."

"You mean the Alzheimer's."

"Yes. Bethie says she doesn't recognize anyone."

"Beth?"

"Ryan's sister."

"Do you recall Ryan's parents ever talking about Pat and Susie?"

"No."

"Or Mike and Liza Kincaid?"

"Who?"

"The people who owned the house that burned."

"No."

"But you knew that Ryan's family owned the lot."

"Oh, sure, Susie's garden, his grandmother's pride and joy. But by the time I showed up, she couldn't garden anymore. Catherine took it over, and truth be told, made it better. Catherine had a real green thumb. But she credited everything to her mother-in-law: Susie's roses, Susie's avocado. Susie's garden."

Ed flashed on the withered remnants. "I'm wondering if any elderly Duffys are still alive, someone who might know about the fire."

"Just Aunt Clara. She's the last of that generation."

"How old is she?"

"Eighty-eight."

So Clara was in her teens during the strike, Ed thought. She had to know about the fire.

"How's she related?"

"Ry's great aunt. Pat's youngest sister."

"Does she live in the city?"

"An assisted-living place on Van Ness."

"You have any contact with her?"

"Quite a bit, actually." Sheila's lips curled into a thin smile. "I love her dearly. Growing up she was Granny Clara to me. She wasn't my real grandma. We're not blood. But when she was a teenager, she babysat my mother and loved her. Attended my parents' wedding. My christening. Then I married Ryan and Granny Clara and I *were* family. She's still sharp as a tack. Remembers what she wore to every St. Patty's party they ever had."

"Were she and Pat close?"

"She mentions him now and again. Susie, too. She lived a few blocks from them for, oh, it must have been fifty years. But like I said, Pat's been dead since I was in high school, and Susie died right after the Loma Prieta." The big earthquake in 1989. "But Clara I visit every few weeks. Billy and I take her to the Plough and Stars. They don't have Guinness where she lives. We were there—" She inhaled sharply. "That night."

Sheila rose and stepped into the kitchen to a laptop on the counter. She wrote on a slip of paper and handed it to Ed. "Her address and phone number."

"She won't mind if I call?"

"Mind? She's a lonely old woman. She'll love the company. Oh, and I gave you Bethie, too. She's the family historian. She might know about that fire."

Ed flashed on the funeral. "Is Clara in a wheelchair?"

Sheila's brow furrowed. "No."

"At St. Paul's, I saw you embrace an old woman in a wheelchair pushed by—" Ed blanked on the name. "Some developer."

"Oh, Molly McCain. Eric's grandmother, old friend of the family. Lived a few doors down from Ryan's grandparents. She's in a nursing home now."

"Did she know them?"

"I assume."

"I understand Eric and Ryan were friends."

"Grew up on the same block, went to St. Paul's together. Eric was a couple years older. Kevin's best friend—that's Ry's older brother. We were all in the same crowd. I was with Ry, but Eric was a real charmer. All the girls loved him. The bad boy with the melt-your-heart smile."

"Bad boy?"

"Oh, you know, cut classes, got in trouble. Eric didn't like school. His father was a carpenter. Taught him the trade. Eric thought high school was a waste when he could make good money working. But his parents made him stay until he graduated—barely. Then he worked construction. Became a contractor, then a developer. Now he's very successful. Whenever my boys mess up in school, I console myself with how Eric was—and how he turned out."

"You still friends?"

"Sort of. After high school, we lost touch. But when Ry started writing about real estate, Eric was making a name as a developer, and he had money to throw around. Used to take us out to fancy dinners. Lobbied Ry about projects—his own and other people's."

"How often?"

"Couple times a year."

"It ever work?" There was the flap about Duffy's support for McCain's Civic Center transit village.

Sheila shrugged.

"Do you have any idea how I might contact McCain's grandmother?"

"Try Eric. I think it's McCain Development."

"At the funeral, I also noticed that you received condolences from Mitchell Callahan."

"Yes. Old friend of Billy's. Actually, Billy's dad's."

"Are you aware that Ryan crossed swords with him over the Armory?"

"No."

"I'm surprised. Callahan wanted to renovate it. Ryan wanted it torn down for a park."

"When was this?"

"Not too long ago."

"Must have been when Ry and I were having our troubles. We barely spoke and I wasn't reading the paper."

Julie nudged Ed. As they rose to leave, the phone rang. Sheila stared at it.

"Watch," she predicted, "another call about the house. Hello?" She rolled her eyes. "No. It's not for sale. No—" Her pitch rose. "The lot's not for sale either. I don't even own them. No." She glowered at the phone. "*Please* stop calling me." She tossed the receiver into the cradle. "Since the funeral, I've been getting two calls a day. Everybody wants Twenty-sixth Street."

"How'd you know the call would be about the house?" Julie asked.

"Friends call my cell."

"That's what happens in a hot market," Ed offered. "The realtors read the obits and call the next of kin. What's going to happen with the house?"

Sheila sighed. "I don't know. Kevin's dealing with it."

"Sorry, who's Kevin?"

"Ry's brother. He's the executor. It's complicated. The one good thing that came out of the divorce was that Ry bought it. Everyone was so happy to keep it in the family. No one wants to sell. But legally, Kevin has a responsibility to the boys' trust to get an income out of it, by selling or renting. But renting it means fixing it up. It needs a lot of work, and the money would have to come from the trust. So I don't know. Kevin's talking to Simon—Simon O'Connor, Ry's lawyer, another grade school friend."

Simon O'Connor. The name rang a bell, but Ed couldn't place it.

"Billy says he'll give Kevin a deal to get it rentable. So we'll see."

"And the lot?"

"The family owns it, including the boys now. When Ry bought

the house, the family agreed to sell the lot and use the money to pay for Catherine's care. But now everything's in limbo. I suppose they'll eventually sell it."

"Which is why the realtors keep calling."

"I guess."

"I'm curious. Did you catch that caller's name?"

She waved a dismissive hand. "Scott Something from Connecticut Whatever."

As they walked back to the car, an icy wind ran its fingers through their hair. Ed zipped up and Julie huddled into a raised collar. Summer in San Francisco.

It was a good bet the caller was from Connecticut Avenue Development, one of the companies on Duffy's utility bill. Connecticut traversed Potrero Hill. Only that was Connecticut *Street*. This was *Avenue*. Odd.

As Ed started the car, he remembered how he knew Simon O'Connor. On the PG&E bill, right above CT Ave. Devel. Duffy had written Simon O'C. It had to be him.

Sheila was right. Death was hard but murder was harder, especially when the killer got away with it. What could Ed do? Just one thing, it seemed: grant Duffy's last request, make sense of the diary. But seventy years after the fact, the chances of that looked pretty slim.

—18—

THE BELL CHIMED, FOLLOWED BY SEVERAL SHARP RAPS ON THE DOOR.

"Can you get that?" Ed called. "I'm changing Jake!"

"I'm slicing watermelon!" Julie yelled back. "Sonya, see who it is."

Sonya scampered down the hall, then veered into the living room. Her parents had trained her never to just open the door. She was to identify the person first, and for those she didn't know, she was to call one of them. Sonya was still too short to use the peephole, but the living room window looked out to the porch.

"It's a man!" Sonya shouted. "A tall man—with no hair!"

"Who is it?" Julie asked through the door, a towel in her hands.

"Police officer. Arson investigations."

Julie opened the door. "Arson?"

He wore a navy blue suit and a striped tie. He introduced himself as Steven O'Farrell, flashed a badge, and asked, "Is this the home of Edward Rosenberg?"

"Yes. What's this about?"

"Is Mr. Rosenberg at home?"

"Why?" Julie still had some of the Bronx in her.

"I need to speak with him." The cop smiled. He looked friendly.

"Ed! Police!"

Ed handed Jake to Julie and invited the officer in. O'Farrell looked around fifty. He had a shaved head and a white goatee.

"Did you say *arson*?"

"I did."

"Are you sure you have the right Ed Rosenberg? I don't know anything about any arson."

O'Farrell stated an address on Twenty-sixth Street. Duffy's house. "You know anything about the fire there last night?"

"What?" Ed's jaw dropped. "No! What happened?"

"Somebody tossed a pineapple lamp through the front window."

"My God!"

"Luckily, a neighbor called 911. But the living room burned."

"Jesus," Ed said. "Julie! Someone tried to burn Duffy's!" He turned back to the arson investigator. "So, why are you here?"

"Sir, where were you last night between eleven and midnight?"

"What? You're accusing *me*?"

O'Farrell looked Ed in the eye. "No."

"Then why the question?"

"Just following up on some information."

"What information?"

"Three days ago, did you visit Sheila Duffy, widow of the owner of that house?"

"Yes. She's a friend."

"Did you ask Ms. Duffy about a fire at that address?"

"No! I asked her about a fire, but not at *that* address—at the house *behind* it, on *Twenty-seventh* Street. But that fire happened seventy years ago."

"I see." His voice softened. "And why the interest in that fire?"

Ed explained who he was, and that he hoped to write a column on the dock strike, how it turned friends into enemies, and how it looked like Pat set the blaze that burned the Kincaid home to the ground. "I asked Sheila if she knew anything about the fire. She didn't."

"I see. But I still need to ask where you were last night."

"You're joking, right?"

"No, I'm quite serious." O'Farrell's eyes were gas-flame blue and burned into Ed's. "Just a formality."

Ed swallowed hard and said, "My wife and I saw a play with

friends. Then we came back here for coffee and dessert. Our friends left around 11:30."

"And after that?"

"I took the babysitter home and went to bed. If you like, I can put you in touch with our friends and the sitter. And the theater. The tickets were will call. They'll have a record."

"That won't be necessary. Do you know anyone who might have reason to burn the Duffy home?"

"No. But it was a pineapple lamp?"

"Yes."

"Like the loft fires. But they've all been big buildings under construction. This is a single-family home."

"Correct."

"So…?"

"That's what I'm trying to determine. Gangs. Copycats. Dumbass kids out for kicks. We don't know. It was a pretty crude device."

"Why Duffy's house?"

"Not clear. But it was vacant and dilapidated. Property like that attracts vandalism."

"You know Duffy was murdered in his living room."

"Of course," O'Farrell said. "But I seriously doubt this has anything to do with that."

"Why?"

"Instinct. I've been a cop twenty-one years. A murderer doesn't return to the scene weeks later and torch the house."

"Unless he wants to destroy something he left behind."

"I talked to the detective and the techs. They went over the place pretty good. I'm betting there was nothing to find." Then he added, "You work for the *Foghorn*. So you knew Duffy through the paper?"

Ed said he did.

"I'm wondering if the fire might have something to do with his job. He wrote about real estate, right?"

"Yes."

"And he supported loft development in the Mission."

"Correct."

"Like the ones that have burned recently—"

"What are you saying? That whoever's been torching the loft buildings decided to go after one of their boosters? Why? Duffy's dead."

"Do the gangs know that? Do they read obits? Do they even speak English?" His questions hung in the air like soap bubbles. Then they popped. "Thank you for your time."

As Ed closed the door, he realized that his armpits felt clammy. "That was weird."

"Is Daddy going to jail?" Sonya asked Julie.

"No," Ed said, a little shaken.

"It's all right, honey," Julie said. "Just a misunderstanding."

Ed considered calling Sheila and giving her a piece of his mind. How dare she! Then he calmed down. Of course the arson squad would talk to her. With Duffy dead, they'd check with his family, including his ex. Ed couldn't blame her for mentioning his visit and his interest in the Twenty-seventh Street fire. He took a deep breath and exhaled.

"Let's have the watermelon," Julie said. "It's really sweet."

"I could use a glass of wine," Ed said. "You want one?"

"Definitely."

—19—

Ed Googled Eric McCain, found his company's site, and e-mailed a request to chat about his grandmother, the strike, and the Duffys' back lot. He hit the send button just as Julie called down to him. It was time for Jake's bath.

Jake splashed happily as Ed washed him, then cooed as Ed dried and diapered him and zipped him into his sleeper. Julie sang him to sleep with a Beatles song.

Back at his computer, Ed clicked into the paper's archive, specified obituaries, and entered the name Sean Callahan. He guessed the old cop was around thirty-five in 1934, so he'd been born around the turn of the last century. If he died before 1970, when the archive went electronic, Ed was looking at another trip to the main branch. But the obit popped up, August 16, 1971:

COP IN FAMOUS PHOTO DIES

> Sean Callahan, the San Francisco police officer captured in a controversial photograph taken during the 1934 longshoremen's strike, died Tuesday at St. Francis Hospital. He was 72. The cause was a stroke.
>
> Callahan was best known for appearing in a photo taken July 5, 1934, Bloody Thursday, the most violent day of the largest labor dispute in San Francisco history. Callahan grabbed Harry Bridges, president of the International

> Longshoremen's Association (ILA), and clubbed him briefly before strikers pulled their leader to safety. Bridges was not seriously injured, but the photo of Callahan raising a club over him became a defining image of the bitter strike that unionized the waterfront. For the rest of his life, Callahan was vilified by ILA supporters and lionized by strike opponents, particularly police officers who battled union members. Two months after the photo was published, Callahan was promoted to lieutenant. In 1936, he became a captain, and in 1939, deputy chief, a post he held until he retired in 1959.
>
> Sean James Callahan was born July 23, 1899, in his parents' home on 10th Street. His father, Sean Sr., was killed during the 1906 earthquake when a neighbor's fallen chimney buried him under a rain of bricks. Callahan's mother, Elizabeth, died in the flu epidemic of 1919.
>
> Callahan finished 10th grade at Mission High School and worked as a laborer until World War I, when he enlisted in the Army. He spent six months in France. When he returned, he joined the police force. On retirement, he was awarded the department's highest honor, the Order of Merit.
>
> Callahan's wife, Alice, died in 1965. He is survived by....

The obit included the famous photo. It mentioned children and grandchildren, among them his son, Mitchell, president of Callahan Construction of South San Francisco.

So beating Bridges made his career. No wonder Pat hated him. But to have that animosity last three generations—that was hard to believe. Except that Duffy and Mitch Callahan had almost come to blows.

The stairs creaked. Julie appeared, looking round-shouldered. Her posture was usually erect. Either she was exhausted or something was wrong. She collapsed into her chair.

"You okay?" Ed asked.

"No." She frowned.

"What?"

"I don't know..." She laced her fingers and rested her chin on them, eyes downcast. Ed recognized the gesture. Whatever was eating her, it wasn't about him, or them. It was about her.

Ed's desk chair was on rollers. He wheeled over to Julie's side of the room. "Give me your foot."

She raised one leg. Ed slipped her shoe off and began kneading the fleshy pad just behind her toes.

"Tell me."

"I'm a terrible mother."

"*What?* No, you're not."

"I was okay when it was just Sonya. But I don't know how to parent two kids. I have no model." She was an only child.

"What happened?"

"Sonya wanted me to check her arithmetic, but I couldn't because Jake was so squirmy. But when I put him down, he screamed. I feel like I'm short-changing both of them."

"No, you're not. But you can't attend to everyone's needs all the time. Don't be so hard on yourself." He worked the ball of her foot, then the heel. "How's this?"

"Nice. Thanks."

"Other foot."

Julie raised it and sighed. "I don't know. With Jake so squirmy, I'm dreading the flight back East for Thanksgiving."

"Did you call Ravi?"

"Yes. He's e-mailing listings."

"As for the flight, there's always Benadryl." The antihistamine had sedative action.

Julie withdrew her foot, leaned forward, and kissed Ed. She sat at her desk and paid bills. Ed returned to his computer. He had e-mail.

"Hard to believe the lot on Twenty-seventh is still vacant," McCain began. He said he'd be happy to talk with the writer of "San Francisco Unearthed" about his Granny Molly and old times in the Mission. But he had a huge deal cooking and a big Planning Commission hearing coming up. Could it wait until he was out from under?

—20—

ED CROSSED THE PLAZA AND WAS STRUCK, AS ALWAYS, BY THE MAGNIFI-cence of City Hall, a junior version of the U.S. Capitol, but classier. He took the steps two at time, emptied his pockets at security, then strode across the polished stone floor under the huge dome into the warren of offices that housed the city's tax-collection operation. Past the century-old walnut cashier cages was a bank of tacky cubicles where civil servants dealt with problems.

Ed took a number and found a seat in the crowded waiting area where people conversed in a half-dozen languages. Eventually, a white guy in jeans and a starched shirt beckoned to him. His badge said Dan Schuster. He had curly brown hair and a trim beard flecked with gray.

Ed flashed his *Foghorn* ID. He explained that he was doing historical research.

Schuster noticed him for the first time. "You write that column, don't you?"

Ed smiled. "I do."

Schuster smiled as they entered his cubicle. "I like it."

Ed explained that a house on Twenty-seventh Street had burned in 1934. He wanted to know who paid the taxes on the property from 1930 on. He'd half expected this functionary to tell him that such ancient records had gone up the chimney long ago; instead, Schuster turned to his screen, tapped the keys, then worked his mouse.

"For that block, the system goes back to 1950."

Ed's heart sank.

"But the records you want are in the city archive. It'll take a day to retrieve them. We can e-mail or fax you. What's your preference?"

"E-mail."

The next morning, at the paper, Ed's computer beeped and he experienced a rare surge of affection for city government. From 1930 through 1934, the taxes had been paid by Michael Kincaid. Then the property was down-zoned from a single-family home to an undeveloped lot. For the next dozen years, Elizabeth Kincaid paid the taxes. From 1947 to 1962, the checks were written by Patrick Duffy. Then by Susan Duffy until 1969, when William Duffy took over. It looked like after the fire, Liza Kincaid had handled the lot, then sold it to the man who'd burned them out.

Ed called City Hall and asked Schuster if property taxes could be tracked by the taxpayer's name. They could. Ed asked if Michael or Elizabeth Kincaid had ever paid taxes on any other San Francisco properties.

Schuster tapped some keys. "Not since 1950. You want the archival information?"

"Please."

"By e-mail?"

"Yes."

Later that afternoon, Ed glanced at his watch. Julie was late. They were supposed to ride BART home together.

"Sorry," Julie said, pushing his door open. "The Symphony."

Every summer, the *Foghorn* sponsored a free Symphony concert in Union Square. Everyone loved it, but for Julie, the PR was a pain. "You ready?" she said. She was antsy. "I've got to nurse. My boobs are bursting."

Ed grabbed his backpack. Then his computer beeped. "One second."

Julie frowned.

A quick glance at the e-mail told him Michael and Elizabeth

Kincaid never owned any other property in San Francisco. After 1946, they disappeared from the city's tax rolls. The diary was right. After the fire, they left town.

—21—

THE KIDS WERE ASLEEP. THE DVD WAS JULIE'S PICK, A ROMANTIC comedy. She poured the pinot and opened the steamy popcorn bag as Ed emerged from the basement.

"Park just got back to me," he said, disgusted. "Duffy's murder is now officially a cold case. Unless something new turns up, it's over."

"Sad."

"It sucks. Imagine how Sheila feels. How do you explain that to your kids?"

Fortunately, the movie was entertaining—a cute guy and sexy girl. Ed and Julie both came away feeling tender toward each other. As the credits rolled, they embraced.

Ed scooped up the empty popcorn bowl and wine glasses and headed for the kitchen. Julie worked the remote, switching back to cable.

"Coming up," a deep voice teased, "BDSM: Bondage, Discipline, and Sado-Masochism. This woman says it's good clean fun."

At the kitchen door, Ed turned. The screen showed a voluptuous woman in a tight black dress. Her hair was also black, except for a lock of white that started at her forehead and snaked behind an ear.

Julie hit a button and the screen went dark.

"Wait!" Ed exclaimed. "Turn it on. I know her!"

"You *know* her?" She shot him a look, but hit the button.

The screen sprang back to life.

"After Duffy's funeral. Remember? On the steps. That white streak. You dissed her outfit."

"No."

Naturally, it was twenty minutes into the show before Ms. White Streak reappeared. The segment began with a close-up of her face, smiling and maternal, then widened to show her in the Cat Woman outfit standing by a contraption out of the Inquisition, and behind her, a wall of whips, riding crops, and multi-tail floggers.

"This San Francisco woman calls herself Mistress Rod," a woman said in voice-over. "She's a professional dominatrix—a 'pro-dom' to those on the sexual fringe. She gets paid—very well, she says—to spank, whip, and verbally abuse men and women, mostly men, who experience a sexual thrill from obeying her commands, and from being punished if they disobey."

Cut to the reporter, a short-haired blonde wearing a beige pant-suit, in front of the wall of floggers. "Some people call this a dungeon, but it's on the seventh floor of a San Francisco office building. In this studio, Mistress Rod says she cracks the whip, literally, over a dozen clients a week." The reporter turned to the pro-dom. "What about your name? Why 'Mistress Rod?'"

The woman smiled, showing perfect teeth. "Spare the rod, spoil the fun."

"Must we?" Julie muttered.

"Shh!" Ed insisted. "I want to hear."

"Why?"

"Duffy."

"What's BDSM all about?" The reporter asked.

"In a word," the pro-dom replied, "*trust.* In every relationship, trust is the basis of intimacy. In BDSM, you trust your partner in ways that go far beyond what people experience in ordinary 'vanilla' relationships. That deeper trust leads to deeper intimacy, and, if you're into BDSM, tremendous pleasure."

Gesturing to the floggers, the reporter asked, "But isn't it abusive? I mean, you *whip people.*"

"Yes, I do," Mistress Rod purred, bringing a cat-o-nine-tails down on her wrist with a gentle slap. "But it's not abusive at all. It's *play*, very special, very intimate play. BDSM is theater, carefully scripted but usually with room for improvisation. It's no coincidence that sessions are called 'scenes,' just like theater. Everyone plays a part and comes away feeling like you do after a good play: fulfilled."

"If it's theater, what are the roles?"

"Dominant and submissive. Subs, or bottoms, trust doms, or tops, to take them to their personal edge of acceptable sensation, but never over it. Doms revel in being trusted so deeply. Ironically, the top is not the one in control. The bottom is. Players negotiate how long the scene will last, how intense any sensation will be, if restraints will be used—everything. They also agree on a 'safe' word. If subs feel at all uneasy, they say the word, and doms immediately stop what they're doing. The safe word I use is 'red light.'"

"But what if someone doesn't play by the rules? What happens then?"

"The same thing that happens on a playground if basketball players don't play by the rules. Word gets around and pretty soon, no one will play with them."

"How can you call it 'play' when subs get hurt?"

"They may get hurt. But they're never *harmed*. At all times, they're in total control.

"Don't submissives enjoy pain?"

"Very specific types of pain administered by a trusted dom in specific, prearranged ways. Subs don't crave pain for its own sake. Like anyone else, they don't enjoy bee stings or getting punched in the nose. They only enjoy what they've agreed to experience within the limits that excite them."

"You draw a distinction between hurt and harm. Please explain."

"I may *hurt* some subs—with their permission, of course. I may give them the gift of intense sensation. But I never cause lasting *harm*. BDSM is a lot like athletics. Say you run a marathon. After twenty-six miles, you're sore. You're hurting. But you're not harmed. In fact, you feel a special kind of exhilaration you can't experience any other way."

Cut to the anchor, a gray-haired black man, who shook his head and turned to the reporter, now seated next to him. "Is it true? No one gets harmed?"

"Hard to say," the reporter replied. "But according to the San Francisco Health Department, last year, city emergency rooms treated two thousand people for athletic injuries. One hundred were serious, and two people died. The number treated for injuries from BDSM? Just twenty-four. One serious. No deaths."

"But many more people are involved in sports," the anchor retorted.

"True," the reporter said, "but these statistics suggest that BDSM is not a significant public health problem."

"The Bay Area isn't the only place where BDSM is popular, is it?" the anchor ventured.

"Oh, no. I Googled 'BDSM.' Seventeen *million* hits all over the world."

Ed clicked the remote and the screen went black.

"On that note," Julie said, "I'm going to bed. You coming?"

Ed was lost in thought. Mistress Rod was the woman on the steps after Duffy's funeral. Presumably, Duffy was one of her subs. "I wonder..." Ed took two steps toward the basement stairs.

"What?"

"The names on Duffy's PG&E bill. One was Rod. I assumed Rodney. But maybe not."

"Ed, it's late."

"I'll be right up."

He descended the stairs, fished out the number, dialed, and got voicemail. A woman. He identified himself as a friend of Ryan Duffy's and left his number.

Julie was removing her contacts when Ed passed the bathroom.

"I was right. The 'Rod' on Duffy's note, it's Mistress Rod."

Julie frowned. "You're not getting involved in the murder investigation, are you?" Her tone was more shrill than she intended. Ed knew what she was thinking. He had a habit of sticking his fingers into dark corners of San Francisco. Sometimes a mousetrap snapped. Julie didn't like it in the past, and now, with two kids, she liked it even less. "*Are you?*"

"No. I'm investigating the diary. That's all."

"Then why are you calling that—*woman*?"

"Because the case is in the freezer. Park's got nothing. This is something, maybe. It's possible Duffy had contact with Mistress Rod shortly before he died."

"So?"

"So I want to ask her if she's talked to the cops."

"And?"

"If she has, fine. But if she hasn't, I'm going to encourage her to. And if she doesn't, I'm going to call Park and tell him that someone who might know something isn't talking—and maybe he should pay a visit."

—22—

A CROWD MILLED AROUND THE TALL DOUBLE DOORS OF THE HEARING room on the second floor of City Hall. Ed and Julie and their neighbors and surrogates, Keith and Calvin, threaded their way into the crowded chamber and looked for Tom Ferguson. They found him toward the back near a huge arched window that overlooked Civic Center plaza. Ferguson waved. He'd saved seats.

Keith and Calvin were an odd couple, Arkansas meets Hong Kong. Keith was Paul Bunyan, big, barrel-chested, and bearded. Calvin was skinny and slight, like a monk in a Bruce Lee movie. Under a leather jacket, he wore a tight T-shirt: I CAN'T EVEN THINK STRAIGHT. Mismatched as they seemed, they'd been together fifteen years, through the failure of Keith's previous restaurant and the shock of Calvin's HIV diagnosis. Sonya loved them. Whenever they stopped by, they always slipped her a few chocolate kisses.

"Welcome to the funhouse," Ferguson said with an impish grin. Julie introduced everyone.

Department Three had once been a courtroom, but the witness stand and jury seating were gone. The bench was lower and longer, with a half-dozen high-backed leather chairs behind it. As the hour approached, the chamber filled. Supporters of the Association of Property Owners and Developers gravitated toward the front. Most wore suits. Several carried large charts and graphs. Supporters of Tenants United for Fairness occupied the rear half of the gallery. They were dressed more casually and carried fewer visual aids.

"Remember the players?" Ferguson asked. His sky-blue eyes were framed by crow's feet.

Ed said he did but his companions didn't.

They all leaned toward the reporter as he pointed out David Heckendorf a few rows away. The president of TUF wore jeans and a black T-shirt with a red headband emblazoned STOP TRANSIT VILLAGES. He was chatting and joking. The rows around the TUF people were filled with neighborhood activists and representatives of dozens of community groups. Down front, Ferguson identified APOD president Fred DeCampo and his staff. A phalanx of developers sat nearby, plus the presidents of the building-trades unions, along with representatives of merchants' associations and the Chamber of Commerce. Finally, peppered around the room and looking decidedly uncomfortable were people from two dozen environmental organizations. Some supported transit villages to reduce sprawl. Others opposed them because higher density meant more congestion.

"Looks like TUF has more people," Julie observed.

"They always do," Ferguson agreed. "The city's two-thirds renters. But APOD has the money—and the influence it buys."

"That stinks," Calvin said.

"That's the American way," Ferguson sighed. "Politicos champion renters' rights around election time, but it costs billions to run a city, and in this town, most of it comes from property taxes. The BART stations downtown are surrounded by towers that produce tens of millions for the city treasury. But out beyond Civic Center, BART stations are surrounded by much smaller buildings—so much less revenue."

"What are you talking about?" Julie countered. "Rents are through the roof."

"Yes, but compared with most other neighborhoods, the Mission is still pretty affordable," Ferguson continued. "Replace a few taquerias with ten-story condo buildings, and the city makes money. Not to mention fewer poor people, so the city saves on social services."

"But doesn't gentrification increase some city costs?" Ed asked.

"It does. But, per capita, new parks and libraries are a lot cheaper than the ER at General."

"So we're screwed?" Julie looked defeated. "Are they just going to roll over for APOD?"

"Not at all. Remember, Planning is accountable to the Board of Supervisors, and TUF has the numbers. If Planning leans too far over to APOD, there's plenty of time for TUF to gang up on the Board to overrule them and maybe even replace some Commissioners. Watch, APOD is going to promise the moon in new tax revenue and TUF is going to threaten the Commissioners with their jobs."

"Isn't that Mitch Callahan?" Ed asked, nodding toward a tall, gray-haired man in a charcoal suit standing near DeCampo.

"The man himself," Ferguson replied.

"You know he tried to take swing at Duffy?"

"Yeah. He's a hothead. And dirty, too."

Ed's eyebrows arched.

"Several times, he's been accused of bribing building inspectors. Every time, he's slithered out of it."

"Really."

"You remember, oh, five, six years ago, some inspectors got arrested on bribery charges and one committed suicide?"

"Vaguely."

"Callahan was implicated in that. But no charges. *Nada*."

"Here's something you may not know," Ed said. "At the hearing when Callahan's people pulled him away from Duffy, Alvarez overheard him say it wasn't just about the Armory. It was about Callahan's father and Duffy's grandfather."

Now it was Ferguson's turn to raise an eyebrow.

"Callahan's father was a cop. Duffy's grandfather was a longshoreman. They mixed it up during the dock strike of 1934. Duffy's grandfather hated Callahan's father for clubbing Harry Bridges."

"Who?" Ferguson asked.

"President of the union."

"And that's why Duffy was against Armory Heights?"

"That's what Callahan thinks," Ed said. "And get this. The only high-density housing near BART Duffy *ever* opposed was Callahan's Armory project."

Ferguson pursed his lips. "Hard to believe that Duffy nursed some grudge of his grandfather's from so long ago."

"Weirder things have happened. The Hatfields and McCoys. Romeo and Juliet. If this feud is real, it gives Callahan a motive. Eliminating Duffy scores one for his father, and as a bonus, Planning might reconsider the Armory."

"I wouldn't put anything past Callahan." Ferguson nodded toward the door. "There he is—the man of the hour, Eric McCain. He's shelled out millions on his Civic Center village, and if this hearing goes his way, he's one step closer to making a good fifty million." McCain strode in with two young people, an Asian guy and a redheaded woman.

"I'll be right back," Ed said, squeezing past Ferguson. He threaded his way through the crowd and caught the developer as he approached the APOD people. "Excuse me," Ed said. "Eric McCain? I'm Ed Rosenberg from the *Foghorn*."

"Yes?" McCain produced a quick smile and a blank look. He was taller than Ed. He wore an expensive suit and smelled of cologne.

"I e-mailed you about your grandmother. The vacant lot behind the Duffy's?"

The light switched on. "Oh, yes."

"I'm hoping we can get together in the next week or so. Is that possible?"

McCain's smile broadened. "Of course." He clapped Ed's shoulder like a politician on election eve and turned to the woman. "Denise, schedule a time with Mister, uh—"

"Rosenberg. Ed Rosenberg."

"Late afternoons usually work best for me."

"Fine." Ed handed a business card to the young woman. "I'm also hoping to talk with your grandmother."

"Shouldn't be a problem," McCain said. "But I have to warn you—" he winked, "Granny Molly's an incredible flirt, God love her." His laugh was big and booming.

"Thanks. Looking forward to it."

McCain and his assistants threaded their way to seats amid APOD. Ed returned to his.

"What was *that* about?" Julie asked, as Ferguson eyed him.

"The diary. McCain's grandmother knew Duffy's grandfather. He's going to introduce me to her. I'm hoping she knows something about the fire."

"What fire?" Ferguson asked.

"The fire that destroyed the house behind Duffy's."

"There was a house?"

Before Ed could explain, the Commissioners filed in: a stooped elderly white woman, an obviously gay white man, a regal black woman, a man who was either Hispanic or Arab, a dignified elderly Asian man, and a young Asian woman with spiky hair who looked barely old enough to vote.

The black woman wielded the gavel. She wore a brightly colored African wrap-around outfit with matching turban and gold hoop earrings. She announced that more people had registered to address the Commission than anticipated, so remarks would be limited to five minutes per speaker. After that, the microphone would be turned off and people were to return to their seats. If they did not, Sheriff's deputies would assist them, or, if necessary, escort them out of the building.

She handed a thick stack of papers to a doughy woman who looked Latina and asked her to distribute them. It was the speaker roster, with names listed in the order they'd registered. They scanned the list. Cal was number 121. If everything ran like clockwork, he wouldn't get his five minutes for ten hours.

"That's midnight," Ed said.

"That's ridiculous!" Julie exclaimed.

"That's democracy in action," Ferguson deadpanned. "Ten hours is nothing. Whenever anyone proposes changes to rent control, the hearings last weeks."

"We have to work," Keith said.

"It's not as bad as it looks," Ferguson explained. "Figure ten percent won't show up. And quite a few won't go five minutes. The Commission will call it a night around eleven. If you come back around nine, you'll be in plenty of time."

"Or not." Julie sounded disgusted.

Calvin looked at Keith. "Maybe I could sneak away."

Keith's expression said he didn't like the idea.

"Suit yourself," Ferguson said. "I'll be here till it ends."

"Let's go," Julie told her entourage. She rose from her chair, worked her way to the aisle, and stomped toward the door.

Ed followed Julie, Keith, and Calvin out of the room. Julie looked steamed. He was not looking forward to the drive back to the paper.

—23—

Beth Duffy Vincent worked in the mall near San Francisco State. They met in the food court, metal tables and chairs surrounded by a horseshoe of fast-food places. Beth's message had said she'd be wearing a white pharmacist's tunic with a Walgreen's badge.

"I have something for you," Ed said. He handed her the three volumes of the diary. "Sheila said you're the family historian."

Beth's eyes widened. She held the notebooks as if they were relics of a saint. "Ry mentioned Grandpa Pat's diary. But after… what happened, I completely forgot about it. Thank you."

"I'm so sorry for your loss," Ed said. "Ryan was a good man. We were friends."

Beth stared off into space. Her gaze was as vacant as an empty chair at Thanksgiving. "We were very close." She pulled out a tissue and blew her nose. "My husband was in Ry's class at Mission High. Sheila was in mine. She was my best friend. Still is."

"Horrible thing."

"Worse than horrible." Her lip trembled. "I still can't believe it." She wiped her eyes, opened the first volume, and flipped pages, scanning her grandfather's scratchy penmanship. "They'll have a place of honor in the shrine."

"Shrine?"

Beth managed a thin-lipped smile. "One wall of my den is covered with family photos and memorabilia. The oldest picture is a portrait of my great-great grandparents, Grandpa Pat's grandparents, taken after the Civil War. I have baptismal certificates going back five generations. ”

“You really *are* a historian.”

Beth blushed. “Well, not like you. I just deal with the family.” She closed the notebook and folded her hands. “Like I said in the e-mail, I know there was once a house behind our house. And I know it burned and Grandma Susie bought the land and planted her garden.”

“The diary is very sketchy. Do you know how your grandparents came to live in the house?”

“It was originally owned by Grandpa Pat’s uncle Connor. He wasn’t well. His wife took care of him—Mary, I think her name was. When she died, Pat and Susie moved in to look after him.”

“Connor and Mary didn’t have any children?”

“They did. But one was a priest. The others moved away.”

“When did Pat and Susie move in?”

“I’m not sure. Around the time of the stock market crash. I have a photo dated 1930, the three of them sitting on the front steps. When Connor died, he willed the house to them.”

“Do you know anything about the house behind theirs?”

“Just that there was one and it burned.”

“It was owned by Mike and Liza Kincaid. You know anything about them?”

“I think they were friends of my grandparents.”

“The diary implies that Liza and your grandmother were related,” Ed said.

“They were cousins, both Keenans. That’s how Grandma Susie introduced her the one time I met them.”

“When was that?”

“At my grandfather’s funeral…” She did some mental arithmetic. “…the early eighties. They came out from Boston.”

So that’s where they went.

“Really? What were they like?”

“Old and frail like Grandma Susie. I was in high school. I don’t remember much about Liza. But Mike made a *big* impression. He was a retired Boston cop. He knew the Kennedys. In our family, President Kennedy was a saint. I couldn't believe I shook the hand that shook the hand."

Ed summarized what he'd learned from the diary.

"Do you think my grandfather set the fire?"

"I do. He had the means, motive, and opportunity. He knew one of the strikers the police shot. He'd just been to the funeral. He was drinking. And he was furious at Mike for clubbing Harry Bridges."

"Another saint in our family."

"But I can't be sure. Diaries lend themselves to confession. But your grandfather didn't write one word about the cause of the fire. He was arrested, charged with arson—"

"Amazing! I had no idea."

"Then the charges…evaporated. I found no record of them being dropped, or of a plea, or trial. They just disappeared, which is very strange. The city was tense. It was occupied by the National Guard. A striker torches a cop's house. You'd think the papers would have been all over it. But they ignored it."

"Aunt Clara may know."

"Sheila said she's still pretty sharp."

"Oh yes, and a real talker, that one. When I visit, I arrange for my husband to call at a certain time. I tell Clara something's come up and I have to go. Otherwise, she'd keep me all day. Speaking of going, I have to get back to work."

They stood up.

Ed said, "I assume you heard about the fire on Twenty-sixth Street."

"Yes. First Ry. Now this."

"Someone boarded up the windows."

"My brothers."

"Any idea who might have…?"

"No. The police say it was neighborhood kids who knew the house was vacant."

"I understand you tried to maintain it, but your mother wouldn't let you."

"Yes. Alzheimer's is awful. Any little change, anything, and she started screaming. Rages like I've never seen, ever."

"I'm sorry. What's going to happen to the house?"

"It's not clear yet. Kevin—my brother—is looking into having the damage repaired. We'll see."

"Your grandfather would roll over in his grave if he knew what the place is worth now."

"I know. Prices have gone crazy."

"Don't remind me," Ed groaned. "We have a small, renovated house in the Mission. We need something bigger. But there's no way we can afford anything."

Beth smiled. "At the store, we sell Lotto tickets."

They shook hands. Ed let go. Beth didn't. Her blue eyes bored into his.

"I just want to say I'm deeply grateful."

Ed assumed she was referring to the diary. "It's yours. It should stay with the family."

"Not just that," Beth said. "The way the paper...didn't mention certain things."

"I'm glad, too."

"Do you know he wanted Sheila to do it with him? Like it was a picnic or something. It's been so hard for her. She feels like she failed as a wife. What she's been through, you don't want to know. All I can say is thank God for Billy."

"She didn't fail," Ed ventured softly. "Some people just ..." He didn't know what to say.

"Sure, we've all said that. But it doesn't change how she feels. Or how I'd feel if it was me."

She shook his hand, said goodbye, and walked away.

As she left, Ed's thoughts returned to their conversation. So Pat and Susie had been *given* the house. Ed had wondered how a dock worker could have afforded such a big place. And Susie and Liza were cousins, and Liza and Mike went to Boston. It was time to call Aunt Clara.

—24—

JULIE AND SONYA WERE SHOPPING. WHEN JAKE WOKE FROM HIS NAP, Ed popped him into the stroller and set off around the neighborhood. The baby craned his neck and took in everything. Across the street, the crazy old nun smoked on the stoop of the Victorian she shared with her widowed sister. Her face was a bleached prune, and she loudly blessed everyone who passed by. Sonya was scared of her, but Ed found her amusing and Jake seemed to like her.

"Bless you, baby," she intoned, blowing smoke. "Remember the fifth commandment."

A block away, a Victorian converted into two flats ages ago was being gentrified—converted back to a single-family home. It was older than Ed's. He guessed the 1870s. It was being painted. The scaffolding was covered with the black netting the city required to trap old lead-paint dust. The mesh made the house look like a cocoon. Soon a butterfly would emerge.

They stopped in front of Sonya's favorite house, an Edwardian whose tiny front yard was festooned with metal sculptures and wind chimes tinkling in the afternoon breeze. Around the corner, the windows of a boxy second-floor flat were covered with posters of marijuana leaves that read LEGALIZE IT.

Ed turned down Twenty-sixth. The plywood had come off Duffy's fire-scarred front windows. New ones had been installed with shiny white sashes. The stickers were still on the glass.

Ed noticed a man standing on the sidewalk in front of Duffy's.

He looked to be in his late forties—tall, clean-shaven, and broad-shouldered, with a full head of silver-blond hair. He stared up at the house.

As Ed approached, he saw a sign tacked to the siding. Jameson Construction. So Duffy's brother and Sheila's boyfriend had come to terms. But the man standing on the sidewalk was not the boyfriend. As Ed drew closer, he realized who he was.

"Eric McCain," Ed said.

The startled developer's head snapped around. He smiled like a salesman and studied Ed's face. "I know you…the *Foghorn*. Rosenbloom."

"Rosenberg. Ed."

"Right. I'm getting you together with Granny Molly. Did Denise set it up?"

"She did. Next week."

"I mentioned it to her. She got all excited."

"Great. And I believe congratulations are in order. Looks like your Civic Center project is getting approved."

McCain snorted. "What makes you so sure?"

"The reporter covering it."

"Who's that?"

"Tom Ferguson."

"Oh, yeah. I know him."

"He's been talking to the Commissioners. Says they like your plan."

"They've been saying that for two years. Meanwhile, I've put up ten million dollars and I'm still waiting." He looked up at the house and sighed. "But where there's life, there's hope—I guess."

"I understand that you and Duffy—Ryan—were old friends."

"Yes," he said softly. "Ry-Bread we used to call him." He pointed to a home down the street. "I grew up there. Ry's older brother, Kevin, was my best friend, but we all played together: me, the Duffy boys, the Flanagans." He pointed to a two-flat place. "Juan Ramierez, and the Liebowitz twins." He nodded this way and that. "See those phone poles?" He pointed. "Those were our goal posts for touch football. In summer, we painted bases on the street and pretended to be Mays and McCovey."

"What about the Duffys' big yard? You ever play there?"

"Oh, no. That was granny's garden." He looked up at the house and shook his head. "So awful. Leaving two kids."

"Yes."

McCain sighed. "I knew Ry bought the place. He invited me over, but business was crazy—dealing with Planning, my other projects. I never…"

Ed swallowed. "I found him."

"Really."

"We were supposed to have brunch. Sheila said you and Duffy stayed friends."

"We did. Not like when we were kids, but we got together—especially after he started covering development." McCain scanned the Duffy home from the drain in the driveway to the peak of the roof. "I haven't been back here in years. So much is the same. But so much has changed. Big Bill—Kevin and Ry's dad—took great pride in the house, kept it up. Now look at it. And back then the block was mostly Irish. Now it's mostly Latino. But not for long. The techies are moving in."

"What brought you here today?"

"My boat."

"What?"

"I have a forty-two-foot motor cruiser. My pride and joy. My therapy. Whenever I can, I'm on the water. But she's in dry dock. Resealing the hull. So I'm landlocked. Ry's passing, seeing everyone at the funeral—I've been thinking about old times. I was at Costco, and I just kind of wandered over here. You?"

"I live nearby."

"I'm up over the hill." He nodded toward Twin Peaks. His tone reached for modesty, but missed. Twin Peaks had huge homes and commanding views. It was where rich developers lived, a place kids who grew up on the streets of the Mission could only dream of.

"I understand the Duffys used to throw St. Patrick's Day parties."

McCain smiled. "Oh, yeah. Big ones. *Huge*. Burgers, sausages, chicken, and steaks on half a dozen grills. And Guinness. Lots of Guinness. Everyone on the block came. And people from St. Paul's. We went every year."

"We?"

"My family and me. It's funny. After Ry's funeral, my sister Gwen pulled out an old album with pictures from a St. Patty's party in the early sixties. Big Bill got the cops to close the street. I was maybe seven. They had a Celtic band. Everyone dancing in the street."

"Your parents still here?" Ed tilted his head across the street.

"Oh no. Retired years ago to San Diego. My father died in '94."

"I'm curious. Do you know anything about the house on the lot behind the Duffys?"

"Just that there was one a long time ago, but that's all. Why?"

"It burned down in 1934. Duffy's grandfather, Patrick, probably set the fire. Burned out the man who'd been his best friend."

"Really? Why?"

"They were on opposite sides of the dock strike of 1934."

"Incredible. I had no idea."

"Did you ever know him?"

"Old Pat? I met him, but that's all."

"Ever hear of Michael and Liza Kincaid?"

"Don't think so."

"They lived in the house that burned. Your grandparents knew them well. When their house burned, it was your grandparents who took them in."

"Then Granny Molly'll have lots to tell. She's still got most of her marbles, God love her. Hey, you like cruising the Bay?"

"Uh, I never have."

"*What?* You've *never* been out on the Bay?"

"Alcatraz. The Sausalito ferry."

"Oh, no, I'm talking about *real* boats. Mine's a honey. Tell you what: when I get you and Granny together, we'll do it on the boat."

"You take a ninety-year-old in a wheelchair out on your boat?"

“Ninety-one. And yes, I take her out—on calm days. Why not? She loves it. Last time she brought a friend. I had two of them in wheelchairs.”

“And you trust the brakes? What if—”

McCain waved a hand. “Pop-up clamps in the decking. Holds wheelchairs tight. Cost a damn fortune, but they work like a charm. Granny loves the water. They had a fine old time. Beats watching soaps in the day room at St. Catherine’s. What do you say? We’ll do it on the boat.”

“Sounds like fun.”

“Great. We’ll do it—as soon as Planning rules.”

—25—

THE 1906 FIRE CHEWED WEST FROM DOWNTOWN, BUT COULDN'T jump wide Van Ness Avenue. As a result, most surviving Victorians stand west of it. For much of the twentieth century, Van Ness was auto row. Dealerships offering everything from Fords to Rolls Royce lined up shoulder to shoulder for a dozen blocks. But as the millennium approached, the car dealers were replaced by apartment developments—and one assisted-living facility.

Her eyes were the watery blue of a swimming pool. The left one drooped, its lid a window shade stuck halfway. Periodically, a tear gathered in its outer corner and left a glistening trail along her cheek until she wiped it.

Clara Duffy O'Brien was short, thin, stooped, and white-haired. Beth was right. Her aunt didn't stop talking from the moment Ed shook her cool hand. Ed listened and asked a few questions. He maintained eye contact, smiled, nodded, and bided his time.

With short shuffling steps, Clara led him into the library. It had bookshelves, magazine and newspaper racks, board games, and a half-finished jigsaw puzzle. In one corner, a circle of elderly women painted watercolors. At a table, two old men played chess.

Clara not only talked nonstop, she also involved everyone within hailing distance. She made a point of introducing the *nice* man from the paper, who writes those *lovely* history articles, who'd come to interview her about her *big brother*, may he rest in the bosom of the Lord.

Clara rambled about the place, the food, how she'd had a *wee bit* of trouble with her roommate, and how her *marvelous* children were now paying extra so she could have a *private* room. She described outings with Beth and Sheila and the *wonderful* visits from her four children who were scattered around the country. Each came once every three months, so she saw one a month. But she saw her ten grandchildren less because they were in school and doing *marvelously*, except for her Atlanta daughter's youngest, who got mixed up with drugs, but was now in rehab and doing *very well*, thank the good Lord.

Eventually, Clara needed a drink. Ed wasn't surprised. He got parched just listening to her. Food was prohibited in the library, so she held Ed's arm and shuffled him to the snack bar, introducing him to everyone. With trembling hands, Clara made herself a cup of tea and urged a cup on Ed. He carried the two cups to a table by a window overlooking the bustle of Van Ness. When Clara took a sip, he made his move.

"I brought you a present."

Out of his briefcase came a gift-wrapped package. The old woman became a kid at Christmas. Her gnarled fingers unwrapped it and folded the paper. You *never know* when you might need wrapping paper. She dabbed her eye and gazed down at a thick document filled with spidery writing.

"Pat's diary," Ed said. "Beth has the original, but I thought you might like a copy."

"Oh my, yes. Thank you," she said, leafing, her good eye opened wide. She sighed. "Pat never had much use for the Palmer method."

Ed recalled it was the form of cursive penmanship that swept the country in the early twentieth century.

"Thank you." She dabbed her cheek and fell silent as if to say, "I'm ready."

"I understand," Ed said, "that Pat was your older brother. How much older?"

"Seven years. I was born in 1916. He was 1909."

So she was eighteen in 1934.

"What was he like?"

"Oh," she sighed, "everyone *loved* Pat. A real Irish charmer, that one. And headstrong he was. Stubborn as a mule. He'd give you the shirt off his back. But if you crossed him, watch out. He held grudges." Ed could think of one. "He didn't pay me much mind till Susie came along and she and I became friends. Then Pat warmed up to me."

"How did Pat meet Susie?"

"She worked in a bakery on Mission. Pat used to go in there."

"Do you know when she was born?"

"A year after Pat, 1910," she said, dabbing her cheek. "She was six years older than me. I *loved* Susie. I had three brothers; she was the sister I never had. I was *thrilled* when Pat married her. I was a bridesmaid. You should have seen the dress. Pale green with lace trim and a matching sash and shoes. That was a *wonderful* day. Beth has pictures."

"Beth said that after your Aunt Mary died, Pat and Susie moved into Twenty-sixth Street and took care of Connor."

"Megan. Auntie Megan. Yes, they moved in. Pat was fixing cars, not making enough for a decent home, and Susie was a natural-born nurse. So it was a match made in heaven. Brendan and I—my husband, may he rest with the Lord—we bought a house around the corner. Uncle Con was a tough old wharf rat, but he loved Susie. Didn't give her no trouble—not until near the end when he went senile."

"He was a dockworker?"

"Underboss."

"What?"

"Every crew had a boss that ran the gang, and an underboss who helped. Nobody was hiring, but Uncle Con's boss said he could get Pat a Blue Book for two cases of Canadian whiskey. It was Prohibition. Bathtub gin was cheap, but real Canadian was very expensive. The family took up a collection and Pat got his job."

"What about Michael Kincaid?"

"Such a *nice* boy. Our mothers were friends. Pat and Mike

started playing when they were in *diapers*. Went all through school together. Mike's father was a cop and got him a job."

"And Liza?"

"*Darling* girl, could sing like an angel."

"I understand that she and Suzie were related."

"Cousins. Keenans. Liza come out from Boston to help her sister, Evie, care for her brood—six kids."

"Do you know how Mike and Liza wound up on Twenty-seventh Street?"

Clara smiled and dabbed her eye. "When Pat and Susie moved in with Uncle Con, Mike and Liza had a flat a few blocks away. That house come up for rent and they grabbed it. After a while, they bought it."

"Pat's diary mentions something about a back fence."

"Oh, my, yes. Tall, it was, big posts and wide boards. Once Mike and Liza bought the house, all four of them wanted that fence down. So they threw a little party and everyone helped. It was the weekend of St. Patty's Day. That was what started their annual parties. Went on for, Lord, fifty years—until Catherine couldn't handle it no more."

"Ryan's mother. With Alzheimer's."

"Yes, poor dear."

"What about the dock strike of 1934?"

"Now *that* was a *very* hard time in the middle of hard times."

"I've read that most longshoremen had to go on welfare."

"Pat never did. Too proud. When work dried up, he worked at St. Paul's and repaired trucks for a bootlegger."

"The diary mentions repairing cars, but not for a bootlegger."

"He didn't do it long. Susie was against it. Even though the police winked, she made him quit. So it was just St. Paul's. Mike tried to get him a job with the police, but they weren't hiring. They were cutting wages. But Mike always seemed to do all right."

Thanks to the bootleggers and speakeasy owners.

"And then the longshoremen went on strike," Ed prompted.

"Yes, they did, God bless 'em. And they won, too, won everything they struck for."

"But the strike turned Pat and Mike into bitter enemies."

Clara wiped her cheek and gazed into her lap. "A *very* sad chapter. Pat and Mike, they were both so Irish. Cursed with the sin of pride, the both of them. And stubborn, too, so stubborn. It gives you cancer, stubbornness does. I saw a doctor on Oprah. He said that. That's what took the both of them, cancer."

"In the diary, Pat says something about trying to get Mike to quit the force, but Mike said he had 'a gun to his head.' Do you know anything about that?"

"Oh, my, yes. There were a lot of Irish boys on the docks, and a lot on the force. Many cops like Mike had their hearts with the boys and didn't want to go making no trouble for them. So when the city put the force against the strikers, a lot of boys didn't want to go. They were threatened. Their families, too."

"Mike was threatened? You know this for a fact?"

"Liza said it. I knew other cops' wives. They said it, too."

"Who threatened them?"

"Their bosses."

"Did you know a police officer named Sean Callahan?"

Clara pursed her lips. "I spit on his grave."

"Was it Callahan who threatened Mike?"

"That's what Liza told me. Mike, too."

"How?"

"Like Mike said, 'A gun to his head.'"

"In that case, you'd think Pat would have been more understanding."

"Some cops quit, Brendan's brother Tommy for one, and nothing happened to them. Pat threw that up at Mike."

"And?"

"Mike said, 'Tommy don't work under Sean.'"

"He couldn't transfer?"

"He tried. But no."

"Still, I find it hard to believe that Pat would cut off his best friend like that."

"Pat held grudges. He wasn't the only one. The strike divided everyone. It was the Civil War—Irish lads on the docks, Irish lads in blue. When it was over, some families didn't speak to each other for years. The union wanted their boys to stand *together*. That meant standing against the other side. And Pat did."

"But the diary says Susie and Liza stayed close. Pat started to rebuild the fence, but Susie stopped him."

"Yes, she did, God love her. And it wasn't easy." Clara bowed her head and said, "Pat—" before cutting herself off.

"What?"

Clara wiped her eye and shook her head. "I'll not speak of it."

"Did he hit her?"

Clara dabbed both eyes. "That was a *very* hard time for Pat and Susie. It was hard for all of us, but especially them. Pat was so bull-headed. And truth be told, there was something else, too."

"What?"

"The green-eyed monster."

"I don't understand."

"Pat was jealous. He was bigger than Mike, stronger, tougher, better looking, more charming. He was the leader, Mike was the follower. But Mike had the good job and Pat was a janitor at St. Paul's. Mike's kids had nice shoes. Pat's had holes in theirs."

"In the diary, Pat says Mike clubbed Harry Bridges."

"Pat told *everyone* that. But Mike swore he didn't, that he was trying to pull Sean *off of* Harry."

"What do you think?"

"Only the Lord knows, and he's not talking."

"What about the fire at Mike and Liza's? The diary implies that Pat or his friends set it. But Pat was strangely silent on the subject."

Clara stared into her tea cup. "Yes. He was. They all were. None of them ever talked about it. Not a one of them."

"Not even to you?"

"Not to me. Not to anyone."

"I assume you pressed them."

"Oh, my, yes. But none of them said a word—not Pat, Susie,

Mike, or Liza."

"So what do you think?" Ed asked. "Did Pat set the fire? He was jealous of Mike. He believed Mike clubbed Bridges. He saw the police kill the two strikers. He knew one of them. He marched up Market Street. And after, he and his buddies got drunk and hurled insults at Mike. It's hard to imagine him not doing it."

"Maybe so," Clara said, "but Pat didn't do it."

"Really."

"My brother wouldn't do something like that. There were babies in that house."

"If Pat didn't do it, who did? Other dock workers?"

"As Christ is my witness, I don't know."

"Pat was arrested for arson, but the charges were dropped. Do you know why?"

"No evidence. It was Mike's word against Pat's."

"So Mike *accused* Pat?"

"He did. Pointed his finger. They put Pat in jail."

"I'm surprised the charges were dropped. Mike was a cop. Tensions were high. You'd think the police would have—"

"They might have, except Liza and Mike moved away. Out of sight, out of mind. Pat went free. And none of them ever talked about it."

"When did Susie turn the lot into a garden?"

"A year or two after. I forget."

"Mike and Liza retained ownership of the lot until 1947, then sold it to Pat and Susie."

"Sounds about right."

"So Liza and Mike sold to the man who may have burned them out."

Clara's eye drilled into Ed's. "Pat didn't set that fire." She finished her tea and set the cup down. "You'll have to excuse me," she said, "I'm feeling a *wee bit* tired."

"Of course. I understand. Just a couple quick questions. Do you remember the general strike?"

"Oh, you should have *seen* this city. Police and National

Guard everywhere. The mayor and governor predicting riots. But *nothing happened*. The working people kept their heads, and the boys *won*. Roosevelt gave them everything they wanted. It was *wonderful*."

"Beth told me that Mike and Liza moved to Boston."

"They did. Took the insurance money and left."

"So maybe there wasn't a gun to Mike's head."

"With the fire, Sean let him go."

"Why Boston?"

"Liza was from there. She had uncles on the police force. They got Mike a job. And you know what he did? Became big in the union. He was ashamed of what he done here. That was his penance. Only Pat never forgave him. *So stubborn*, my brother."

"Pat knew?"

"Oh, sure. Susie and Liza kept in touch. After the war, Mike wanted to bury the hatchet. But Pat wouldn't. Stubborn as a mule, that one."

Clara got a second wind and chattered about her dental problems and her love of ballet—a cousin took her to performances. And Sheila and her *nice young man*, Billy—from St. Paul's—took her to the Plough and Stars to watch the Irish dancing.

"I understand that you were there the night Ryan—"

"Yes." Her face clouded at the memory. "I had a *wee bit* too much Guinness. Sheila had to help me into the car when she drove me home."

At first, Ed didn't register what she'd said. Then he realized the implications.

"*Sheila* drove you? Where was Billy?"

"Off somewhere. Sheila drove. I remember, because I sat in front. When it's Sheila and Billy, I sit in back."

Ed inhaled sharply. "Do you know where Billy went?"

"No. Off with friends, I suppose."

"Do you remember what time Sheila drove you back here?"

"I can't be sure. I was a *wee bit* tipsy. Maybe around twelve."

Ed's heart pounded. Sheila and Billy were off the suspect list because a throng had seen them dance the night away. But around the time someone took a statue to Duffy's head, Billy was not on the dance floor.

—26—

Ed called Detective Park and told him what Clara had told him. "Strange. Several witnesses swore he was at the bar dancing. You said the old lady was drunk. Maybe she got it wrong."

"Maybe. But she specifically recalled sitting in the front seat beside Sheila. When Jameson's there, she sits in back."

"All right. I'll take another look."

Ed gave him the address.

A few hours later, Wheelwright e-mailed:

> Guess who has a history of assault. Park went back 10 years, and Billy Jameson was clean. But 18 years ago, he was arrested after slugging an umpire at a softball game. Jameson was called out at first, but thought he was safe. Got probation. The next year, he's arrested at a bar. Took a pool cue to someone's head. Judge says: jail or AA. He joined AA, got sober, and from all accounts, hasn't touched a drop since. Started his construction company. Solid citizen, but still—it's not much of a leap from hitting a guy with a pool cue to doing it with a statue. Nice work. If the cops nail Jameson, you're a lock for a Mayor's Commendation.

On the way home, Ed and Julie ran into Wheelwright at the elevator.

"Oh, Ed," she said, "I just sent you another e-mail. Jameson's clean. The old lady was right about riding in front—because Jameson was stretched out in back with an upset stomach. She didn't remember that. One too many. When they got her home, Jameson felt well enough to help her into the building. The night guy remembered him."

The elevator door opened and they stepped into the crowded box.

"Julie keeps telling me I should stick to history," Ed said.

"But does he *listen*?" Julie asked.

"Hey, it was a solid tip," Wheelwright said. "You did the right thing." The elevator opened and everyone streamed toward the exit. "Did you get the DNA report?"

"Yes. Thanks, I guess."

The final report showed no matches.

"You know what it means," Wheelwright said.

"The freezer," Ed replied. "That really sucks."

—27—

WHEN MISTRESS ROD CALLED, ED WAS AT THE CHILDREN'S PLAYground in Golden Gate Park. It was Saturday afternoon, sunny and warm with a cool breeze, sweatshirt weather. Julie was running errands with Jake in tow. Ed had Sonya and a couple friends. The girls were getting a little old for the playground, but they begged to go anyway. They especially enjoyed the carousel.

Ed had once written a column about it. Golden Gate Park was originally hundred-foot sand dunes and saw grass. Inspired by Woodward's Gardens, the park's original visionary, William Hammond Hall, reserved a corner of his 1871 design for a merry-go-round. Hall was succeeded by the John McLaren, who loved the carousel idea and envisioned a grand European model with carved, lacquered horses gliding up and down to calliope music. But his budget allowed only crude horses fixed in place. When the 1939 Golden Gate International Exposition closed in 1941, its carousel, built by master craftsmen in Buffalo, was moved from Treasure Island to Children's Playground. In 1990, it was restored magnificently, a jewel of the park. Sonya adored it.

Ed bought a fistful of tickets and told the girls to have fun. He retired to a bench and was deep into the *Sunday Times* Book Review when his phone chimed. It took him a moment to realize who "Rod" was. He explained his connection to Duffy, that he'd seen her at the funeral and on TV, and that among Duffy's effects, he'd found her number.

"So tragic," she said softly. "Such a sweet man."

"Yes," Ed replied.

"I still can't believe it." Mistress Rod's voice cracked.

"Me neither. I hope you don't mind if I ask you a few questions. Duffy and I were friends. But I had no idea…what he was into. I'm trying to understand. You mind?"

"Not at all."

"I'm curious. How did you hear about the funeral? The news didn't mention it."

"The police told me."

"At one of the clubs?"

"No. I called them."

"I don't understand."

"I don't go to the clubs much anymore. But I was teaching the intro class at Roissy and saw Ryan's picture on a flyer. That's how I found out. I called them right away."

"What'd they ask you?"

"Who I was, how I knew him. They got interested when I mentioned Little Girl."

"Who?"

"Ryan's sub. She has a high-powered job, so she uses a handle."

Ed recalled that Duffy played the dom with the gal who'd been in Seattle when he was killed. He flashed on his friend spread-eagled, his skin waxy. "So he was dominant with her, but submissive with other—?"

"Oh, no. He was a total dom."

"Always?" Ed asked. "*Never* a sub?"

"Never. He didn't have a bottom bone in his body."

Ed couldn't believe his ears. "Did the police say anything about how he was found?"

"No."

"What *did* they tell you?"

"Just that whoever killed him was into BDSM."

Evidently, the blanket the cops had thrown over the clubs had holes.

"Daddy!"

Ed looked up. Sonya was blissfully gliding up and down on a leaping tiger.

Ed waved back, while informing the pro-dom that he'd found the body. He described the scene.

"But that's impossible," Mistress Rod insisted. "He couldn't have been bound."

"Well, he was. Wrists and ankles tied to the furniture. And a big ball gag with leather straps."

Mistress Rod said, "No way. He was a dom. Never a sub. *Never*."

"So…?"

She paused before replying. "Was he wearing cuffs?"

"Handcuffs? No."

"No, wrist and ankle cuffs. Nylon sleeves that wrap around and attach with Velcro—with D-rings for the ropes."

"No. Nothing like that."

"So the ropes were against his skin?"

"Yes. Why?"

"Ryan always used cuffs. *Always*."

Ed's heart began to race. He exhaled slowly. "Would you mind telling me how you're so sure of all this?"

"Because that's how I taught him. Cuffs are safer than skin contact. You say he was naked?"

"As the day he was born."

"Ryan always stayed clothed. The sub didn't, but he did. *Always*."

Like a carousel rider grabbing for the brass ring, Ed reached for a conclusion, but couldn't snag it. "What are you saying?"

"Don't you see? The scene was a hoax. Ryan was a sub, a role he'd never play. He was naked, which he'd never be. And he wasn't wearing cuffs, which he always used."

"Daddy!"

Sonya's smile swept past him like a searchlight.

"So the killer set things up to throw the police off?"

"Evidently. But he had no idea how Duffy played, so he set it up all wrong."

"I don't know. How would the bad guy even know Duffy was into it? Did he have the gag lying around?"

"He kept it in a suitcase. It was Saturday night—I imagine he was on his way out to play. The suitcase was there. The murderer found it and put it to use. Only he didn't know what he was doing."

"I don't know."

"You have a better explanation?"

She had a point. The medical examiner ruled it kinky sex gone bad, but he didn't know Duffy. The pro-dom did.

—28—

Sonya changed her mind about Monopoly when her after-school program acquired five copies and launched a tournament with prizes—gift certificates to a pizza place. To play, kids had to show one piece of completed homework to Learning Center Director Hector Ramirez. They raced through their schoolwork to claim seats.

To keep things moving, Hector changed the rules. You didn't drive the competition into bankruptcy. You just had to be the first to assemble two monopolies with one hotel each.

This turned the game into a frenzy of acquisition. Cash reserves be damned. Players offered several parcels for one if it meant closing a first monopoly, and even more for a second. Then they mortgaged everything to build the hotels that won the game.

Ed wasn't sure he liked the new rules. But Sonya did. She jumped in with both feet, and won one of three third-place prizes. She also acquired a passion for the game and its new hip-hop rules.

"Daddy," Sonya ventured cooly, "I'll trade you Marvin Gardens for States Avenue."

Ed surveyed her holdings. "Don't you own Virginia and St. Charles?" The trade would give her a monopoly.

"No," she squealed, squirming.

"Funny. I distinctly recall you buying Virginia."

"And St. Charles, too," Julie said smiling.

"No way!" Sonya replied, indignant. "See?" She waved a fan of cards.

"Well," Ed said, "if you don't own Virginia and St. Charles, why trade? Marvin is worth twice as much."

"Uh," Sonya stammered, "the *color*. Marvin Gardens is yellow. I hate yellow. States is purple. *That's my favorite color.*"

Ed and Julie laughed.

"Come on, honey," Ed said. "I *know* you own them."

Sonya produced the two cards from her lap.

"Aren't you supposed to keep your cards on the table?" Julie asked. "Isn't that how they play at the club?"

"Yes," Sonya replied, casually covering some of her property cards with Monopoly money. "But sometimes they fall on the floor—*accidentally*."

"Or into your lap?" Ed prompted.

"Or under the board," Sonya added.

"Or under your money," Ed pointed.

"Doesn't Hector watch?" Julie asked.

"Sure...."

"But..."

"He can't watch five games at once. And sometimes he has to do other things."

"So when Hector's distracted, you—"

"Not just me, Mom. *Everyone*."

"There's a word for that." Ed tried to sound more avuncular than stern. "Cheating."

"*No, it isn't!*" Sonya insisted. "That's how you play. You have to remember what everyone has. If you don't, you're a chump. You snooze, you lose."

More phrases picked up at the club, along with swear words in four languages. Sonya clearly had the potential to become a rampaging capitalist. When they first played, Ed and Julie did their quiet best to help their daughter develop monopolies without her knowing. Now Ed feared that if he glanced out the window, by the time he looked back, his watch might be missing.

"Well, you can forget States," Ed said. "No way I'm giving you a second monopoly."

"But Daddy, you'd be closer to winning, too!"

"Forget it."

Sonya rolled the dice, landed on one of Julie's properties, and had to pay. They circled the board. Then Jake started fussing, and Sonya's bedtime loomed. Julie decided to wrap things up. "Tell you what: You have Vermont and Oriental and need Connecticut. I have Atlantic and Ventnor and need MG. Let's trade."

Sonya considered her mother's proposal. "But if I give you MG, you get your second."

"And you get *yours*."

Sonya counted her money and eyeballed Julie's stack. Sonya's properties were less valuable, but the modified rules favored them. Hotels were cheaper. Plus, it was Sonya's turn. She could build a hotel before she rolled, and next time, with any luck, get another and win. "Okay."

"Here's Connecticut," Julie said.

"Here's MG."

Something about "MG" struck a match in the dark cavern of Ed's memory.

Sonya won. Julie hustled the kids upstairs. Ed put the game away and ran the dishwasher.

"Ed!" Julie called. "Reading!"

He and Sonya were into a Nancy Drew. She read a few pages, then Ed read a few as his favorite girl in the whole wide world snuggled into her covers.

"Coming!" he called back. As he climbed the stairs, he realized where he'd seen "MG": on Duffy's paper, along with VT Ave. Partners and CT Ave. Devel. He assumed they referred to Potrero Hill. But those were streets. These were *avenues*. If MG was Marvin Gardens, everything made sense. All three had names inspired by Monopoly.

—29—

Ed believed Mistress Rod. Duffy's final scene must have been a hoax.

But Detective Park would not be so easily persuaded. Ed had already sent him on one wild goose chase based on the warped recollections of a tipsy old lady. He could imagine how Park would greet this new lead. Not to mention that the pro-dom's conclusion raised questions about the effectiveness of police work at the sex clubs. Before he called Park, Ed needed to satisfy himself that Mistress Rod was credible. There was only one way to do that: pay her a visit.

The building was near the Museum of Modern Art, a short walk from the paper. There was no name on the door of the seventh-floor suite, just the number she'd given. He keyed the code. The lock clicked.

Ed stepped into a small, carpeted waiting room with wicker chairs and *Smithsonian* and the *New Yorker* on a coffee table. The walls were adorned with posters of harpsichords.

Mistress Rod opened the inside door. Her black hair and white streak were arranged in a French braid. About forty, she was a little shorter than Ed, plump but poised. She wore a fluffy turtleneck, slacks, and sandals.

Ed fumbled for his wallet with clammy hands.

"Forget that."

"But I'm taking your time."

"This isn't a session. We're just talking. Anything I can do to help."

"Thank you." Ed slipped his wallet back into his pocket.

Mistress Rod ushered him through the door into her studio. Blackout blinds covered the windows. The lights were off. Candles shimmered.

"I have clients later," she said, motioning to the candles. "I was setting up. I'll turn on the lights."

Ed recalled the room from the television piece: the floggers and Inquisition contraptions. Two chairs occupied a corner. She motioned him to sit.

"Do you have a name other than Mistress Rod?"

She laughed. "That name has been very good for business. Subs adore it. But you can call me Veronica."

She was sweet—in a whips-and-chains sort of way. Ed relaxed.

"I have a feeling that's not your real name either."

"Correct."

Across the room, Ed noticed a door with a sign: Exit. Veronica followed his eyes.

"My clients appreciate discretion," She explained. "They enter the way you did, but leave through that door. It leads to a stair that takes them down one floor, where they catch the elevator. No one sees them."

"What about the neighbors? Don't they *hear* things?"

Another laugh. "Oh, no. There's soundboard. No one hears anything."

Ed's eyebrows arched. "Soundboard?" It had to be underneath the walls, carpet, and ceiling. To build the studio, someone had to take the room down to the studs, install the board, then put it together again.

Veronica read Ed's mind. "I have an arrangement with the management company." Her smile said someone high up was a client who'd provided the studio. "Officially, I teach harpsichord." Hence the posters. She glanced at her watch. "I have a client in forty minutes. I need about fifteen to get ready, so—"

"I understand. This won't take long. I'm just trying to understand Duffy's relationship to—" he gestured, "all this. How well did you know him?"

"We were friendly. I coached him and Little Girl through a few scenes—"

"His submissive."

"Yes, a very enthusiastic sub."

"Did he use his real name…?"

"As far as I know. He did with me."

"I'm surprised he was so open." If Walt had found out, Ed imagined he would have been on the receiving end of some corporate whipping.

Veronica shrugged. "There's no predicting it. Ryan was more public than many. He once told me that when he finally realized who he was, it was like opening a door into a new world."

"What do you mean you 'coached' them?"

"How much do you know about BDSM?"

"Just what I get from the media."

"I see. Do you know what a munch is?"

"No."

"That's how Ryan and Little Girl met. It's an informal get-together for unattached doms and subs. Usually in a private room at a restaurant. Comfortable and discreet. People wear tags—doms black, subs blue. Ryan and Little Girl started talking and decided to play. They began like most people, pretty light: corsets, heels, collars, spanking, light flogging. But after a while, they wanted to try bondage. Especially Little Girl. She was really into it. Only she was nervous. Ryan didn't know the ropes." Ed smiled. Mistress Rod just kept talking. "So they asked if I'd coach them."

"When was this?"

"Oh…" She calculated. "Couple years ago. I agreed, with my usual conditions. We had three or four sessions."

"Conditions?"

"Ryan wasn't certified in first aid. I told them I wouldn't see them until he was."

"First aid? Why?"

"Safety. Tops have to know what they're doing, and what can go wrong if they're not careful."

"But doesn't first-aid training take awhile?"

"Eight weeks."

"So you have *prerequisites*?"

"Believe me, I didn't need their business. But if a dom I train hurts a sub, I can get sued. That's never happened, and it's never going to. Because I'm careful."

Ed glanced at the wall of whips. "Couldn't you just have them sign a release?"

"Sure. But it's not just about covering myself legally. Subs rarely suffer harm, even when doms don't know what they're doing. First-aid training just helps people make the most of their scenes."

"I don't understand."

"It helps subs relax and feel more trusting. The more trust, the deeper they can go into sub-space."

Sub-space? The last time Ed had heard the term, he was watching *Star Trek*. "Uh—"

"The emotional place where submission becomes transcendence."

Beam me up. Ed felt like he'd been transported to a parallel universe, one that looked like his, but was very different. "You lost me."

"Submissiveness isn't about pain and humiliation for their own sake. It's about *using* intense sensation to go deep into spirituality."

"You mean like religion?" This parallel universe was light years away.

"No, more like what you feel when you fall in love—total connection to the other person."

Ed tried to hook the idea and reel it in, but it got away. His expression showed it.

"BDSM is about connection—deep, intimate connection. For subs, total surrender feels liberating. Before coaching them, I also insisted on having coffee with Little Girl to make sure she trusted Ryan. That he knew her edge and could hold her there without going over."

"But didn't they have—that word?"

"Safe word. Of course. But deep in sub-space, no one wants to invoke it and interrupt the scene. So we met. She felt comfortable proceeding. If anything, she was the one pushing things."

"Into bondage."

"Yes."

"So what exactly did you teach them?"

"Mostly knot-tying."

The only knot-tying Ed ever had done was in Cub Scouts. "Like square knots?"

"Yes. A lot of new doms think they have to learn dozens of knots. But if you use wrist and ankle cuffs with D-rings, you only need a few: square, surgeon's, cinch, maybe lark's head."

"How did you wind up at Duffy's funeral?"

"After our sessions, I ran into them at Roissy a few times. Eventually, they began assisting in my intro classes—"

"Assisting?"

"I would lecture, then Ryan or I would demonstrate on Little Girl. When I heard, I called her right away. By that time, they were lovers as well as play partners. She'd been out of town. She was devastated. I asked if she was going to the funeral. She wanted to, but didn't know where or when. The police told me, so I told her. We went together."

Ed recalled standing on the church steps and noticing the woman with the white streak. He didn't recall seeing another woman with her.

"I know you've already spoken to the police," Ed said, scanning her face. "But would you mind talking to them again?"

He figured she'd refuse. Prostitutes steered clear of cops.

"Why?"

"They don't know that I walked in on a hoax. If I tell the detective, he won't believe me. But I think he'll believe you."

"All right."

"That was easy."

She smiled. "Like I said, anything I can do to help. I have no problem with the police. My business is legal."

"It is? It's not…?"

"Prostitution? No. I never have sex with clients. I just dominate them. I'm a 'fantasy-play consultant.' And even if we had sex, this is San Francisco. The police don't like soliciting on the street, but they don't care what happens behind closed doors—unless it involves kids or trafficking."

Ed thanked Veronica or whoever she was, then headed for the exit. But with a hand on the knob, he turned back.

"Uh, one more question. Being submissive. What kind of person—?"

She smiled. "You'd be surprised. Most of my clients are powerful men—corporate executives, government officials. Where I used to live, my steadiest client was a congressman. They spend their lives being decisive, giving orders, making things happen. They have enormous responsibilities. Someone once said that power is the ultimate aphrodisiac. That's true for some, but not for everyone. Wielding power can be a burden. So they come to me for an emotional vacation. Here they have no responsibilities—they don't have to make any decisions. They're not *allowed* to. Here they can play with what they don't ordinarily experience: feeling powerless. Of course, with safe words, they're ultimately in control. Does that make sense?"

"Not really." He couldn't imagine licking Mistress Rod's spike-heeled boots, much less paying for the privilege.

"Well, if it ever does," she smiled, "you have my number."

As the door clicked behind him, Ed had as many questions as answers. But none of that mattered. What mattered was what Park thought. Ed felt confident the detective would consider Mistress Rod credible.

Only Park didn't call her. He listened politely as Ed explained the ruse in Duffy's living room. A hoax? So what? It only proved that the perp was clever. Park already knew that. Duffy's living room was clean, except for unidentified DNA. Sub? Dom? Thanks, but no thanks. Park had other cases. Unless someone stepped forward with a name or DNA match, Duffy was on ice.

—30—

IRISH STRIKERS BATTLING IRISH POLICE. THE FEELINGS ON BOTH SIDES ran cold and deep. Almost seventy-five years had passed since Bloody Thursday, yet when Clara heard the name Sean Callahan, the sweet old lady stung like a scorpion—"I spit on his grave." Her brother must have felt even less charitable, especially after watching Callahan club Harry Bridges. But what about Sean Callahan? How did he experience the strike? And how did he keep his men in line, men like Pat's former best friend? One person might know: Callahan's son, Mitch, the hot-tempered developer.

Callahan piqued Ed's curiosity for another reason. In Park's notes, he said he'd left his daughter's at eleven. But Duffy might have been killed as late as twelve. Callahan refused the cheek swab, and the DA wouldn't try for a court order, which struck Ed as somewhere between odd and dropping the ball—or maybe not wanting to antagonize a contributor. Ed checked the city's campaign finance site. Callahan gave the DA's political action committee a hefty annual contribution, and twice that during election years.

Ed needed a map to find the street tucked into the hillside above West Portal. The house was a white colonial with fluted columns. On a block filled with Spanish haciendas, it looked like it had been shipped out of Virginia.

The man who opened the door was seventy-six but looked much younger. He stood erect. His full head of sand-colored hair showed little gray. As he led the way past a kitchen out of *Sunset*, Ed had to hustle to keep up.

The large living room had leather furniture, a Persian rug, a huge TV, and windows that overlooked a pond with water lilies. On the wall beside the television hung a large print of the famous photo.

"There it is," Ed said.

"Yes," Mitchell Callahan said. "Join me in a Guinness? One of those days."

Ed nodded.

"Maria!" Callahan called, motioning his guest into a buttery leather chair.

A middle-aged Filipina appeared. "Yes, Mr. Mitch?"

"Two Guinness. And do we have nuts or pretzels?"

"I look."

"My wife passed away two years ago. Leukemia."

"I'm sorry," Ed said.

Callahan nodded. "Her last few months, Maria helped out. Now she takes care of me."

"One of those days?" Ed prompted, feigning commiseration. Later, Ed planned to ask some obnoxious questions. Leading up to them, he hoped to persuade his host that he wasn't just another asshole reporter.

"We've got a project in Pacifica. Seventy-five apartments and twelve thousand feet of storefronts and offices. Today was pour day—the foundation. You know what a special concrete inspection is?"

"Seismic?"

Callahan smiled. "Very good."

Ed's renovations had involved a seismic upgrade, which meant foundation work, a structural engineer, tons of rebar, and lots of money. It also meant that the concrete pour had to be supervised by an independent verifier to make sure the contractor did it properly.

"The inspector's supposed to show up at eight. We've got cement mixers lined up two blocks. The guy doesn't show—car trouble. I have to pick him up. But it worked out; we poured and he signed."

"*You* picked him up? You didn't send an assistant?"

Callahan laughed. "I *am* the assistant. When my wife got sick, I sold the business to my nephew. But after Jeanette passed, I was bored, so I went back, helping Doyle. I was glad to drive the inspector. Chatted him up. It helped."

Like Ed was doing with him.

The housekeeper set a tray before them, mixed nuts and two glasses of dark liquid topped with creamy foam. Callahan handed one to Ed using his right hand. Ed flashed on Park's notes. Whoever whacked Duffy was a rightie.

Callahan raised his glass, nodding toward the photo. "To my father." They both swallowed.

"Beautiful home," Ed said.

"Built it myself," he said with pride. "The old man wanted me to be a cop. But growing up, hearing his stories—the nastiness, greed, and stupidity—I decided I'd rather pound nails."

"You've done very well."

"Can't complain. But no matter what you do, it's nastiness, greed, and stupidity."

"I hear you."

"So," Callahan said, "about the picture, why are you interested?"

"A diary just surfaced. The writer was there on Bloody Thursday."

"Cop? Striker? Or observer?"

"Striker."

"Let me guess: he hated my father's guts."

"He did. That's why I called. To hear the other side—to the extent that you know it."

"I'll do you one better." Callahan smiled. "You can hear from the man himself."

"What?" Ed exclaimed. Sean Callahan had been dead thirty years.

"Before my father died, my sister sat him down and taped his life story. Four cassettes. I dug them out. Found the part you're interested in."

"Incredible! What a treat."

Callahan reached over to a wall unit that held books, family photos, and a cassette deck.

"Dad," a woman said, "talk about 1934, the strike."

Sean Callahan's voice was labored but firm. "It was an old story, the good guys against the bad, God-fearing men against godless Communists and their dupes. They had Russia. They were fixing to take Europe. And they were big here, too. It was the Depression and people were hurting. They took advantage of them. On the docks, it was Bridges."

"Harry Bridges?" the woman prompted.

"Aye. Evil, Bridges was. Doubly evil. A goddamn Communist, and Irish to boot. That stuck in my craw. But he had the gift of gab. Talked real pretty and duped the longshoremen, had them eating out of his hand, eating his poison like it was cake."

Callahan recounted his delight when the mayor put the police at the disposal of the Industrial Association. He was spoiling for a fight, and so were his men. They wielded their clubs proudly.

"What about the photo, Dad? When did you first see it?"

"The Friday after Bloody Thursday."

"How'd you feel?"

"I was of two minds. On one side, I was mighty proud. There I was, standing up to the Communists, by God, giving them what for."

"But?"

"I just wish the photographer waited another second. He caught me with me billy raised. But if he'd 'a waited, the world woulda seen me giving that son of a bitch what he deserved. I only got one hit before they pushed me off, but I bet Bridges hurt for a while."

"Who pushed you?"

"Strikers. We was outnumbered. It was just me and three of my men. Had to be a dozen strikers come at us to rescue Bridges. A couple more seconds, and I'd 'a saved the government all they spent later trying to deport him."

During the McCarthy era, the government had branded

Bridges a Communist and tried to ship him back to Australia, but lost. Bridges died in San Francisco in 1990.

"Did you have any idea the picture would become famous?"

"None. I was just doing me duty. It was the strikers made it famous. They blew it up, put it on posters, and marched them up Market Street."

"The funeral parade?"

"Aye. But you didn't see any marches for the cops who caught hell. Don Clancy got stabbed. Fritzy Schultz got ribs broke. Jimmy O'Hara lost teeth."

"How do you feel about the picture now?"

"Proud. When I'm gone, I want each of you kids to have a copy. Hang it up. Look at it. Remember your Dad and what he done."

Callahan turned off the tape. "I did like he asked. Hung the picture."

"I'm curious," Ed said. "He implies that everyone under his command was as enthusiastic as he was. Did he ever talk about that?"

Callahan looked quizzical.

"Lots of police knew strikers, had friends on strike. Maybe they didn't want to go up against them. Did your father ever talk about having to lean on any cops to fight the dock workers?"

"Not that I recall. But in 1934, I was five years old. By the time I was old enough to ask my father about the picture, it was years later. Why?"

"Because the diary I mentioned says that some police didn't want to fight the strikers, that they were threatened, their families, too."

"I don't know anything about that. Who wrote this diary?"

"Patrick Duffy."

Callahan smirked. "Of the St. Paul's Duffys?"

"Yes."

Callahan sneered. "Fuckin' Duffys. Old Pat hated my father's guts. During the strike, he tried to run our family out of St. Paul's. He couldn't, so his family and their union friends shunned us—when they weren't attacking me in the schoolyard."

"Who attacked you?"

"Billy Duffy. Pat's son. Two years older than me. He and his cousins and friends jumped me more than once." He smiled at the memory. "But I was scrappy and I had friends, too. I gave as good as I got."

"Billy. Wasn't he the father of—"

"Ryan Duffy, of your newspaper. Yes. The Duffys hold grudges—forever. Ryan held one against me for what happened on the docks between my father and his grandfather."

"Your plan to develop the Armory."

"You know about that?"

"I know you proposed a hilltop village and he wanted Woodward's Gardens."

"That's right. He went on and on about how the North Mish needs a park. But when his old buddy Eric McCain proposed a bigger development only a few blocks away, he didn't write one goddamn word about any park. Oh, no, he was all for it. And McCain's going to get his village, mark my words."

"That must have annoyed you."

"I was furious. The little prick knew they'd never tear down the Armory. It's on the National Register, for God's sake. He just wanted to fuck me because of my father and his grandfather."

"I heard it you took a swing at him."

Callahan's eyes bored deep into Ed's. "How'd you hear that?"

"A reporter who was there."

"Well, it's true. I went for him. Usually, I keep a cooler head. But my wife was dying. I snapped."

"Are you still interested in developing the Armory?"

"Sure. But we have projects for a good eighteen months."

"And after that?"

"We'll see how the wind blows."

"What do you mean?"

"In the eighties, Planning voted unanimously not to develop the Armory. In the nineties, it was 7-2. On our proposal, 5-4. They'll come around. Eventually."

On his way out, Ed noticed something he'd missed on the way in. A niche in the front hall contained a plaster statue. Only this one was still in one piece.

—31—

THE SKINNY ALGERIAN KID BEHIND THE COUNTER AT THE FRONT Page gave Julie a shy smile as he handed her a spinach salad. He continued to eye her as he pushed a grilled chicken sandwich to Ed. They slid their trays down the rails.

One of the TVs suspended from the dining room ceiling was tuned to CNN. A perky blonde was saying, "...the nation's most expensive housing market—the San Francisco Bay area."

"I just lost my appetite," Julie said.

Ed leaned close. "But think of all our equity." At the end of the line, he paid the counter kid's mother.

At a table by the window, they were planning an outing with the kids when Tom Ferguson appeared holding a tray and grinning. "Good news."

Ed motioned to pull up a chair.

"No transit village near you—"

"*Yes!*" Julie looked heavenward and raised two fists in triumph. She and Calvin had returned to the hearing and he'd testified.

"—and McCain won big in Civic Center. His parcel qualifies. They're letting him go twenty stories with minimal setbacks. Monster buildings. He was a kangaroo on a trampoline."

"What do you mean, 'qualifies?'" Ed asked.

"He owns enough of the block. In Civic Center, a developer has to own no less than three-quarters of a block, with its closest point no more than two hundred feet from BART. And he's got it."

"What about Twenty-fourth Street?" Julie asked.

"Anything beyond Civic Center has to be much smaller—ten stories, seven set back—"

Julie inhaled sharply. "But that's awful!"

Ferguson held up a hand. "*But* any village near you has to occupy no less than *one entire block*."

"So?"

"That's a lot of property. Most blocks in the Mission are pretty big, and they're divided into small lots. So dozens of lots per block. It's virtually impossible to buy up a whole block."

"But don't big developers have tons of money?" Julie asked.

"Sure," Ferguson explained, "but property within two hundred feet of your BART station just got a lot more expensive—and you don't even want to think about the last few lots."

"You lost me," Julie said.

Ed picked up the explanation. "Owners close to BART now know that any transit village developer has to buy their lot. They'll hold out for huge bucks. The closer a developer gets to owning a whole block, the more expensive the remaining lots become."

For Julie, it was sinking in. "So, no village. Thank God. I have to call Calvin." She pulled out her phone.

"For sure?" Ed asked.

"For the foreseeable future. Of course, APOD is already scheming to make things easier for developers out your way. But the vote was eight to one. They have to change a lot of minds. No one controls a whole block within two hundred feet of your BART station. I checked. I don't see how anyone could build a village near you."

Julie dialed, eying Ed. "But I still want to move—eventually."

"Fine. But now there's no rush."

—32—

Ed Googled Callahan and came away more confused. The developer donated generously to civic causes, but had a notoriously short fuse. APOD had awarded him Developer of the Year, but he'd been implicated in the building-inspection bribery scandal. He was not indicted, but he was a big contributor to the DA. Ed found him affable, even charming. But the night of Duffy's murder, he had no witnesses to his whereabouts between eleven and midnight, and he'd refused the cheek swab.

Ed spun away from his screen and considered the diary. It would make a fine column, maybe even a Sunday magazine piece. But his thoughts kept drifting back to Duffy on the living room floor. Who else did Ed know who knew Callahan?

He climbed the stairs and found Julie considering the TV listings. "We haven't seen Henry and Franny in ages."

"Funny, I was just thinking about them."

Ed grabbed the phone.

They became friends with Henry and Franny Levy when their daughters attended preschool together. But the girls wound up at different elementary schools, so the couples saw less of each other. Franny was a real estate lawyer. Henry was an architect for the Affordable Housing Coalition.

They met at Tadich Grill, a venerable bistro in the Financial District. Founded in 1849 as a coffee stand on a wharf that became a street when Yerba Buena Cove was filled in, Tadich's was the oldest surviving restaurant on the West Coast.

Franny had olive skin, dark curly hair, and huge brown eyes behind big glasses. Henry had a fair complexion, vestiges of sandy hair, and a small gold post earring. She was outgoing and gesticulated when she spoke. He was more reserved, but had a wry sense of humor.

A Latino kid in a starched white jacket set a basket of sourdough before them. It was as crusty as their waiter.

As usual, Ed and Julie split everything. The Levys weren't splitters. Franny ordered sand dabs.

"Just so you know," the waiter explained, "the sand dabs are not filleted."

"I know," she said. "Not a problem."

"I hate picking bones out of fish," Julie said.

"It brings back fond memories for me. My father took us fishing as kids."

"Jews fishing?" Ed asked. The closest his family ever came to a rod and reel was Go Fish.

"Where do you think lox comes from?" Franny retorted. "Someone has to catch the salmon."

Ed laughed. "No one in my family."

"Or mine," Julie concurred.

"Franny can fillet anything," Henry said.

"Back in Minnesota, we had a cabin on a lake. Went fishing all the time."

They chatted about the kids, then Ed turned to Henry. "I've been watching your senior housing project go up by Mission Playground." The playground was a favorite of Sonya's, and Jake enjoyed the baby swings.

"So far, so good," Henry replied, raising two sets of crossed fingers. The development involved eighty one-bedroom apartments and a street-level produce store, cleaner, hair dresser, and medical clinic.

"Your design?"

"No." Henry's lips formed a thin smile.

"These days Henry's more of a developer," Franny said.

"I'm really a mediator." He sighed. "A mediator of institutional dysfunction."

"That's a mouthful," Julie said.

Franny explained, "Henry's spent way too much time lately juggling the Mission Neighborhood Council, the Mayor's Office on Housing, and the Community Banking Alliance."

"Which means I get shit from everyone." Henry smiled.

"You must be nervous about the fires."

"Now *there's* an understatement," Franny said.

"It's been awful," Henry explained. "The CBA's threatening to pull financing unless we post guards round the clock, but we have no budget for that. Meanwhile, the Neighborhood Council's broke, and the Mayor's Office doesn't want to set a precedent."

"Leaving you—?" Julie asked.

Henry shook his head. "Getting shit from everyone. Fortunately, the Council has ins with the gangs. They're trying to convince them that our project *isn't* gentrification. It's housing for their *grandmothers*."

The waiter brought the entrees. Franny made a shallow incision in her fish, peeled back the skin, and exposed flaky meat. She probed a bit, got a purchase on the spine, wiggled it, and, with a flourish, lifted out the entire skeleton.

"Wow," Julie said, applauding.

Franny smiled. "Nothing to it."

"Speaking of real estate development," Ed asked, "on the phone, you mentioned you know Mitchell Callahan."

"Sure," Franny said. "Big developer."

"You know him?" Henry asked.

"Talked to him recently." Ed explained about the diary and the Duffy-Callahan feud.

"I knew Ryan," Henry said. "Nice guy. Very supportive of us. Terrible what happened. As for Mitch Callahan…" His voice trailed off.

"What?"

"I know lots of people who have stories. None end happily. He's an ass."

"What about Eric McCain? You know him?" Ed explained that he'd grown up on Duffy's block.

"Not personally. But I respect him." Henry took a bite of salmon. "His Civic Center village—very creative."

"How so?" Ed asked, spooning up some cioppino.

"You know how developers combine small lots into big parcels?"

"No."

"*As quietly as possible.* If you do it under one name, word gets out and sellers demand more. So developers hide behind a bunch of LLCs—"

"What?" Ed inquired.

"Limited liability companies. Like corporations, but not as complicated. Good for real estate development. The LLCs buy up the lots using a variety of names and the sellers never know it's all one buyer."

"But how would they find out? When we bought our house, we knew nothing about the seller."

"Commercial's different," Henry explained. "The numbers are much bigger. The city's involved. And people gossip like crazy. So developers hide behind LLCs. The city's been dancing around a transit village in Civic Center for years. Since day one, all the owners in the area have been thinking they'll get a windfall. But something always derailed it—zoning, school fees, neighborhood opposition, you name it. So the owners' hopes have been dashed several times."

"I represent one of them," Franny said. "Cynical like you wouldn't believe."

"Meanwhile," Henry explained, "with all the drama, the owners over there—printers, plumbers, auto repair guys, two dozen of them—they got to know each other. Which made things worse."

"Why?" Ed asked.

"Developers hate organized sellers—"

"Why?" Julie asked.

"Strength in numbers," Franny explained. "They demand more money."

"And they *get* it," Henry said. "Way up there. Then, oh, seven, eight years ago, McCain shows up. No bullshit. No hiding behind LLCs with Monopoly names. He tells the owners, 'God knows if the city will ever approve a village. But I want to build it and to do that, I need your land. So I'll option your property right now—give you decent money renewable annually if you play ball. If the city ever approves the village, I exercise my option and buy your property at a set price—three times its current appraised value."

"You lost me," Julie said.

"McCain paid each owner twenty thousand dollars a year—big bucks to the mom-and-pop shops down there."

"Whoa," Ed said. "With two dozen owners, that's almost half a million a year for eight years. That's pushing four million—and just for the right to buy them out for tons more money?"

"Yes," Henry explained, "but four million looks pretty shrewd when you consider that he nailed down the entire parcel."

"Only now he has to pay them even more."

"Sure. But the price is firm, part of the original deal. No muss. No fuss. McCain goes to the capital markets, folds the cost of the land into his financing, and he's ready to break ground."

Ed recalled Ferguson mentioning that McCain had sunk millions into Civic Center property.

"So what does he wind up paying?"

"Around fifty."

"Fifty *million*!" Julie exclaimed. "That's a fortune."

"True. But when his village is built, he stands to clear at least that, probably millions more."

Ed whistled.

"It gets better," Henry explained. "Once McCain bought the options, the owners loved him. They saw real money every year, with more at the buyout. Of course, the neighborhood activists made a big stink. But with the owners waving flags for McCain, the opposition lost its poster people—no little victims getting screwed by the big, bad developer. That helped a lot with the city. Of course, it still took McCain and his APOD buddies years to get the thing approved—"

"Welcome to San Francisco," Franny said.

"Other developers said McCain was insane. Now he looks like a genius."

Ed reflected on running into McCain in front of Duffy's. The developer hadn't mentioned any of this. All he talked about was Duffy, old times, and his boat. Now, with the money he stood to make from his transit village, he could trade his forty-two-footer for an aircraft carrier. Then Ed remembered something Henry mentioned. "What did you mean by LLCs with Monopoly names?"

Henry glanced at Franny, who replied, "An in-joke in real estate. Everyone names their LLCs after properties in Monopoly. I just closed a deal for Baltic Avenue Associates. Last month, it was Ventnor Ventures. Over the years, I must have done a dozen deals for LLCs called Park Place, Boardwalk, New York Avenue, even Pass Go Properties."

"Funny," Ed said. "Right before he died, Duffy had contact with groups called Vermont Avenue, Connecticut Avenue, and Marvin Gardens."

"See? They love Monopoly."

Their plates were cleared. The waiter presented the dessert menu. They ordered one chocolate mousse cake with four spoons and various coffees.

"You mind another real estate question?" Ed asked.

"Of course not. What?"

"It's about Duffy's house. He and his siblings own back-to-back properties running from Twenty-sixth to Twenty-seventh. Duffy bought the family home on Twenty-sixth. The other lot's vacant. Before Duffy bought the house, the family had calls from developers interested in the two properties. But as soon as one sold, they stopped calling about the other. They all wanted both or none. Then after Duffy died, the calls started up again—for both lots. So here's my question: What's so magical about the pair? Why isn't anyone interested in just the one?"

Henry smiled at his wife.

"Because," Franny said, "a single lot is a 'contractor special.' Guys who build on single lots are contractors with enough capital to get a construction loan. Trust me, in this market, if the family puts that lot up for sale, someone will snap it up. But developers go after larger parcels—more profit in them."

"A *lot* more," Henry added.

"What's the big difference," Ed asked, "between one lot and two?"

"On a single lot zoned residential, you're limited to three units—four if you set back the top floor. But on two adjoining lots, you can build *ten* units, and with a little finagling, up to twelve—assuming you can knock down what's there."

Ed nodded. "Ah, yes. The knock-down controversy."

From the 1950s well into the '70s, developers demolished so many Victorians that activists pressured the city to set up a Landmarks Preservation Board. Developers had to win Landmarks' approval before razing anything more than eighty years old.

"That part of the Mission is a preservation district," Franny said. "To knock down that house, a developer would have to take it to Landmarks—unless it's DBRR."

"What?"

"Damaged beyond reasonable repair."

"Meaning?"

"It's structurally unsound, or an eyesore, or severely damaged by flood, fire, or an act of God."

Ed's bite of cake stopped in midair halfway to his mouth. "There was a fire at Duffy's a couple weeks ago. Pineapple lamp through the living room window."

"Does the house look like it might collapse?"

"No. It was a small fire. Just the living room. It's being repaired."

"Then it's not DBRR."

"The police say it's gangs," Julie said. "Evidently, they get off on torching vacant homes."

"Maybe," Franny said, sipping her cappuccino. "But in my experience, vacant homes adjoining vacant lots have a funny way of burning down."

—33—

ED, JULIE, AND SONYA STOOD ON A SLOPING SIDEWALK IN FRONT OF a large craftsman-style home on a quiet byway in Glen Park. The sheet said it had been built in 1935 and completely renovated. The description read like a wine label.

Jake fidgeted in the backpack, kicking Ed and pulling his hair. Between popping the pacifier into his mouth and retrieving it when he spit it out, Julie reminded Sonya about open-house etiquette.

"I know," she interrupted, rolling her eyes. "No talking till we get back to the car, then I can tell you what I think."

Julie smiled.

"But I *already know* what I think."

Ed and Julie knew, too. Sonya loved their house and didn't want to move.

"We're not moving, honey," Julie retorted for the fiftieth time. "Just looking."

"But if you're looking, you *want* to move. I *don't*." She stuck out her lower lip and folded her arms.

It was shaping up to be a long afternoon. After this place, they had four more.

"We know how you feel," Ed said. "We just want to see what's available. The sooner we finish, the sooner we get to Mitchell's."

Ed and Julie exchanged a guilty look. Neither of them liked bribing Sonya, especially with ice cream. But sometimes there was no other way.

Mitchell's was the last vestige of nineteenth-century dairy farming in Noe Valley. In those days, the Mitchell family made ice cream as a sideline to milk and cheese. Developers bought the farm before World War I. In 1953, two Mitchell descendents began making ice cream using the old family recipes, and sold it out of a hole-in-the-wall scoop shop in the Mission. Mitchell's Ice Cream quickly became a local landmark.

"Think about a cone with Irish coffee and cinnamon snap," Julie suggested.

That mollified Sonya.

The house had new everything. The kitchen had been expanded. A master bedroom suite had been added. The yard had been terraced and landscaped, and a two-car garage had been inserted underneath, with a bonus room behind.

They climbed to the wide front porch. Sonya spied a swing and jumped on it. They admired the view—the Mission and, in the distance, downtown. Inside, the kitchen was straight out of a magazine, with a large eating area leading to a deck that overlooked the yard. The three original bedrooms were on the small side, but the master suite was huge with two walk-in closets and a bathroom with double sinks and fancy tile.

Sonya tugged at Ed's sleeve and whispered, "Which room would I get?"

"We're just looking," Ed reminded her.

"But what if—"

"The one at the top of the stairs," Julie said. "Or the one next to it."

"But they're *too small*!"

"Shh," Julie admonished.

"Actually, they're not," Ed whispered. "They're pretty much the size of your room now, but with a great view."

On the way out, they lingered on the front porch as Sonya frolicked on the swing.

"I love it," Julie said.

"Me, too. Unfortunately, they're asking two fifty more than we can afford. And I'm guessing it'll go for over asking."

At the foot of the stairs, they turned into the garage. It could accommodate two cars side by side. In back, a door led to a large room with a skylight and half-bath.

"It's perfect," Julie sighed. "We'd even have our room downstairs. I wish…"

"Me, too." He squeezed her hand. Maybe something would work out.

Ed didn't notice a sign tacked to the garage siding: Jameson Construction. As they stepped back into bright midday light, a broad-shouldered man with thinning blond hair was speaking to a woman in a sweatsuit and cowboy hat. The man pointed to the garage. Ed was barely aware of them, but when the woman saw him, her jaw dropped. She marched up to him and slapped him hard across the face. The blow sounded like a firecracker. "You son of a bitch!"

"What the—?" Ed recoiled, wide-eyed.

"Sheila!" Her companion grabbed her by the shoulders and pulled her back a few steps. "Get a grip!"

Sonya cowered behind her mother, who looked aghast. It all happened so quickly.

Sheila Duffy shook herself free from Billy Jameson and shouted, "*How dare you* accuse Billy! Like we haven't had enough trouble."

"Sheila!" Jameson demanded. He pulled her two steps back from Ed.

"It's Ed Rosenberg," she spat. "From the paper. He put the police on you."

At that, Billy turned to Ed, and puffed up like someone had taken a bicycle pump to him.

"Hey, I'm sorry," Ed said, backing up a step. "I really am."

"The police were *all over* Billy!"

"I'm truly sorry, Sheila. It was a misunderstanding."

The other open house visitors gave them a wide berth. Jake sensed the tension and began whimpering.

"Your aunt swore it was just the two of you driving her home that night. That Billy wasn't there. What was I supposed to do? *Not* call the police?" Then to Jameson, "I had no idea you were lying down not feeling well. Clara didn't remember that. I'm sorry. Please accept my apologies."

"Just stay out of our business," Sheila sneered. "Two seconds after their father is killed—"

"I should bill you for the day I lost," Jameson said.

"—my boys have to see the police *interrogating Billy*?"

"Get in the truck." Jameson pushed her up the hill toward a pickup with Jameson Construction stenciled on the side. She was about to say something when his eyes bore down on her. He pointed toward the truck. She turned and stomped up the hill.

"I was just trying to help," Ed called after her. "The case is going cold. Do you want the killer caught or not?"

Sheila opened her mouth, but didn't reply. She climbed into the truck and slammed the door.

"I'm sorry," Ed said to Jameson. "I really am. I hope the cops weren't too rough on you."

"Cops don't bother me," Jameson mumbled, "but it cost me a day."

"Bill me." Ed reached into his wallet and offered Jameson a card.

Jameson looked him up and down, then said, "Forget it."

"I was just trying to help. Really."

"Yeah, well, whoever did it, we all want him caught." Jameson turned and took a step toward his truck. Then he turned back. "Is it true that the case is going cold?"

"That's right. The cops have nothing. It's in the fridge on the way to the freezer."

Jameson shook his head. "I knew Ry since we were kids."

"I know. He and I were friends. Maybe Sheila told you."

"It's been really hard on her."

"I can imagine."

"No. You can't."

Ed wasn't about to argue. He looked at his feet. He expected to see Jameson's running shoes turn up the hill, but they stayed put. Ed's gaze returned to Billy's face. "So you renovated this place?"

Jameson grimaced, torn between anger at Ed and pride in his work. Pride—and years of AA—won. "Subcontracted the garage and bonus room."

"Great job." Ed's enthusiasm was just a tad forced.

"Big job for us. The entire foundation. I was showing Sheila."

"Nice skylight."

"Thanks. My suggestion. The owner liked it."

He turned toward his truck. Ed's eyes followed him. In the side mirror, Ed could see Sheila in the passenger's seat, arms folded across her chest tight enough to break a rib. Suddenly, Jake felt very heavy on his back.

"You know what?" Ed said, "I could use a break. Let's hit Mitchell's now."

"Yay, Daddy!" Sonya's frown became a big grin as she raced down the hill toward the car.

—34—

WHEN ED RETURNED FROM GROCERY SHOPPING, JULIE LOOKED LIKE she wanted to pack a suitcase and catch the first flight to anywhere, *alone*. Jake had been crying nonstop.

"Would you take him?" she scowled. "I'm losing it. I'll deal with the groceries."

Jake was into one of his weird crying jags. Julie had tried everything to no avail, so Ed said, "Hey, buddy, let's take a walk."

He worked Jake's arms into his jacket and stepped into a bright, breezy afternoon. The crazy old lady was on her porch smoking. Jake reached toward her, seeming to recognize her. His crying cooled to a whimper. When she called, "Bless you, baby," he fell blessedly silent.

Jake bounced in his seat and pulled Ed's hair for a block. Then he stopped. He was dozing as Ed turned down Twenty-sixth Street and strolled toward Duffy's.

Next to the house, on the sidewalk in front of the Mexican bakery, a dark-haired young man hosed perforated rubber mats. His tight *Jim's Gym* T-shirt flaunted the physique of a body builder.

Jake was dozing so it was safe to stop moving. Much of Duffy's façade had been replaced with new siding, trim, cornices, and dentition. That didn't come cheap. And it would have to be painted—also pricey, which meant the family had decided to sell. For a rental, they wouldn't do all that.

Jake woke up and began burbling. The aroma of fresh-baked

cookies hooked Ed by the nostrils.

"You want a cookie, Jakey?" He was starting on solid food. Ed stepped into the store. "Sure you do."

The Latina woman at the counter smiled. Ed pointed at a thin pancake-size cookie covered with white glaze. "Are they soft?" he asked.

"*Si*," She nodded. "Soft and chewy."

"Okay, one of those and..." Ed nodded toward the bin of Mexican croissants. "One of those." They were less flaky than their French counterpart, but contained just as much butter.

Ed gave the cookie to Jake, who immediately got down to business. He was putting his wallet away when the body builder laid a stack of mail on the counter. Ed turned to leave, then stopped and took another look at the top envelope. It looked like a bill. What caught Ed's eye was the return address: Atlantic Avenue Properties, LLC. A Monopoly name.

"Excuse me," Ed said to the young man and older woman, presumably mother and son. "Is Atlantic Avenue Properties your landlord?"

The woman pretended not to hear. The young man gave Ed the hairy eyeball.

"I don't mean to pry," Ed said, "but I'm with the *Foghorn*. I'm investigating changes in Mission real es—"

The body builder brightened.

"The *Foghorn*? Did you know Ryan Duffy?" He tilted his head to the house next door.

"Yes. We were friends."

"Us, too. Awful."

"I'm curious," Ed said. "How long has Atlantic Avenue owned your building?"

"I don't know, couple years."

The return address was a P.O. box.

"You ever talk to anyone from there?"

The young man looked Ed up and down.

"Are you taking over Ry's story?"

"What story?"

"Right before he was killed, Ry asked me about our landlord. Wanted to know if we ever met anyone from Atlantic."

"And?"

"No. We knew the old owner. Nice guy. Then one day we get a letter saying he sold to Atlantic, and if we have problems, call a number."

"Have you called?"

"Yeah."

"And?"

"Got a machine."

The number was part of the return address. Ed memorized it.

The body builder stepped outside and dragged rubber mats into the store.

Ed took a bite of croissant and continued on his way. A few doors down, he noticed a skinny young woman wearing a studded dog collar leaving GarbAge, a boutique for those who dressed only in black. In the window, the mannequins had tattoos, pierced nostrils, and chartreuse hair. The sign read, "WIDE OPEN."

On a hunch, Ed stepped inside. The plump woman behind the counter wore a black leotard with a lavender scarf that matched her hair. The side of her neck bore a small tattoo, the head of a unicorn. Her quizzical look said men carrying babies rarely shopped there. "Can I help you?"

"I hope so. I'm from the *Foghorn*. I'm looking into recent changes in the Mission. Are you the owner?"

Ms. Unicorn nodded.

Ed asked if she owned the building or rented.

"Rent."

"You mind if I ask who the owner is?"

She smelled of tobacco and marijuana. "SLH."

"Someone's initials?"

"A company. Short Line Holdings."

Another Monopoly name. Ed felt his heart pounding.

"You ever meet anyone from the company?"

She appraised him the way the body builder had. “I already told the other guy.”

“What other guy?”

“From the *Foghorn*. He wanted to get hold of SLH.”

“You remember what he looked like?”

Her description sounded like Duffy. Ed’s heart beat like a bass drum. “I’m guessing you never met anyone from SLH.”

“That’s right.”

“You have a phone number?”

She touched a few keys and read seven digits—different from the ones Ed had just memorized.

“If you call,” Ms. Unicorn said, disgusted, “don’t hold your breath waiting for a call back.”

Outside, a bird squawked and Jake tried to imitate it, flapping his arms like wings. Ed concentrated on what he’d heard. So, shortly before Duffy died, he got interested in the owners on his block. The Levys said real estate people loved Monopoly names, but this was getting ridiculous. Five Monopoly names: three on Duffy’s list, the bakery, and now this place. What had Duffy been thinking? Ed wished he knew.

—35—

THE LUNCH CROWD AT RED'S JAVA HOUSE WAS THINNING. IN A CORNER by a window overlooking a dilapidated pier, Ed nursed iced tea. He'd written about the place, a little waterfront shack by the massive Bay Bridge anchorage. During the 1930s, Red's had been a dock worker hang-out, a favorite of Harry Bridges. Now it catered to downtown office workers who wanted a cheap lunch with a bay view.

The door swung open and Eric McCain wheeled his grandmother in. She was so bundled up—thick sweater, wool hat, and blanket across her lap—she looked buried alive. McCain wore a 49ers jacket over an incipient potbelly and a captain's cap over graying blond hair. His cheeks were on their way to jowls.

"Granny Molly," McCain shouted into an ear fitted with a hearing aid, "this is Ed Rosenberg, from the *Foghorn*. Remember? He wants to hear about Patrick Duffy and the dock strike and fire."

The old woman stirred. She had wispy white hair, watery blue eyes, and dentures that looked too big for her. She raised a bony arm. Her hand moved as if beyond her control, making corkscrews in the air. Her skin was translucent, like waxed paper with vegetable oil. In Ed's hand, hers felt cold.

"Pleased to meet you," she said. "I remember it all, a terrible time, but wonderful, too."

"Why terrible, Granny?" McCain asked.

"Oooo, the Depression. Hard times."

"And why wonderful?"

"Oooo, I was young and beautiful, the belle of the ball, and all the lads wanted to dance."

McCain nudged Ed and whispered, "Her memory is good, but her imagination is better."

Across the cafe, a booming baritone called, "Good golly, Miss Molly!"

It was a fat man behind the counter. He had a long gray pony-tail that emerged from a red babushka. "There she is! What'll it be, doll? The usual?"

The men working the griddle and fryer waved and shouted greetings.

Molly beamed a thousand watts. "Yes, dear boy, the usual. And how are you lads?"

"Much better since you arrived," the fat one said. "When are you going to wise up and marry me?"

Her wattage doubled.

McCain wheeled her to the counter. "She always gets chicken salad on a roll," he said softly, "and a beer. Has maybe two bites, but finishes the beer."

The guy at the griddle had faded tattoos and a three-day beard. "He can't live without you, Molly! Can I be best man?"

McCain leaned toward Ed. "Whenever I take her out on the boat, we stop here. They make a fuss. She's in heaven."

McCain ordered a cheeseburger, Ed a grilled chicken sandwich. The cooks plied Molly with suggestive banter as they packaged the order. McCain paid. Ed protested. McCain waved him off and motioned for him to carry the food so he could push the chair. At the door, McCain rearranged the blanket across his grandmother's lap. She looked up at Ed, her hand doing the corkscrew. "About Patrick and Michael. There's more to that tale than meets the eye."

"Really? What?"

She was about to reply, when McCain interjected, "Get the door, Ed, would you?" By the time he looked back, Molly was dozing.

A warm sun shone but a nasty breeze slapped their cheeks.

McCain pulled his grandmother's hat tighter. She dozed as he pushed her down the Embarcadero toward the ballpark. Behind cyclone fences and NO TRESPASSING signs, derelict piers jutted into the bay. There was talk of redeveloping two near Red's into a huge cruise ship terminal and high-end mall. Meanwhile, with the Embarcadero freeway torn down, the crumbling warehouses that once squatted in its shadow had been razed. In their place stood million-dollar condos with bay views and a short walk to downtown through the new waterfront park.

"So," Ed said, "congratulations on your transit village."

"Thanks," McCain said with a rueful smile. "Now we have to build the thing. The clock's ticking."

"What clock?"

"The building permit. Cost two million. Has a time limit. If we don't pass final inspection in four years, we have to renew it—for another two mil."

"Who's 'we'? I thought it was your project."

"Me and my staff. When I got into this business, it was just me and my first wife doing small buildings. Permits? You just showed up at the building department and paid your fee—and maybe a little on the side." He winked. "Now my projects are huge and the bureaucracy's insane. I've got a finance guy, an office manager, two secretaries, a permit expediter, plus a lobbyist who's spent years leaning on Planning to get Civic Center approved. Not that I'm complaining. I've done *very well.* But dealing with the city? You don't want to know. It's a wonder anything gets built."

"I heard what you did, offering those options. Very creative."

"How'd you hear about that?"

"Friend of mine works for the Affordable Housing Coalition."

"Yeah, well, I've never assembled a parcel that way before. But it was the only way. The people down there, they'd been through the mill. They were fed up and wanted to cash out, but no one could close a deal. I gave them what they wanted, good money annually and a nice big chunk when the thing finally got approved. The staggered payout is working very nicely. The stars just kind of aligned."

"Staggered payout?"

"*How* they cash out: 60-20-20."

"Uh…"

"I'm buying those lots for three times their appraised value back when the owners signed the deal. But they don't get it in one lump. They get 60 percent now. Another 20 when everyone signs the title transfers. And the final 20 when everyone vacates. They just got their first payment. Now, if anyone tries to screw me, it's not just my problem. The other sellers get screwed, too. So they gang up on any holdout for me. And nobody gets their final payment until *everyone's* out."

"Efficient."

The stadium loomed. The huge warehouses on several piers were being transformed into offices, skyscrapers on their sides. Molly's wheelchair hit a bump, and Ed heard metal clang coming from a duffel bag hanging from the wheelchair handles. "What's in there?"

"Gear," McCain said. "What they say is true: boats *really are* a hole in the water where you throw your money." He had a big, booming salesman's guffaw. "I love my boat. But she's just like a woman—it's always something. Now it's a new starboard handrail. My weekend project."

"You know Mitch Callahan, don't you?"

"Sure. Known him for years."

"You mind if I ask what you think of him?"

"Why?"

"Oh, a few years ago, he and Duffy got into it…"

"Over the Armory. I remember."

"You know Callahan almost slugged him?"

McCain smiled. "No."

"At the final hearing, he went for Duffy. Had to be restrained."

McCain shook his head. His smile widened. "I'm not surprised."

"Why?"

"Mitch has a short fuse."

"You've heard this? Or you know it for a fact?"

"Oh, I know. *Personally.*"

"You mind telling—"

"Oh God, it was…ages ago. I was just out of high school. Had a carpentry job on a crew of his. You know what a stringer is?"

"Isn't it the frame for a stair?"

"Right. Cutting them is a little tricky. I was young and green. I'd helped cut them, but never done one myself. So I fucked it up. Had to get new stock and redo it. Mitch found my first try in the garbage and went nuts. Screamed. Fired me. Ordered me off the site. When I didn't move fast enough, he grabbed a hammer."

"He threatened you?"

"Not really. It was just to let me know he was serious. Next day, he called and hired me back. Mitch is like that: a hothead, but underneath, a decent guy."

A decent guy who had an hour unaccounted for and wouldn't take the swab.

A forest of masts rocked back and forth. Ed had driven past the South Beach Marina many times, but never noticed its size or opulence. There had to be a couple hundred vessels moored at its slips, mostly sailboats that looked like they could run to Hawaii and motor yachts the size of Ed's house.

Next door in McCovey Cove, two dozen kayaks bobbed in the chop, bleacher bums in boats. They had radios tuned to the game and nets ready. They were hoping to snag home run balls swatted out of the park into the water.

McCain unlocked a metal grill that read No Trespassing. "Granny." He nudged her awake. "Ready for the ramp?"

"Ooooo, yes, dear."

McCain tilted the chair back and rolled down a metal ramp that ended on a floating wooden walkway. Ed followed. Thirty yards away, the Embarcadero hummed with traffic, and beyond it, the stadium was sold out. Yet the marina was silent and, except for them, deserted.

"It's so quiet," Ed observed, "and it's the middle of the afternoon in the middle of the city."

"Isn't it great?" McCain said. "This is a weekend marina. Only a few of us take our boats out during the week. This way."

Ed followed as McCain pushed the chair left, then right, along a boardwalk maze on pontoons. He felt like he was traversing a waterbed.

"Thar she blows," McCain said, nodding toward a huge gleaming craft. He called it a boat, but that was like calling an eighteen-wheeler a truck. A dinghy was lashed to a platform off the stern. Above it, the name was painted in swirling script. *High Rise.*

McCain locked the wheelchair. He scrambled up plastic stairs, unzipped a canvas flap, opened a hatch, and pulled out a ramp. He clipped it to cleats and rolled the chair on board.

As McCain clamped the wheelchair to the decking, Molly's hand corkscrewed at Ed. "About Patrick and Michael and the fire. I know why Pat did it. And it's not what you think."

—36—

McCain unzipped more canvas, opening the cockpit. He climbed to the helm and shouted instructions to Ed. Molly smiled. The engine rumbled. McCain negotiated the labyrinth of the marina. Then they were out on the bay.

They anchored on the city side of Treasure Island, Molly's favorite view. Ed passed out lunch. McCain was right—Molly was less interested in the sandwich than the beer.

"So, Granny," McCain said between bites, "What about Patrick Duffy and the fire?"

"Oooo," she replied, cheeping like a bird. "I shouldn't say. I really shouldn't."

"What do you mean?" McCain boomed, grinning. "That's why Ed's here—to hear the tale." He rolled his eyes.

"But you might think the less of your old Granny."

McCain laughed. "Impossible. Nothing could change how I feel about you, especially not something—what? Seventy years ago?"

"All my life I've been a good Catholic, but I'm not perfect. Granny's done things she's not proud of, God forgive me." She closed her eyes, crossed herself, and lapsed into silence.

McCain made a show of begging. "Please tell us. Please."

Molly's wrinkled face blossomed with an impish grin. "All right. If you must know." Her hand corkscrewed. "Here's the truth of it: Michael was in love with me. Then Patrick fell in love with me."

"*What?*" Ed and McCain gasped in unison.

"Patrick was jealous. Between that and the strike, that's why he done it."

Ed and McCain looked at each other wide-eyed.

"You had an *affair*?" McCain asked.

"Oooo, nothing like that." Molly said. "I loved your grandfather. I was always true to Donovan. *Always*, as God is my witness. But he was on the road. I was young. A girl gets lonely."

"Your husband was on the road?" Ed asked.

"Fresno to Redding," Molly said, her hand doing the corkscrew. "Two weeks a month."

"Sold irrigation equipment up and down the Valley," McCain explained.

"I worked at St. Paul's. I was Father O'Rourke's secretary. And Michael, he used to come 'round the rectory."

Ed said, "Michael Kincaid."

"Yes."

"So, if you didn't have an affair," McCain asked, "what happened?"

She folded her hands. "It was like this. Michael wasn't happy at home. Liza wasn't very good to him in the way men like. Michael needed comforting. He was such a charming young man. And so handsome in his uniform."

"So you—*what*?" McCain pressed, literally on the edge of his seat.

"We did what young people do. We fooled around a little. But I swear to God, I never betrayed my marriage vows. Never. You've got to believe your old Granny."

"I believe you." McCain winked at Ed. "So you and Michael fooled around. I'm curious. Where? In the office? Your house?"

"God forgive me." Her hand corkscrewed in front of her face. "In the sacristy."

"The what?" Ed asked.

"A side room off the main church," McCain explained.

"And what about Patrick?" Ed asked. "How did he fit in?"

"I always liked Pat, but not *that* way. He worked on the docks.

When times got hard, he worked at St. Paul's. That's when it happened."

"What?"

"Patrick walked in on Michael and me. And Pat wanted me, too."

"The three of you? Together?"

"Oooo, no. He wanted me to stop with Michael and take up with him. But I wasn't interested. He didn't like that."

"So he burned Mike out in a jealous rage?" Ed ventured. "What about the strike?"

"Pat could make his peace with one or the other. But not both."

"So Pat was furious with Mike over the strike. Then things with you pushed him over the edge?"

"As God is my witness."

"Amazing," Ed said.

"Granny, I had no idea."

"I don't mind you knowing, Eric. But don't tell your mother or your aunt. Promise me."

He smiled at Ed. "I promise."

"I mean no disrespect," Ed said, "but I wonder, is there any way to confirm this? Any—I don't know, *anything*?"

"I still have the love notes."

"*Love notes?*" Ed and McCain exclaimed simultaneously.

"Mike used to leave little notes on my desk. Pat, too. I kept them."

"Can I see them?" Ed asked.

"I don't mind."

"Where are they, Granny?" McCain asked. "At St. Catherine's? Or with Dottie?"

"Who?" Ed asked.

"My aunt."

"I forget," Molly said. "Somewhere."

—37—

McCain rolled Molly off the boat and along the floating walkways to shore. By the time he pushed her up the exit ramp, she was asleep.

"'Fooling around'?" Ed asked. "What did she mean? If she never broke her vows…"

"They didn't fuck," McCain said.

"So…what?"

"God knows. The question is, how far beyond kissing?"

"Maybe he felt her up."

"Jesus. This is my grandmother."

"I know. But…"

"She's said many times that when she was young, she was a little wild. Everyone was. It was Prohibition."

"So maybe Mike got more than a quick feel. Could you ask her?"

"Oh, right." McCain shook his head in disbelief. "Now, Granny, let me get this straight. Did you yank his shank? Did you blow him? Did he finger you?" McCain shook his head. "I'm not going anywhere *near* there—if it even happened. Granny never let the truth get in the way of a good yarn."

"So she's exaggerating?"

McCain laughed. "She's a bullshitter from way back. Especially when she's been drinking."

"What about the love notes?"

"I'll hunt for them. But they could easily be a bit of the old blarney. I packed her things when she moved to St. Catherine's. I didn't see any love notes. But I'll look, and I'll ask my aunt."

McCain's Mercedes was parked nearby. He lifted Molly out of the chair and slipped her into the passenger seat. He clicked her belt, then folded the chair and stowed it in the trunk.

"So?" McCain said. "You like the boat? Getting out on the Bay?"

"Loved it."

"Want to come out again some weeknight? Bring the family."

"Uh, sure, but—"

"What?"

"You must have lots of important people—"

"Actually, no. I have a hell of a time getting people out, especially weeknights."

"I'd like to…. It's very generous of you…"

"But?" McCain's brow furrowed.

"Well, you're this major big deal, and I'm one of the little people."

McCain laughed. "Fuck that. I'm just a carpenter who got lucky."

"In that case, sure. I'd love to."

"Great. I'll check my schedule. Denise will call you."

Ed was a few steps past and saying goodbye when McCain called to him. "Have you heard anything about the investigation? Ryan's, I mean?"

"It's on ice. The cops have nothing. I found out the kink was a hoax, but they don't care."

McCain's jaw dropped. "*What?*"

"The police said it was kinky sex gone bad. But it wasn't sex at all."

"I—I don't understand. The *Foghorn* didn't say anything about—"

"Him being bound and gagged. You're right. The paper suppressed it. There was a kinky scene, but it was faked. To throw off the cops."

McCain's eyes opened as wide as eggs sunny-side up.

"Duffy was a top, the dominant, the one who gives the orders. But when I found him, he was tied up like a submissive. He was also naked. But he never undressed for his scenes. The sub did, but he didn't."

McCain leaned in. "How do you know all this?"

"I interviewed the woman who trained him in BDSM technique."

"But the police don't care?"

"No. It doesn't change anything. They had no leads before I told them, and they still have no leads."

"So you're involved in the investigation?"

"Put it this way: I'm trying to keep it out of the freezer."

—38—

On reflection, Ed decided the old woman's tale had to be as tall as the Transamerica Pyramid. The proof was in the diary. If Pat had lusted after Molly and burned with jealousy over her dalliance with Mike, it seemed likely he'd have written about her. But Molly was hardly mentioned.

After they put Jake to bed, Ed read Sonya a few pages of *Little Women*, and Julie sang the goodnight song, this time Motown's "My Girl." Then they descended the stairs to their sanctuary. Julie booked plane tickets for Thanksgiving, then added snaps to a corduroy outfit she'd been making for Jake. Ed opened the diary with fresh eyes, looking for anything he might have missed.

Pat did mention that Molly was Father O'Rourke's secretary. *Little Molly O'Hara is now Molly McCain, all growed up and married. Back in school she was a plain Jane who never said a word. Now she's a looker whos got some spunk especially after a pint.*

A toilet was running in one of the church bathrooms. *Molly called me to fix it. The float ball was gone. Some fool kid probly stole it. Had to get a new one at Clancy's.*

One afternoon on Twenty-sixth Street, Pat chatted with Molly's husband, Donovan, as he watered the shrubbery in front of their home. Donovan's Packard had developed a rattle. He asked Pat to take a look. Meanwhile, Donovan complained about Molly. She was giving him grief about his time on the road. *Susie would never stand for it. He leaves her all alone in that big house with the babies.*

Seems lonely, Molly does.

Once Pat mentioned Mike flirting with Molly. *I come in the office and Mike's joking and Molly laughing goin on about how clever he is. Later Mike tells me he's had thoughts about her a man shouldn't have in church.*

The final mention had to do with the fire. After the house burned, the Kincaids took refuge at Molly and Donovan's.

That was it. Nothing about Mike and Molly doing more than innocent flirting, let alone pawing each other in the sacristy. Nothing about Pat feeling attracted to her. Nothing about Pat feeling jealous of whatever Mike had with her. And not a word about love notes.

It was certainly possible that the diary wasn't private, that Pat feared his wife's prying eyes. But Molly claimed her fling with Mike made Pat burn with jealousy, that it struck the match that kindled the fire. If so, Ed would have expected Molly to get more ink. McCain was probably right. His grandmother had an overactive imagination.

On the other hand, if Molly made it all up, why invent love notes that never existed? It was one thing to exaggerate an old flirtation, quite another to claim she had evidence. Ed had a feeling that McCain would tear apart his grandmother's things looking for the notes—not for Ed's sake, but to satisfy his own curiosity.

Still, the weight of the evidence pointed to an old woman's wishful thinking. If any buttons had come undone in the sacristy, if Pat and Mike had really been rivals for Molly's affections, even if Pat feared Susie might read the thing, Ed figured the diary would have said *something*.

Of course, a trove of seventy-year-old love notes would change his mind. But Ed was willing to bet they wouldn't turn up. He decided to give McCain a week before calling.

—39—

Eddie is nine, and the big table is set for Passover. He's crouching in the little alcove by the back stairs in the antique kitchen of his grandparents' huge old house in White Plains. The kitchen is crowded with a dozen women wearing aprons over fancy dresses—Eddie's indomitable grandmother, his mother, aunts, and adult cousins all chattering at once while stirring chicken soup, making matzoh balls, chopping nuts and dried fruit—preparing for Seder. Marvelous aromas fill the room: chicken, brisket, kugel, farfel, and the few pieces of homemade matzoh his grandmother bakes every year, personally commemorating the Exodus. Eddie prefers matzoh from the box, thin and light, with a reliable crunch and those endless rows of perfectly straight pinholes. His grandmother's is a thicker, lumpier biscuit, but it wouldn't be Seder without it.

The second hand sweeps around the old clock over the stove. Eddie is hungry. When will Nana call everyone to the table? He knows it will be a long haul until dinner. His grandfather will chant every word of the Hagaddah in Hebrew and expect everyone to follow along. Every few pages, he will stop and ask one of the grandchildren for the next word. The right answer earns a toothy grin and a silver dollar. A wrong answer brings a stern look and an admonition to pay closer attention.

Eddie, his brothers, and cousins also have another responsibility—the Four Questions: Why is this night different from all other nights? Every year, they chant the traditional melody. Then they recite the answer. We were slaves to Pharoah in Egypt.

As Eddie watches Aunt Gertie peel a fat horseradish root, the kettle begins to whistle, but none of the women notice.

As the whistle grows more shrill, Eddie smells smoke. Something is burning. He gazes at his grandmother's oven, a clawfoot relic with chipped white enamel. Plumes of smoke issue from it. The chicken! The brisket! But the adults don't notice.

The kettle shrieks. The smoke grows thick and acrid. It fills the kitchen. The women remain oblivious. Eddie opens his mouth, but no words emerge. He lunges for his mother, but can't move.

Ed sat up in bed. Smoke filled the air. A siren wailed. Something was burning. *Another fire nearby?* And that sound. *A smoke alarm.*

He pulled the chain on his bedside lamp. A haze muted everything. Smoke! It filled the room. He grabbed the clock—2:40. He shook Julie. She moaned.

"Something's burning," he snapped. Fully awake now, his chest in a vise from smoke and fear, he jumped from bed and wrapped himself in his robe.

"Oh my God!" Julie gasped. "The kids!" She sprang from bed.

The hall was smokier than their bedroom. Ed hoisted Sonya, blankets and all, into his arms and maneuvered her out of her room as Julie lifted Jake from his crib.

On the staircase, Ed heard crackling. *Flames!* But he didn't see any. He also heard a dull thudding as if someone were pounding a bass drum across the street. Downstairs, the smoke was thicker, the crackling and thudding louder, but still Ed saw nothing burning. *What the hell?* Meanwhile, vicious smoke clawed at his throat and chest. Sonya stirred in his arms. Was someone calling his name? The voice was not Julie's.

"Move it, Julie!" Ed yelled up the stairs. "*Out! Now!*"

"Coming!" Julie screamed, hugging Jake close and grabbing as many photo albums as she could carry in one arm.

The thudding grew louder. Ed groped his way through thick smoke to the front door. Outside, someone was banging on it.

Ed flung the door open and found Keith from next door.

"Thank God!" he said, pulling a squirming Sonya away from

Ed, and hustling her down the stairs. "Cal! They're not dressed! Get some robes! Blankets!"

Ed coughed as he guided a dazed Julie and the baby down to the sidewalk. A fire truck pulled up. A half-dozen people jumped out wearing the big hats and long coats. They moved quickly, some grabbing axes, other unfurling a hose. A man with a droopy blond mustache approached them.

"Everyone out?"

Neither Ed nor Julie could speak. The enormity of what might have happened began to dawn on them.

"Yes," Keith said.

"You're sure no one's still inside."

"Yes."

"What the…?" It was all Ed could manage.

"Your garage is burning," the firefighter said. "Now, please. Step across the street." It was not a request.

Calvin appeared with arms full of blankets, which he wrapped around Ed, Julie, and the kids as Keith herded everyone out of the firefighters' way. Sonya wriggled out of Keith's arms and rubbed her eyes.

"What's happening, Daddy?" she mumbled, coughing.

"The garage is on fire." *Am I dreaming?*

Ed's words were drowned by the crash of axes shattering wood. The garage door was suddenly kindling. Two firefighters wearing oxygen rigs hustled the hose into the smoky darkness. Water spattered everywhere.

Sonya burst into tears and ran for her mother, wrapping her arms around Julie's waist and burying her face in the Navajo blanket Calvin had draped over her.

Ed took a deep breath of cool night air thick with smoke. Julie passed Jake to him and hugged Sonya. Husband and wife looked at each other in disbelief. They were in pajamas, robes, and blankets standing on the street in the middle of the night watching their house burn.

"We're okay," Ed said. "We're all here and nobody's hurt."

"Yes, thank God," Julie sputtered, petting Sonya's hair. "But the house..."

Behind them, curtains parted, and a window rose. A neighbor called "What's happening?" They told her.

"We got home and saw smoke," Calvin explained. "We called 911. They got here fast."

"How can we ever thank you?" Ed gushed. "You saved our lives."

"Lucky we work late."

A firefighter approached, a big African-American woman. "Fire's out. We stopped it in the garage. But your car's a mess. And the room above will need a new floor." She glanced heavenward. "Someone up there likes you. Another ten minutes and—"

Something about the way she left the thought unfinished uncorked Julie's tears. "Our house," she cried. "Our beautiful home." Her tears triggered Sonya's.

Ed held Jake tight and wrapped an arm around Julie's shoulder, pulling her toward him. Sonya came along with her.

"It's just a house," Ed said, trying to convince himself, his voice trembling. "We're okay. No one got hurt."

"You're very lucky," the firefighter said. "Do you have a place to stay tonight? You can't stay here. But I need to tell Arson where to find you."

"Stay with us," Keith offered. "We have plenty of room—"

"And half a blueberry cheesecake left over from tonight," Calvin added.

It took a moment for the woman's words to register. "Arson?" Ed asked.

"Looks like," the firefighter explained, holding out a shard of glass flat on one side, textured on the other. "A piece of a pineapple. We found it at the base of the wall with the biggest burn. The damage fans out from there."

A pineapple lamp? Ed felt himself leave his body and float up into the tree canopy. From the upper branches, he gazed down on their little group. Across the way was their once-beautiful home, its garage door smashed, charred blackness inside. There was the fire engine, its lights flashing. Around the truck, firefighters coiled hoses and stowed gear. Up and down the block, curtains opened as neighbors roused by the commotion peered out, shouting words of thanksgiving that everyone was okay.

"But we won't know for sure until Arson gets here," the woman said.

Her words brought Ed back down to the sidewalk.

"Who would *do* such a thing?" Calvin lamented.

Ed flashed on Duffy's house. But the gangs didn't torch single-family homes. Or did they?

Calvin took Jake from Ed and cooed to the baby as Keith opened his big arms wide and shepherded everyone toward their place. Ed looked over his shoulder at the home they'd spent so long renovating. Four colors of new paint were blackened by smoke. Above the garage, their living room had to be wrecked. As for the garage itself, gazing into its blackness reminded Ed of the inside of his grandmother's oven.

He remembered his dream, the old kitchen and all those Seders so long ago. Why is this night different from all other nights? He clamped his eyes shut, choking back tears. The question now had a new answer.

—40—

JULIE AND CALVIN SETTLED THE KIDS TO SLEEP AS ED AND KEITH met the police car that pulled into the driveway of a blackened home. The cop had a shaved head and a white goatee, the same guy who'd interrogated Ed about the fire at Duffy's.

"So we meet again," the arson investigator said, extending a hand. "Sorry about this." The words sounded simultaneously automatic and heartfelt.

"Thanks," Ed replied. "No one got hurt." That was his mantra, the only thing that kept him sane. *Is this really happening? When do I wake up?*

"That's what counts," the cop said.

Ed introduced Keith. The arson investigator shook his hand and said, "Steve O'Farrell."

"My partner and I called 911," Keith said.

"Someone else called, too. You know who?"

Ed and Keith looked at each other and shrugged.

"Must have been another neighbor."

Shining a large flashlight, the arson investigator stepped into the garage. The door had been reduced to splinters. O'Farrell stepped here and there, testing the floor with the sole of his shoe. Ed heard crunching.

"The door had a window?" O'Farrell asked.

"Yes," Ed said, using his hands to mime the dimensions, six by twelve.

"They punched it out and tossed it in."

"The pineapple lamp?"

"Yes." O'Farrell stepped deeper inside the black cavern. His beam circled what could have passed for a coal mine. The garage reeked of smoke and charred wood. Ed could hardly breathe. One side of the minivan was incinerated. The circle of light settled on the concrete floor at the base of the plywood wall where Ed hung garden tools. The wall was charcoal, the tools barely recognizable. More crunching underfoot. O'Farrell crouched and scooped up black lumps. Glass.

He handed a piece to Ed. "See? Smooth on one side, lumpy on the other. Definitely a pineapple." He displayed a flat half-moon of sooty glass. "See this? Half of the base. And this—" He held up a metal disc, a jar lid with a nipple. "This is the top. The wick fits in here."

"Goddamn those pineapple lamps," Keith hissed.

"Looks like they got it at Cole Hardware." O'Farrell displayed the other half of the base. The jagged glass had part of a label affixed: COL HAR. Cole Hardware, a fixture in the Mission for decades, operated out of a cluttered storefront a few blocks from Duffy's.

"Just like the other fires," O'Farrell said, sour-faced. "Seems the gangs support local merchants—or, more likely, steal from them."

Ed's jaw tightened like a vise. He wanted to wrap his hands around the neck of the prick who'd tossed that lamp and squeeze until his eyes bugged out and he stopped gurgling. On second thought, strangling was too good for him—or them. A slow roast over a big fire, that's what they deserved. Burning at the stake. Poetic justice.

"Lucky for you," O'Farrell said, "they don't know what they're doing." He trained his flashlight on the most blackened wall. The beam traced a V fanning up from the concrete floor. "See the char pattern?"

Inside the V, the plywood was burned through. Outside it, the wall showed less damage.

Ed gazed at the wall, but instead of charcoal, he saw four coffins being lowered into cold ground, two large, one half-size, one tiny. He clenched his teeth so hard he thought they might shatter. Then he consciously opened his mouth as wide as he did at the dentist. His jaw felt sore.

O'Farrell holstered his flashlight in a metal loop on his belt. "In the movies," he explained, "the partisans light a rag stuffed into a bottle of gasoline and whoosh—" His hands gestured up and out. "Nazi tanks explode. But that's not how Molotov cocktails work. To get a good burn, you have to saturate the target with fuel. Only the final bottle has a fuse. It ignites everything—fire all over the place. But these assholes don't know that. They only used one lamp, and got a V-shaped burn, and a slow-spreading fire. Lucky for you."

Ed forced himself to breathe. *They were alive. He and Julie and Sonya and Jake—they had survived.*

"The responders said you were vacating as they arrived. Did you hear the glass break?"

"No. We were asleep. The smoke alarm woke me." And his dream. Ed didn't believe in a gray-bearded God enthroned in heaven, or even in a disembodied universal Oneness. But from somewhere out there in the cosmos, his grandmother, dead twenty years, had reappeared as his guardian angel.

O'Farrell nodded. "With only one bottle, it takes time for the fire to spread, and it throws a lot of smoke."

Ed saw the mourners gathered around four holes, passing shovels, taking turns, shaking their heads, wiping eyes.

They left the garage and returned to the sidewalk.

"Do you have any enemies, Mr. Rosenberg?" O'Farrell asked.

"None that I know of."

"What about your wife?"

"No."

"Any problems with the neighbors?"

"No," both Ed and Keith said in unison.

"Everyone loves them," Keith said. "Especially since they painted. Dressed up the whole block."

"Have you ever filed a complaint about neighbors making noise? Motorcycles? Dogs? Stereos? Loud parties?"

"No," Ed said.

"Any nasty graffiti on your home or sidewalk?"

"Never."

"Your paint job looks new. Is it?"

"Yes." New—and ruined.

"When was it finished?"

"Last month."

"Any problems with the painter?"

"No."

"You paid him in full?"

"Yes!"

O'Farrell pointed to a run of smooth new concrete beneath the garage-door opening. "Looks like new foundation here. Grade beam?"

"Yes."

Grade beams were a hallmark of seismic engineering. In earthquakes, buildings fail above the largest opening—in homes, above the garage door. To prevent this, a deep trench was dug under the opening, filled with rebar, bolted to a reinforced door frame, and then filled with concrete.

"When did you do it?"

"Four, five years ago."

"Beside painting, you do anything else to the house recently?"

"Some window frames had dry rot. We replaced them before we painted."

"What about that contractor? Any problem?"

"No."

O'Farrell played his beam around the remains of Ed's car. "Any problems with your auto mechanic?"

"No."

"Thing is, we don't see much arson in single-family homes. It happens—family feuds, grudges. But most often it's businesses that get torched. Usually by the owner. The place is on the ropes and the guy figures he'll cash out with insurance money. Mostly, I see grease fires in restaurant kitchens. They try to make it look accidental, but they don't know what I know."

Keith, a restaurateur, opened his mouth, then closed it.

"Same MO as on Twenty-sixty Street," O'Farrell said. "One lamp through a window. Same V-shaped burn. Only there, they tossed it into his living room—no window in that garage door."

"You think it's the same people?"

O'Farrell snorted. "If you call gangs people. Both fires look like the work of dumbass kids. Maybe some kind of gang initiation. We've had more gang activity in the Mission lately. Did you see the article in the paper?"

Ed grunted, recalling the piece. He'd dismissed it as lousy reporting by a dweeb who didn't know the Mission from Mount Tam. Now he wasn't so sure.

"The guy on Twenty-sixth Street wrote articles supporting loft development. What about you?"

"I wrote a column comparing the loft fires to the ones that destroyed early San Francisco."

O'Farrell's eyes bored into Ed's. He felt like a third grader who'd just blurted an answer everyone knew was ridiculous. "You think Duffy and I were *targeted*?"

"You tell me."

Ed found it hard to swallow. Did gang members read the *Horn*? Did they even speak English? And how would they find him? His address was unlisted.

"The two of you ever get hate mail?"

"Duffy got tons of it."

"About lofts in the Mission?"

"About everything. Take sides on development, and people jump all over you."

"What about you? Any hate mail lately?"

"Not really."

"What does that mean?"

"After my piece on the fires, some jerks sent e-mails applauding the fires. 'Die, yuppie scum.' That sort of thing."

"You have those e-mails?"

"My editor does." A few short years ago, back when people wrote letters to the editor on paper, Ed had displayed the most flattering and vituperative in his office. But compared with penmanship or typing, printouts didn't pack the same visual punch, and he'd stopped.

"Good. E-mail's traceable."

Ed sighed. "Probably to some Internet café."

"Maybe," O'Farrell said, "but you wouldn't believe how stupid most criminals are. I wouldn't put it past them to use computers in their homes. And if they did, I'll nail them." He was the cat eying rats.

It was four in the morning. Keith yawned. The glow from the streetlight was still hazy from smoke.

O'Farrell shook Ed's hand, reiterated condolences, and urged him to call if he thought of anything else. "And when you rebuild, I have a suggestion. Hammer-proof plastic for the garage window. It's unbreakable." He said he'd send along a copy of his report and let Ed know if anything turned up—but that the odds were against it.

As O'Farrell drove away, Keith said, "Best not to leave your garage open. You have anything to cover it?"

Ed looked stricken.

"No problem," Keith said. "We have plywood."

"You're the greatest," Ed said, his voice cracking. He saw the mourners walking away as the cemetery guys finished the shoveling. His eyes filled with tears. He wiped them with the sleeve of his robe.

"Going weepy on me won't work," Keith said, laying a hand on Ed's shoulder. "You still have to help with the plywood."

In spite of everything, Ed smiled.

Julie was right. They had to move. As quickly as possible. The Mission was too dangerous, too weird. They were risking their children's lives—as she was certain to remind him *ad nauseum*.

But before they could move, they had to repair the house, and secure it. He liked O'Farrell's idea—hammer-proof plastic for the garage window. While they were at it, Ed decided, the living room windows could use plastic as well. No sense risking what happened at Duffy's.

The cop made sense. Only two single-family homes had been on the receiving end of pineapple lamps and both owners worked for the *Horn*. There had to be a connection. The gang angle was too easy. The paper regularly excoriated Latino gangs—the Norteños and the MS-13—but none of those reporters had ever been awakened by shrieking smoke alarms.

Ed had other connections to Duffy: their friendship and the diary. But how did they add up to a burned-out garage? Ed had no idea. All he knew was that his house was a mess and he'd run out of arguments against moving.

—41—

WITH SAN FRANCISCO'S VACANCY RATE NEAR ZERO, IT WAS IMPOSSIBLE to find a short-term rental for a displaced family with two kids whose house had just burned. Landlords hated fires. If they'd been burned out of one place, who was to say it wouldn't happen again?

They struck out on Craigslist and fell into a well of dispair. Then they e-mailed everyone they knew and got lucky. The father of one of Sonya's classmates owned a six-unit place on Bernal Hill. A two-bedroom had just been vacated. As a rule, he didn't do short-term rentals, but he knew Ed and Julie from the school's parent group and made an exception.

The building sat on Bernal's homey main drag, Cortland Avenue, about a half-mile from Fair Oaks. The location worked. It was farther from Jake's day care, but closer to Sonya's school. Beyond that, it was a sad, boxy, stucco affair, devoid of charm, perched on steel posts above dingy carports that attracted wind-blown litter. Cortland was considerably noisier than their sweet little side street. The kids had to share a room. The bathroom smelled of mildew and had broken towel bars. The windows rattled, and the kitchen had a wheezy fridge, no dishwasher, little counter space, and barely enough room for the four of them to squeeze around their transplanted table. But it was affordable, available immediately, and they could leave whenever they were able to return home. Ed had never felt so grateful.

Considering that the fire never made it out of the garage, their house was a mess. Everything reeked of smoke. Most of their clothes could not be salvaged. They had to buy a truckload of replacements. To Ed, this was a time-consuming chore. But to Julie, it was a knife to the heart. Beyond a woman's bond to her wardrobe, she'd sewn many of her outfits and the kids' herself. She shed bitter tears as Ed grimly stuffed the contents of her closet into big plastic garbage bags. She didn't smile for what seemed like weeks.

The insurance agent took photos and the company agreed to cover the repairs. But as the contractors produced estimates, the company balked.

"What about my *full replacement* coverage?" Ed asked his agent.

"I'm just telling you what they told me."

Ed called the customer satisfaction office. Sorry, the woman told him. That's our final offer. Of course, if you disagree, you're free to pursue legal remedies.

Ed slammed the phone down. He imagined a dozen new ways to kill a human being, most of which violated the Geneva Conventions. He fumed for a week, then decided he had better things to do than dick around with lawyers. *This is why we have savings.* He swallowed hard and ate the difference.

Meanwhile, they set up the apartment, settled the kids into the new routine, and made lists of items they would need when they were able to reoccupy their home—or, preferably, move.

Evenings and weekends, one of them entertained the children while the other toured open houses. The search went horribly. Even with a generous estimate of what their repaired home would bring, everything they could afford was no bigger than what they had. And eating the insurance shortfall depleted their reserves, meaning less for a down payment.

Julie cried, grieved, and moped. She talked about antidepressants but never went to the doctor. She railed at Ed about his arson columns and his investigation of the fire behind Duffy's house. Then she apologized. Meanwhile, Ed flipped like a three-way switch among silence, sarcasm, and rage. He snapped at the kids and at Julie. They alternately shunned physical contact and clung to each other the way flood victims embrace tree branches. But slowly, their lives returned to some semblance of normal—except for agonizing about who tossed the pineapple and why.

"It *has* to have something to do with Duffy," Julie insisted.

"I agree," Ed said. "But what? You think Sheila or Jameson did it because I put Park on him?"

"Sheila, no. Billy, maybe."

"O'Farrell says he was in San Jose at his brother's."

"What about gangs?" Julie asked.

"Possible. But it doesn't make much sense."

"What does?"

"Got me."

"So what do we do?"

"What we're doing," Ed said. "One foot in front of the other, and keep our eyes and ears peeled."

Ed arranged for the paper to run some old columns. He reminded Marilyn Bishop that he was still interested in writing about the publishers using the typesetters to slant coverage of the dock strike. She reiterated her objections. The piece made the *Horn* look bad. And with the paper losing money, this was no time to wash dirty laundry in public. Ed figured as much. Ordinarily, he would have fumed. But with the fire and everything, this slap in the face felt more like a mosquito bite.

Late one afternoon, the body shop called him at work. "It's good as new. When can you pick it up?"

Ed checked his watch. "How about an hour?"

He called Julie and announced that after work they would drive home in their brand new old car.

"Great. Another little step."

"Yes. We'll get there."

In the cab to the body shop, Ed's phone chimed. The screen offered no name, just a number he didn't recognize.

"Ed!" a cannon of a voice boomed. "Eric McCain. You want to go out on the bay Thursday night? The Giants have fireworks. From the water, it'll be spectacular. Bring the family."

Ed checked his calendar. “Sure. I’d love to. Let me check with Julie. What about the love letters? Anything?”

“No. I looked. My aunt looked. Not that I expected to find anything. Ol’ Granny’s imagination ran away with her.”

—42—

DAMN, THE TOWEL BARS. ED PARKED OFF THE EMBARCADERO AND strolled toward the ballpark in deepening twilight. The stadium lights turned on. The crowd roared.

Ed had planned to buy towel bars on the way to picking up the kids. But the daycare called to say that Jake was running a fever, and could someone please come get him right now? Julie was at an event with her phone off, so it fell to Ed. He left work early, got Sonya at the Youth Center, then collected Jake, who cried and fussed all the way home. Ed gave him some Tylenol and plopped him in the wind-up swing, which helped a little. But Jake was still miserable, and Sonya had started complaining of a scratchy throat. They were all invited out on McCain's boat, but there was no way Julie would take a feverish infant. When she got home, Ed offered to reschedule. But she said she'd stay with the kids and he should go.

The marina was deserted. McCain met Ed at the gate, and locked it behind them. From the kangaroo pouch of his windbreaker, he produced two Anchor Steams. They popped caps and clinked bottles. "To victory over Design Review!" McCain said. "Fuck those fools."

"What happened?"

"They tore me a new one this morning. They were supposed to green-light Civic Center. Then some turd-brain decides we need more parking. Four stories underground isn't enough. He wants five. Asshole. You have any idea what going down another floor costs?"

Ed couldn't imagine. "What'd you do?"

They approached *High Rise*, the only boat with lights on.

"Called everyone. Full-court press. My lawyer screamed at his boss and he caved. But I was all set to take the staff out to lunch. Guess what we wound up eating—*Tums*. Finally, three o'clock, we got the green light. Which is why I'm so happy to get out on the boat tonight."

They climbed aboard.

"What now?"

"Finalize financing. If it comes through—and I don't see why it shouldn't—we break ground in a few months."

"Congratulations." Ed raised his bottle.

"Thanks." McCain cast off. "And you? How are the house repairs?"

"Coming along. But I hate my insurance company. Fuckers just jacked my rate. I can't switch, though. No one else will touch me because I just got a big claim. It's maddening."

"Life's a bitch. But on the water, it doesn't seem so bad."

Bottles in hand, game on the radio, they motored out of the marina and headed under the Bay Bridge and around Treasure Island. Dusk turned to dark. Downtown became a forest of giant sequoias with lights. For Ed, the effect was magical. What if a forty-niner could be transported into the twenty-first century to this spot? What would he think? Probably that he was drunk. Which was what Ed was becoming as his host handed him another cold one.

McCain piloted them back under the bridge to a spot off McCovey Cove. "Dropping anchor." A gusting breeze kicked up a chop. The boat rolled.

"A toast!" Ed said. "To *you*, Eric. For introducing me to your grandmother. And for taking me out on the bay. You're right. It helps."

McCain smiled. The boat bobbed. Seagulls soared overhead. A

thick tongue of fog extended through the Golden Gate and across the Bay to Berkeley. Occasionally, they could hear cheers from the ballpark.

"And to Ryan," McCain said, raising his bottle, "a true friend who passed too soon."

"To Duffy," Ed agreed. He swallowed another swig.

"Any news?"

Ed shook his head. "No. Whoever did it is getting away with murder."

"Damn shame."

The game ended. The Giants lost. Then suddenly, above the stadium, it was the Fourth of July. A shell exploded and the sky filled with shimmering streamers of multi-colored light. A cavalcade of booming rockets followed.

"Speaking of Duffy," Ed shouted above the din, "You mind a quick real estate question?"

McCain zipped his jacket against the stiffening breeze. "What?"

"It's about his house and lot. Three LLCs contacted him right before he died, presumably to buy the two properties. All the LLCs had names out of Monopoly. A friend of mine's a real estate lawyer. She says everyone loves Monopoly names for real estate LLCs. Meanwhile, the bakery next door to Duffy's is owned by an LLC with a Monopoly name. So's a boutique nearby. Five Monopoly names. Feels weird to have so many. What do you think? Do real estate people love Monoploy names *that much*?"

McCain inhaled sharply, then exhaled slowly. His chin jutted toward Ed. "You know the names of these LLCs?"

Ed ran them down.

"How did you get them?"

"Duffy left three on a paper I found. I got curious. I asked the store managers about their landlords and came up with the other two."

"And how do you know they're after the property?"

"Sheila told me. They've been calling her."

"Really." McCain drew another sharp breath. "I'm surprised

you care."

"Well, I'm interested in the 1934 fire. One thing just led to another. Happens when you're a reporter. You become a professional snoop."

"I see." McCain looked pensive, then brightened. "Well, your lawyer friend is right. Real estate people love Monopoly names—especially real estate *lawyers*. They're the ones who draw up LLCs."

Above them, the sky was ablaze with glittering spinners, puffballs, waterfalls, and Roman candles in a dozen colors. They stood in the stern. Ed was vaguely aware of McCain stepping behind him.

Suddenly Ed felt beefy paws clamp around his collar and belt. Before he realized what was happening, McCain picked him up and threw him overboard. Ed flailed and splashed into cold black water.

Ed surfaced, flailing. Bobbing in the boat, McCain looked down on him and smirked, his face illuminated by fireworks. "Professional snoop? Not anymore, *asshole*."

Then he disappeared.

The water was cold. Ed struggled. His clothes dragged him down. How could McCain—? But there was no time think about that. His legs were going numb. He had to swim for shore. He took a deep breath and started kicking.

Overhead, the fireworks were an artillery barrage punctuated by machine gun fire. Nearby, Ed heard another sound, metal on metal, a winch pulling a chain. Then the boat started up. Off to the right, the water was bathed in light. McCain had floodlights. The boat wheeled around. The lights blinded Ed. The boat was heading right for him. The engine's low rumble became a high whine. It was coming *fast*.

Ed thrashed, desperate to swim out of its path. But his clothes made that difficult. The water was frigid. And he'd been drinking. Before he could react, the huge hull was on top of him, followed by vicious twin propellers that tore up the water and anything in it.

—43—

THE BOAT WAS ON TOP OF HIM. SOMEHOW HE FLIPPED TO HIS BACK, kicked off the hull, and escaped the meat grinders. He swam to McCovey Cove and tugged at the arm of a startled Vietnamese man in a kayak, who towed him to shore and pulled him out of the water. The concrete felt oddly warm. He dug his nails into its veneer of sand and grit. *I'm alive.*

The kayaker rolled him over. "You're not bleeding. Doesn't look like anything's broken. I'm calling 911."

Ed's eyes focused. The man's face was round and huge, like the full moon near the horizon. The fireworks were over. The sky was dark, the night silent, but the world was spinning. Ed labored to breathe. He dug his fingernails into the concrete to steady himself. *I'm alive.* The next thing he remembered was being rolled into the emergency room at General.

—44—

The black woman at the Hall of Justice ushered Ed into a stuffy windowless room just large enough for a small table and four folding chairs. "He'll be with you in a moment."

The fluorescent light buzzed. A video camera hung from a corner of the ceiling. Three of the walls had once been yellow. Now they were just grimy. The fourth was a mirror. Ed assumed it was one-way glass.

Detective Curtis Fluker, a black man of around fifty, entered in a cloud of cologne. His suit was sharp. His hair and mustache showed gray. He placed a manila folder on the table in front of him.

"I already told you everything last night at the hospital," Ed said. "Why'd I have to come here? Did you arrest McCain?"

Fluker shot him a sour look. "No. We didn't."

The pot of Ed's patience boiled over. "Why *the fuck* not? He tries to *kill* me, and *no arrest*?"

Fluker glanced into the mirror, then his eyes returned to Ed's and held them. "That's right. No arrest."

Ed started to speak, but Fluker raised his hand like a traffic cop. "McCain says it never happened. Says you never showed up."

"Bull*shit*. He took me around Treasure Island. We anchored off McCovey Cove. Right after the fireworks started, he threw me overboard and tried to run me down. *Just like I told you*."

Fluker was a study in inscrutability. "How long were you in the water?"

Ed did not expect the question. "I don't know…ten minutes. Fifteen. As long as it took to swim in. Why?"

"And how long until the ambulance arrived?"

"What does it matter?"

"It matters."

"I don't know."

"I checked with 911. Down by the stadium, response times average eight minutes."

"Okay. So what?"

"And how long from the time you got into the ambulance until the doctor saw you?"

"Who knows? A half hour. Forty minutes. What does—?"

"So, you're in the water ten or fifteen minutes. You wait eight for the ambulance. And it's thirty to forty until you're seen. So we're talking an hour, give or take, from the time of the alleged incident until—"

"*Alleged?* Jesus Christ. *You think I made it up?*"

"Mr. Rosenberg, at the hospital, do you recall them drawing blood?"

"Uh…"

"Look at your elbow creases."

His right elbow showed a recent puncture wound. "Okay, so they drew blood. So what?"

"Blood alcohol. Yours was 0.07. You were almost legally drunk. And that was a full hour after you claim—"

"It's *not* a *claim*. It's *true*!"

"Given your weight and the rate of alcohol metabolism, I'm estimating that at the time of the alleged incident, you were around 0.09, maybe higher. Mr. Rosenberg, are you an alcoholic?"

"No!"

"Binge drinker?"

"No!"

"In that case, it's safe to assume you have don't have much tolerance. With a level of 0.09, you would have been pretty loaded."

"He had beer." Ed meant to be matter-of-fact, but his tone had an edge of pleading. "We had a few."

"No one at the marina saw you. How do you explain that?"

"No one was around. The place is dead weeknights."

"You say he tried to run you down."

"He *did*."

"That you kicked off the hull."

"Yes."

"With your feet?"

"Yes!"

"But you weren't wearing shoes."

"That's right. They were dragging me down, so I—"

"So your feet were bare."

"Socks."

Fluker extracted a piece of paper from the folder and passed it to Ed. It bore the logo of San Francisco General Hospital. "So his boat is coming at you at high speed, and you kick off in stocking feet. Take a look at page two. They examined your feet. Nothing broken. No significant bruising. How do you explain that?"

"I don't know. Maybe I kicked off my shoes after. I forget. Why do I feel like a suspect?"

"Because, Mr. Rosenberg, we have no evidence of a crime—except possibly filing a false police report."

"*What?*"

"McCain says you never showed up."

"He's lying."

"The fireworks started at 9:05. He called your cell at 9:13. Says he asked where you were. Then he called your home. Spoke to your wife. Said you never showed. I've verified those calls."

"Don't you see? He was setting up an alibi."

"Possibly. Or maybe you went down to the water, got plastered, and fell in."

"Why on earth would I do that?"

"You tell me. There's no physical evidence of you setting foot on the boat."

"No fingerprints?"

"None. I was down there with the tech this morning."

"Then he wiped it clean."

Fluker eyed Ed. "I stuck a hand in the engine compartment. It was cold."

"The bay's cold. It cooled off!"

"Or it never ran." Fluker glanced at the mirror. "McCain says he hasn't taken it out since last weekend."

"What about DNA? That could show I was on the boat."

Fluker flipped through the file and pointed at a page. "You were on the boat before, with McCain and his grandmother. We find DNA, it doesn't prove you were there *last night*."

Fluker nodded at the mirror. The door opened. In walked Detective Park. "Mr. Rosenberg."

"What are you doing here?"

"Helping a fellow detective with a hit-and-run that may or may not have happened."

"It happened. It *fucking* happened *exactly like I said*."

Fluker shrugged. "We have no physical evidence."

"Well, *get some*!"

Park tried to smile but didn't succeed. He spoke softly, the good cop. "You've been under a lot of stress. You found a dead body. You were questioned about the fire on Twenty-sixth Street. Then your home was firebombed. That kind of stress makes people do things they don't ordinarily do. Like drink too much. And fall off piers."

"I don't *believe* this. I *didn't* make it up. I swear to God. It *happened*. Just like I said."

"Fine. But right now it's your word against his," Fluker said. "Only your word involves serious charges—assault and attempted murder—with no evidence to back them up."

"He's lying. Don't you see? McCain's full of shit."

"Maybe," Park sighed. "But tell me: What's McCain's motive? Why invite you out on his boat to toss you overboard and try to kill you?"

"Isn't it *your* job to figure it out?"

"Our job," Park retorted, "is listening to people lie to us."

Ed opened his mouth, but Fluker beat him to it. "Talk is cheap. Before we make an arrest, we need evidence we can take to the DA. We don't have any. You're accusing a solid citizen of attempted murder. Now I'd love to yank a rich fuck out of his country club and cuff him. But answer me this: Why would a guy like McCain try to kill you? Why would he give a *flying fuck* about you?"

—45—

"THE CAR'S LOADED," ED SAID.

"We may have to come back and get something."

"Then one of us will come back. But we need to be here as little as possible."

"I'm scared," Julie said. "And I don't think I can keep it from Sonya."

"I'm scared, too. McCain's *out there*. He could…Where's the reservation?"

She named a hotel by the airport. "There's an indoor pool. We can sell it to Sonya as a vacation. I just wish I knew how long—"

"Until the cops come to their senses."

"I'll deal with Jake. Make sure Sonya takes her jacket and backpack."

—46—

ED POINTED THE CAR UP THE STEEP INCLINE AND MANEUVERED through narrow winding streets, headed for an address he hadn't been near in years. They traversed the Mission side of Twin Peaks, homes from the 1960s with huge windows and views of downtown and the East Bay. Cresting the hill, they descended into the older, more stately enclave above Haight Ashbury, homes from the 1920s with views to the north: Alcatraz, Angel Island, the Marin headlands, and the Golden Gate Bridge.

Julie looked at Ed as he worked the wheel, negotiating the maze of twisting streets. "So, how are you feeling today?"

He glanced her way. "Same."

"You mind telling me what's going on in there?"

His expression mixed approach and avoidance. "My mind's a blender on liquefy."

"And?"

"And I'm *pissed*. Did you see the Real Estate section this morning? The picture of McCain and his staff—all smiles—celebrating their transit village with a big bash at Farrallon? That mother*fucker*."

"Let's hope it keeps him *very busy*."

For the first time in a week, Ed chuckled. Then he sighed. "I don't know. It's like an out-of-body experience. Like I'm watching it all happen to me. I mean I hardly know the guy. How *could* he—? And the police! How *could* they—?"

She kneaded his quad. "The important thing is you're still here with us. We're all together."

"It's too much," Ed mumbled. "The condo fires. Duffy's death. His fire. *Our* fire. And now *this*." He shook his head and lapsed into silence. He turned right and curved left, then pulled up next to a new Jaguar and backed into a tight space. "I'm not really in a party mood."

"Me either," Julie said, "but we promised. You okay?"

"I guess so."

Before he could open the door, Julie reached across and took his hand in hers, raised it to her lips, and kissed his palm. Ed observed his wife, really noticed her. Her eyes were a deep well of anguish. He pulled her close and nuzzled her neck. "I'm sorry, babe. I really am. How did I get myself into this? My word against that *cock-sucker's*."

"It's not your fault. You're the *victim*. Remember?"

"Yeah. I just wish the cops saw it that way."

Holding hands, they ascended the hill past enormous homes lined up like a fleet of battleships.

"Any more thoughts about *why*?"

"None. I hardly know the prick. One day he's introducing me to his grandmother. The next, wham."

"What could he possibly have against you?"

"No idea. But I'll tell you one thing. He lucked out with his alibi. He had to figure you'd know where I went. Anything happens to me, you'd say I was meeting him. He's the prime suspect, the last guy to see me alive. So he kills me then says I never showed. When my body washes up, it looks like I got drunk on the way to his boat, fell in the water, and drowned—a poor schmuck under too much stress. That didn't happen, but his story still works. I never showed up. I'm all stressed out. I tie one on, fall in the bay, and climb out spouting a drunken hallucination."

The champagne brunch was a benefit for the Affordable Housing Coalition. Henry Levy had invited them. The featured guests were the lieutenant governor and "a noted entertainment celebrity."

The house sat on the downhill side of the street. From the outside, it was modest, a one-story, tile-roofed Spanish affair. But when the door swung open, the place was enormous, several stories built down the hill, with killer views from the Bridge to Sausalito. Henry and Franny met them in the foyer, which was almost the size of Ed and Julie's first floor and considerably more opulent: dark wood, Persian rugs, and original art illuminated by recessed spotlights.

Julie's eyes widened. "This house is incredible!" she gushed, embracing Franny as Ed shook Henry's hand. "Who lives here?"

"J. Craig Buschman," Henry said. "President of our board."

"This woodwork is amazing," Julie exclaimed. "These carpets. And the art. Is that...?"

"Yes," Henry said, "Diebenkorn,"

"That's nothing," Franny said. "Let me show you what's in the library. You'll flip." She hooked elbows with Julie and led her away.

Franny and Henry knew nothing about the "alleged incident" and that's how it was going to stay.

Ed accepted a baby lamb chop from a server in a tuxedo, then turned to Henry. "I took the kids to Mission Playground. Your building looks almost done."

"Final inspection in two weeks," Henry said, "God willing." His eyes turned heavenward.

"Who's the celebrity?"

Henry lowered his voice. "Sean Penn."

Penn lived in Marin and supported several good causes.

"Really? Is he here?"

"Not yet. But let me introduce you to some people."

The host, who went by Craig, was in his seventies, a tall, regal, white-haired patrician dressed in a suit that made Ed think of golf at St. Andrews. Hearing Ed's name, he launched into his family saga. His great-grandfather had traveled the Oregon Trail and settled in Portland in 1845. Four years later, he became a forty-niner, one of the first wave of non-Californians to arrive at the diggings. He hated mining but loved San Francisco. He returned to Oregon, chartered a ship, and ran lumber down the coast to the instant city that kept burning down and rebuilding with his wood. He invested his profits in a startup called Wells Fargo.

"Lovely neighborhood, Ashbury Heights," Ed observed.

"Yes," Buschman agreed. "We had some dark days in the early seventies when the Summer of Love turned into the Winter of Hard Drugs. Several neighbors sold out and moved. But not Alma and me. That pioneer spirit. A dozen of us got the neighborhood organized. By the late seventies, things turned around. Now it's never been better. The house two doors down just sold. What they got, it's obscene."

After a sumptuous brunch and the speeches, everyone wrote checks and lined up to shake hands with the guests of honor. Penn was charming. Julie swooned.

As things began to break up, they found themselves in a corner of the vast living room picking out landmarks through floor-to-ceiling glass: the park, the church at USF, Sausalito, Belvedere, and Tiburon.

"I never tire of this view."

Ed and Julie turned to see Buschman showing it off to a young couple. The husband was a vice president at Google, the wife a biggie in the Junior League. With a laugh, he added, "I also get to spy on the neighbors." He pointed down the hill to a home on the block below. "General manager of the Opera." He indicated the mansion to its left. "UCSF chancellor. And that—" He pointed at a huge French Chateau. "Big developer. Apartments around Civic Center BART."

Ed's eyes met Julie's. "You mean Eric McCain?"

Buschman turned their way. "You know him?"

Ed replied with studied neutrality, "We're acquainted."

"Nice guy," Buschman said. "His wife, too. I run into him on Cole Street. At the bakery. The hardware store."

At the mention of a hardware store, Julie nudged Ed. "Towel bars."

"Oh," Buschman bubbled, "no problem. Cole Hardware will have them. They have everything."

Ed started. “Did you say Cole Hardware? I always thought ‘Cole’ was a family name. They’re not just in the Mission?”

“Oh, no. Cole Street’s the original store. Been here longer than I have, since the early fifties.”

Fragments of the pineapples thrown into their home and Duffy’s bore labels from that store. Ed had assumed that the Latino gangs patronized the one in the Mission—or shoplifted from it. Now he saw another possibility.

Down the hill, the sidewalk in front of the homey old hardware store brimmed with grills, charcoal, lawn furniture, bedding plants, fertilizer, and garbage cans. They found towel bars and a cutting board. Julie stood in line as Ed wandered around, searching for something else. It should have been with the grills and patio stuff, but it wasn’t. Ed went looking for a clerk. But before he could collar one, in the back by some sheet metal, he found what he was looking for.

—47—

ED FOUND MCCAIN'S WEB SITE AND PRINTED HIS PHOTO, THEN RACED back to Cole Street.

He flashed the photo at the two cashiers, girls in green vests. He mentioned pineapple lamps. They shrugged and shook their heads. An Asian teen stocking plumbing supplies said he'd never laid eyes on him. A white kid mixing paint took a long look, then said, "No."

Ed worked his way toward the rear of the store. A middle-aged Hispanic man was stocking light bulbs.

"Oh, yeah," he said, "Lives up the hill." The plastic badge pinned to his vest said Ernesto Hernandez.

"Do you recall him buying any pineapple lamps lately?" Ed's heart thumped like a bass drum.

Hernandez eyed him with leisurely Latino suspicion. "What's this about?"

Ed smiled and slipped the man twenty bucks. "A little practical joke. Neighbor to neighbor. Guy's a friend of mine."

Hernandez pocketed the cash. "Well, your friend's weird."

"How so?"

"He come in, wants a pineapple."

"That's weird?"

He nodded.

"I don't understand."

"Warmer neighborhoods, okay. The Mission, Potrero. But the

Haight's foggy and cold. Maybe you grill out. But you eat in. Not much call for pineapples. So we keep them in back."

"Okay, so he buys some—"

"No. That's why he's weird. He buys one. Just one."

"You lost me."

"One don't do much for bugs. You gotta ring the area. You need four, five. I tell him. But no. One's all he wants. Then he come back, buys one more."

Ed's heart cranked it up to the drum part in "Wipe Out."

"Just one?"

"Right."

"You remember when?"

Hernandez didn't recall, somewhere between recently and a while ago. But the clerk was fairly certain the two purchases had happened a week or two apart within the past month—which dovetailed with Duffy's fire and his.

Ed flashed the photo one more time. "And you're sure this is the guy?"

"Oh, yeah. He come in a lot. Hey, what kind of practical joke you pullin'?"

Ed smiled. "A good one."

—48—

WAVES CRASHED INTO FOAM ON OCEAN BEACH. IT WAS A COOL, SUNNY summer afternoon. The sand was alive with dogs, Frisbees, kites, and beachgoers young and old on blankets and folding chairs. Beyond the breakers, figures in wetsuits waited on their boards, maintaining position, scanning for the next set. Up ahead, Cliff House balanced precariously on its promontory. In front of them, Sonya and her friend, both barefoot, romped and squealed and splashed in the water, chasing the ebbs, fleeing the flows. Ed had Jake in the backpack. Julie ambled beside him, holding his hand.

"I still don't understand why you don't call the police."

"Because I've got nothing to give them."

"You have him buying the lamps."

"That's not a crime."

"From Cole Hardware."

"They have four stores."

"Right when Duffy's house and ours—"

"I'm not sure about the dates. And if they didn't believe me about the boat, why should they believe me about this? It just looks like I'm out to get him—which, of course, I am. But as far as the cops are concerned, I've got squat."

"So what are you going to do?"

"I know what I'd like to do. But you wouldn't like it."

"What?"

"Toss a couple pineapples through his window."

"You're right. I don't like it."

"Don't worry," he replied softly.

"So what are you going to do—really?"

"The only thing I can do. Keep my eyes open and my ear to the ground."

"But he's still out there." And we're still in a hotel. "He could—"

"What do you want me to do? We either obey the law or take it into our own hands. Which would you prefer?"

"Mommy! Daddy!" Sonya and her friend, Emmy, ran up, jumping up and down, and pointed at a short brown man in a Raiders jacket struggling to push a small cart through the sand. "Can we get ices? Can we? Can we?"

Mexican ices. The vendors were all over the Mission, but this guy had ventured far afield. Ed glanced at Julie, who nodded.

"Sure." He dug into his pocket and handed them a bill. "What flavors does he have?"

"I'm getting mango!" Sonya shouted over her shoulder as she scampered off, kicking sand behind her.

"Strawberry!" Emmy yelped, following at a gallop.

Julie snuggled up into Ed's arm. "I keep wondering why? People don't kill for no reason."

"I wish I knew. I've had all of three conversations with the prick. Ran into him outside Duffy's. Interviewed his grandmother. And that night. That's it."

"And the two of you talked about—what?"

He inhaled, then sighed. "I told you. The diary. The Duffys. Him growing up on Twenty-sixth Street. His grandmother. His doubts about her story. And his transit village."

"That's all? You didn't talk about anything else?"

During previous rides on this merry-go-round, he'd dismissed the question. This time, he heard it. *Was* there anything else?

A bright sun glinted off the water in a million diamonds. The tide was coming in. A wave broke and a tongue of water rushed up to the dry sand in front of them. They skirted it, approaching a bivouac of blankets and lawn chairs where middle-aged couples were dishing food onto paper plates. They had a boom box. Ed caught Springsteen.

Poor man want to be rich
Rich man want to be king
And a king ain't satisfied till he rules everything

They were on the boat drinking beer and watching the fireworks. They toasted Duffy. Suddenly Ed remembered what else they'd discussed.

—49—

JULIE WAS READING HER BOOK CLUB BOOK IN THE CRAMPED HOTEL bedroom when Ed entered after tucking Sonya in. "She asked about the house and moving—again."

Julie looked up. "Anything new?"

"Not really."

"She's anxious. Going to open houses was bad enough. But now, with the fire, the apartment, and winding up here, she feels homeless."

"Me, too."

"Me three. You talk to Lu?"

Luis Bejarano was their contractor.

"Ran over at lunch. It's coming along. The new joists are in, subfloor tomorrow. Oak next week."

"And painting?"

"Scaffolding goes up Monday. Jeff and Ian start Tuesday. They should be done with the façade and ready to do the living room by the time Lu's finished."

"I can't wait to go home," Julie said.

"I hope we can."

"I had no idea how much I'd miss the house. I mean, I still want to move. But it's home. I hate the apartment. And this place is worse."

Ed left the bedroom, crossed the dark front room where the kids were sleeping, and stepped out to the hall. He pulled out his phone and dialed the Levys. Franny answered.

"Got a real estate question for you. How can I find out who owns an LLC?"

"Who? As in a person?"

"Yes."

"May I ask why?"

"Oh, just curious about the groups nosing around Duffy's house. Are there records in City Hall?"

"No. LLCs don't file with the city. They file with the state."

"So?"

"You can try the Secretary of State's Web site, but you probably won't find anything."

"Why not?"

"Because that's how the world works. If an LLC is member-managed, that is, by a person who's involved, the Secretary of State has the name and contact information, and it's public. But one reason real estate people like LLCs is that it's easy to hide ownership. You make the manager a second LLC that's managed by a third one or a corporation. People can dig forever and never find a human being."

"So where does that leave me?"

"Up the proverbial creek—unless you know someone who's willing to talk."

Ed returned to the bedroom, opened his laptop, and Googled the Secretary of State. He found the LLC database, and all five came right up. Each listing specified a manager, but in every case, it was another LLC. He looked them up. Their managers were other LLCs. He worked back a few steps. Same deal—LLCs piled on top of each other like bricks in a wall shutting him out.

—50—

Ed finished a column marking the anniversary of the Fatty Arbuckle verdict. In early Hollywood, the Fat Man was a major star and a frequent gossip-column item because of his devotion to starlets, booze, and partying without the encumbrance of clothing. In 1921, San Francisco police arrested him for the murder of an actress, Virginia Rappe, who'd died during a night of drinking, drugs, and debauchery in the actor's suite at the St. Francis. The trial was a sensation from coast to coast. In San Francisco, it dominated front pages for weeks. The actor was acquitted, but the scandal destroyed his career.

Ed loved the Arbuckle story. It had, sex, drugs, glamour, and death overlooking Union Square. But he couldn't stay focused. He and McCain had discussed LLCs—those that wanted Duffy's property, and those that rented to the stores. Now it turned out that LLCs were locked up tighter than Fort Knox.

Ed called APOD. No one had heard of any of them. He tried the Residential Builders Association and other real estate organizations. Same story.

Finally, he called Rodney Wong, an old high school buddy of his *Foghorn* friend, Tim. Wong was a computer genius who billed himself as a private investigator. Actually, he was a hacker for hire.

"LLCs?" he said with uncharacteristic skepticism, "I don't know, man. They're a bitch. How far back did you go?"

"Three managers."

"I can go back further, but no guarantees. I've never had much luck with LLCs."

Later, Ed was about to rendezvous with Julie to pick up the kids when Rodney called.

"Sorry, man. No names."

"How deep did you go?"

"Fifteen layers."

"Shit."

"But all five of your LLCs are related, part of a group of like three dozen that all manage each other. I'll e-mail you the list."

—51—

ED'S STEPS ECHOED OFF THE POLISHED STONE FLOOR UNDER THE HUGE vault of the City Hall dome. Stepping into the Assessor's office, he took a number and joined the polyglot multitude in the waiting area. A Chinese woman emerged from the warren of cubicles and called his number, but he let an elderly white woman go ahead. An Indian woman with a red dot on her forehead called his number and again he deferred to a couple speaking Russian. Finally, a familiar face appeared.

"Remember me?" Ed asked.

Dan Schuster hesitated. "Uh..." Then he flashed a dimpled smile. "The *Foghorn*, right? The history guy."

Ed smiled and nodded.

"Hey, I liked your Fatty Arbuckle story. The John Belushi of his day."

"Kind of."

On the way to Schuster's cube, Ed explained that the story about the Kincaids' lot had morphed into a more ambitious feature on development trends in the Mission, how investment groups were buying property. "So I'm looking at that whole block," Ed said. "Can you tell me who pays the taxes on each lot?"

"No problem." Schuster worked his keyboard like a concert pianist. "Voila."

Over the previous five years, most family owners had sold to investment groups. Now, in almost every case, the taxes were paid by an LLC—and every one of them appeared on Rodney's list. Only two lots were still family-owned.

"I'm surprised," Schuster said. "I know LLCs have been buying in the Mission, but this is ridiculous."

"Can you print the map and the list of taxpayers?"

Schuster hit a few keys and presented Ed with sheets of paper.

Ed felt like he'd just had a double espresso. He took the City Hall steps three at a time. Heading toward Market Street at a run, he pulled out his phone and dialed Tom Ferguson. "Refresh my memory. If a developer wants a transit village out beyond Civic Center, didn't you say he has to own the whole block?"

"Correct."

"Suppose I told you that LLCs probably controlled by one guy own every lot on Duffy's block—except Duffy's house and the lot. What would you think?"

"What do you mean, '*probably* controlled'? Are they or aren't they?"

"I'm pretty sure they are."

"How? It's impossible to find out who owns them."

"Let's just say that sources assure me."

"Then I'd guess he wants to build a transit village."

"Now suppose Duffy wouldn't sell."

"Why wouldn't he? He was sentimental but not stupid. In that situation, he could have gotten an incredible price."

"I'm guessing he had no idea his house and the lot were the last two on the block. Let's say sentiment won out and he refused to sell—at any price."

"What are you saying? That Duffy was killed for his house?"

"Yes."

"Jesus, Ed. That's pretty wild, even for San Francisco. Who's the developer? Do you know?"

"I'm fairly certain."

"So?"

"Sorry. Can't."

"Have you told the cops?"

"Not yet."

"Why the hell not? This is page one. Pulitzer Prize."

"I don't have it nailed down. And the cops think I'm a flake."

"So you *don't* know that one man owns all the LLCs."

"Not with evidence that would stand up in court."

"What *do* you know?"

"That eventually shit stinks. But let's say this asshole could build a village on Twenty-sixth Street, how much profit are we talking?"

"A lot."

"A hundred million? Or five hundred million?"

"Probably somewhere in between. Three, maybe four hundred—except for one thing. You said Duffy's block, right? Twenty-sixth to Twenty-seventh, Mission to Valencia."

"Correct."

"Off the top of my head, I'm not sure that block is close enough to BART to qualify. Where are you?"

"Civic Center. About to jump on Muni to the paper."

"Meet me in the third floor conference room. We'll look at the maps."

—52—

Ed found Ferguson hunched over the huge table poring over a street map the size of a bed sheet.

"Sorry, Ed," he said. "The numbers don't work."

Ed stopped in his tracks.

"It's beyond the radius. That block is too far from BART. It misses by a good twelve feet."

Ferguson stood up, holding a ruler, looking like he'd just chewed a lemon. Ed was speechless.

"This," Ferguson said, gesturing to the huge creased paper unfolded over the conference table, "is the B-SUM map. Bureau of Street Use and Mapping, the most detailed map the city produces. Transit villages can't be more than two hundred feet from a BART station. That means two hundred feet from any spot on the *plat-form*, but the nearest corner of Duffy's block is two hundred twelve feet away. That block can't be a village. Sorry."

Ed swallowed hard. "Show me."

Ferguson lay the ruler on the map. He was right. The corner of Duffy's block closest to the platform was a dozen feet beyond the magic radius.

"Maybe," Ed mused, "he thought they'd extend it."

"Unlikely. Ever since APOD first floated the idea of transit villages, it's always been two hundred feet."

"Why?"

"Because Planning's very sensitive about approving high rises out in the neighborhoods. Hell would freeze before they extended it. And I don't see your mystery man spending zillions on the slim chance that they would."

"Could he build something else?"

"Sure. But if it isn't a transit village, he's restricted to four stories. Not worth it."

Ed was out of arguments.

"How sure are you that your guy killed Duffy?"

"Ninety percent."

"Based on?"

"He tried to kill someone else."

Ferguson's blue eyes bored into Ed's. "Anyone I know?"

"Sorry, Tom."

"I see." Ferguson slapped his palm with the ruler and scanned the map. Then he bent down and looked more closely. "Wait a minute."

"What?"

"I wonder..." Ferguson smoothed the paper with both hands, then carefully turned it over and searched some more. "Hmmm... See this circled 'U' at the end of the Twenty-fourth Street platform?" Ed leaned in and looked where Ferguson was pointing. He saw the symbol. "That designates a utility area, an underground yard where BART stores equipment."

"So?"

"Take a look. Only two stations in the city have them. See? Embarcadero and Twenty-fourth Street. For a transit village, maybe a utility area counts."

"But you said two hundred feet from the platform. A storage area isn't the platform."

"True, but you never know."

Ferguson pulled out his phone.

"Hey, Carlos, Tom Ferguson, from the *Foghorn*. Listen, I've got a strange question..."

Carlos didn't know, and referred him to someone else. Two referrals later, Ferguson asked for Jimmy Yee. He listened, and nodded, then his face lit up.

"You're sure? It's in the regs? Yes, e-mail me. Thanks! Really appreciate it." Ferguson flipped his phone shut.

"That was the head of Planning regulations. A BART station terminates at the end of the platform—unless there's a utility enclosure, in which case, it extends to the end of that. The utility area at Twenty-fourth Street is twenty-five feet long. So Duffy's block is thirteen feet *inside* the radius."

—53—

"THAT'S MCCAIN'S MOTIVE," ED TOLD CATHERINE WHEELWRIGHT. "Four hundred million dollars. He was *so close*. He could *taste* it."

The waitress at the French bistro near the paper brought their plates: salmon for Julie, *a croque monsieur* for Ed, and *cassoulet* for their guest. Wheelwright spooned up sausage and beans and chewed slowly.

"All he needed was Duffy's house and the lot. So he had some flunkies call, saying they're from his LLCs, and offering to buy them. I bet he figured it was a slam dunk. He knew Duffy was into real estate. Why wouldn't he take a big fat offer for the house and lot? Only McCain didn't figure on Duffy being sentimental. He had no idea what his old buddy was up to. But he knew that anyone looking to buy the two properties was going to knock down the house and build ten units across the two lots. He didn't want to see his childhood home go. McCain got frustrated. One night, he paid Duffy a visit. Probably talked up old times then offered him the moon. But Duffy wouldn't bite. McCain snapped and went for the statue. Then I showed up telling him the BDSM was a hoax, and asking too many questions about the LLCs. That's why he tried to kill me—twice."

"Whew," Wheelwright said, sipping iced tea. "Quite a theory."

"Too bad I can't take it to Park. I have no credibility with him. But he likes you. He'll listen to you."

"He's a hardass, as you know. No telling if he'll bite."

"Give him this." Ed handed her the lot map and the names of all the tax-paying LLCs, plus Rodney Wong's findings that they all owned each other.

Wheelwright scanned the documents. "Interesting, but I know what Park's going to say. Interlocking LLCs doesn't prove that McCain owns them."

"But look at the big picture. I ask him about a few of them, and next thing I know, he's tossing me in the bay."

Wheelwright's expression walked a tightrope between support and skepticism. "Even if he owns the LLCs, that doesn't prove he killed Duffy."

"There was no forced entry. Duffy let the killer in. He knew the guy. And the BDSM was a hoax. Who would he open the door for? How about an old friend?"

Wheelwright's expression tilted toward doubt. "But McCain already has Civic Center. He's going to clear, what—fifty million dollars over there. Why risk screwing it up?"

"Financial pressure. Ferguson says he had to spend at least fifty million buying up Duffy's block. Even for a guy made of gold, that's real money. I bet he's leveraged to the max. Civic Center's chump change. The big money's in a transit village near Twenty-fourth Street. Not to mention bragging rights as the baddest developer in town. I don't think he went over to Duffy's intending to kill him. But without the house and lot, he's nowhere. He upped the ante. Duffy said no. So he offered a fortune and Duffy still refused to sell. That's when McCain lost it—just like he lost it on the boat when I started asking questions about the LLCs."

Wheelwright spooned another bite, chewed slowly, and swallowed.

"And let's not forget the pineapples," Ed said. "The arson investigator found Cole Hardware labels on glass fragments at both Duffy's and our place. Go over to Cole Street. Talk to Ernesto Hernandez. He'll tell you. They don't sell many because the Haight's cold. When they do sell them, people buy half a dozen to keep bugs off their decks. But McCain bought one—just one—right around the time of Duffy's fire. And one more right before ours."

"We could have died," Julie said, "all of us. The kids."

"Intriguing," Wheelwright said, "but circumstantial. First thing Park's going to ask is where I got this. And when I say Ed Rosenberg…" Ed stabbed a chunk of cantaloupe. "What you've got won't stand up in court. Park needs something he can take to the DA."

"He's sitting on it. The DNA from the statue. I'll bet anything it's McCain's."

"Oh, great." Wheelwright rolled her eyes. "Park's going to love that."

Julie's brow furrowed. "What's wrong with DNA?"

"On TV, they snap their fingers and DNA solves the case. In real life, it's not that simple."

"Why not?"

"Because it's not easy to collect—or analyze. The state lab's way backed up. And their funding's been cut. Didn't you read my story?"

"But it's already collected," Ed pressed.

Wheelwright sighed. "Listen. DNA works great for exonerations. A prisoner gives a sample. Even if the DNA from the crime scene is funky, it's not that hard to show differences. And if there's *any* difference, the guy couldn't have done it. But it's a lot more complicated to use DNA for a *conviction*. You have to show an absolute match. If the sample's funky, you're toast."

"All Park has to do is tell McCain that he's sitting on a shitload of unidentified DNA from Duffy's, then ask for a cheek swab. See how he reacts. I bet he freaks."

"Even if he does, I'm not sure—"

"Please," Julie implored. "He almost *killed* us. And he's still *out there*. He could do it *again*." Tears filled her eyes.

"Cathy," Ed said softly, "Park won't listen to me. But he'll listen to you."

Wheelwright chewed her lower lip. "There's something else. It sucks, but it's real. The glory."

"What do you mean?"

"If this pans out, who gets the credit? Cops hate amateur investigators—especially when they're right. Makes them look bad."

Ed watched Julie wipe her eyes. "I don't give a shit who gets the credit. I just want my family safe."

Three days later, Ed was working on a piece about the 1969 Indian occupation of Alcatraz when Wheelwright pushed his office door open and leaned in. "Park just arrested McCain."

—54—

"IT'S *WONDERFUL* TO BE HOME," JULIE SAID AS THEY CLIMBED OUT OF bed and opened the curtains to a sunny Sunday morning. "I slept *great.*"

"Me too," Ed replied, inhaling a deep, delicious breath. The horrid smell of smoke was gone. He slipped into his robe and descended the stairs. In the living room, the new oak floor sparkled. He opened the front door and crouched to pick up the paper. Early on a Sunday, Fair Oaks was silent. He felt moved by its quiet charm. The trees appeared greener, the Victorians more stately. And their four-color paint job looked good as new.

In the kitchen, Julie popped Jake into his high chair and placed a handful of grapes before him. Sonya poured milk into a bowl of Cheerios. Ed pulled the paper out of the bag and fished out A-news.

LONG STRANGE TRIP
FROM BUILDER TO KILLER

Wheelwright's profile dominated the front page. It recounted how dogged police work—with a tiny assist from a pair of *Horn* writers—had brought McCain to justice, and how he'd pled to second degree and was looking at a long stretch. Then it traced his early years on Twenty-sixth Street and his transformation from carpenter to contractor to major developer, and how his obsession with acquiring Duffy's entire block led to the murder of his childhood friend. The piece included photos of McCain with three mayors and a governor—and at his arraignment. The paper also reprinted the lot map Schuster had given Ed. Topping it off was a sketch the cops found when they searched McCain's office, an architect's concept of a forest of apartment towers rising above Twenty-sixth Street.

But the article omitted a few details Park had filled him in on. After McCain threw the pineapple into their garage, he called 911. At that point, it seemed he hadn't wanted to kill Ed, just preoccupy him so he'd lay off the murder. But on the boat, when Ed asked about the LLCs, McCain panicked and tossed him overboard.

"What about *your* piece?" Julie reached for the magazine. The cover reprinted the photo of Sean Callahan with his club raised over Harry Bridges. FRIENDS TO ENEMIES: The Untold Story of Lifelong Friends on Opposite Sides of San Francisco's Most Violent Strike.

Ed's piece recounted how Pat and Mike met as toddlers, became inseparable, married cousins, and took down the fence between their back yards—until the strike drove them apart, destroyed the Kincaid home, and sent Mike and Liza into exile.

Ed was able to fill one gap. In 1946 in Boston, Mike signed papers transferring his ownership interest in the Twenty-seventh Street lot to his wife for the sum of one dollar. Soon after, she sold the lot to Susie Duffy for $1,500. Neither Pat nor Mike had anything to do with the transaction.

Ed quoted Aunt Clara: "In those days, women didn't buy and sell property—and certainly not Irish wives of dockworkers and cops. But Liza and Susie did. That's why everyone called the back lot 'Susie's garden.' It really *was* hers."

Unfortunately, Ed was unable to crack the toughest nut: who torched the Kincaid home? Probably Pat, but Ed had no proof. It was frustrating, but some historical questions couldn't be answered.

They paged through the article, lingering over old sepia photos supplied by Duffy's sister, Beth: Pat and Mike on a St. Paul's Little

League team in 1919, at their ninth grade graduation in 1923, and with their young wives on a picnic blanket in Dolores Park. Pat with his cargo hook, Mike in his uniform. News photos of the strike.

Ed turned to the final page and smiled.

A sidebar occupied half the page: "SF Newspaper Publishers Paid Typesetters to Override Editors." It was the column Marilyn Bishop had killed.

Ed said, "Can you believe what I have to do to get a piece in this fucking paper?"

"Ooooh, Daddy," Sonya said, looking up from her cereal. "Bad word."

"I know, honey. But sometimes no other word will do."

They dealt sections. Ed got first look at news, business, and sports. Julie took the rest. They were on their second cups of coffee when the phone rang. Ed answered. It was Tim Huang. "Get on your computer."

"Why?"

"Go to the YJR site."

YJR was *Yale Journalism Review*, the nation's leading journal of media commentary, criticism, and gossip.

Ed scurried downstairs and clicked to the site. On the home page, the headline jumped out at him: "*Foghorn* Spotlights Dark Past." The piece summarized his article on the typesetters selling out to the publishers.

"I can't believe it," Ed said. "How'd they get it up so fast?"

"How do you think?" Tim said. "Bishop knows someone there and pitched him as soon as the magazine went to bed."

"They didn't call me."

"It gets better. Look at the fourth graf."

There was Bishop pontificating about the need for self-criticism in journalism. "This is a story that had to be told. We encourage our writers to practice cutting-edge reporting, no matter where it leads."

"I'm nauseous," Ed said. "How'd you know about this?"

"She e-mailed department heads this morning."

"I can't believe it," Ed said. He called to Julie. "Come down! You've got to see this."

"She kills your idea," Tim said, "and then takes credit for it—like she went to bat for you."

"Bitch."

"Precisely the sentiment that's growing on the board. I don't think she's long for San Francisco."

Ed lingered over the paper, then paid a few bills. Julie took Sonya to Sunday school. When she returned, she seemed positively giddy. She gave her husband a big wet kiss and said, "I love our house."

Ed looked into her eyes. "You love our house—as in you're glad to be home? Or you're reconsidering moving?"

Her smile was sheepish. "I think moving can wait."

Ed spent the afternoon buying new garden tools and hanging them from new nails hammered into the new garage wall.

"Daddy!" Sonya called down the basement stairs. "Phone!"

It was a woman. "Mr. Rosenberg, this is Beth Duffy Vincent, Ryan's sister—"

"Beth!"

"Everyone's in shock about Eric. I've known him my whole life."

"That must be hard."

"It's awful. But it's comforting to know what happened, knowing the guilty will be punished. I called to thank you. The article said you helped the police."

"I did what I could."

"Everyone *loved* your article. You made my grandparents come alive."

"Thank you. I liked your photos."

"No, thank you. Aunt Clara's a celebrity at the home."

"She's a very sweet lady."

"Reading your article, I kept thinking: We lost Ryan, and that's horrible beyond words. But in a way you brought our grandparents back to life, and that's so sweet. I remember how Grandpa Pat rarely set foot in Susie's garden. Wherever Ryan and my grandparents are now—" Her voice cracked. "I think they're smiling."

"I hope so."

"Listen. There's something else I'd like to discuss. Can we get together?"

—55—

"DADDY!" SONYA CALLED, BOUNDING DOWN THE STAIRS AND INTO their huge new decrepit old kitchen. "When are we going to *Carnaval*?"

"Soon as I unload these cans into the pantry."

"What's a pantry?"

"A closet in the kitchen where you store food that doesn't have to be refrigerated."

"But I want to go *now*!" She jumped up and down. "It's *started*! I want to see the parade and the dancers and the costumes. And I want a *lumpia* and a *churro* and ices and a chicken stick!" She put her hands on her hips and thrust one out, a junior version of her mother.

"Me, too, honey. We'll go soon. You won't miss a thing. You want to get there faster? Run this toilet paper to the upstairs bathroom."

Sonya grabbed the box and scampered up the stairs.

It was wonderful—and strange—all of a sudden to have two bathrooms. And a fourth bedroom, a pantry, and big back yard. All the rooms were twice the size of their counterparts on Fair Oaks, and the basement could even accommodate a pool table. Of course, the kitchen and bathrooms were a disaster. Much of the rest of the house, too. But at least this time, while one bathroom was torn up, they could use the other.

Ed looked out to the rotting back porch. It had to be replaced.

He was hoping to extend it, maybe glass part of it in. Julie was making plans for the yard: a swing set, passionflower around the perimeter, a little lawn, and TLC to bring back the Meyer lemon and Santa Rosa plum.

Ed glanced over the new back fence. The contractor who'd bought Susie's garden was well into a four-story condo building.

Ed's phone rang. The screen said Keith.

"We're next door at the bakery. Y'all mind if we stop by?"

"Keith! Sure. Please."

"Julie! Sonya!" Ed called upstairs. "Keith and Calvin!"

Sonya was down the stairs in a blur. She flung herself at the two men and received a bag of cookies fresh out of the oven. Keith and Calvin were both wearing suits.

"Can I have a cookie, Daddy? Can I? *Please?*"

"Sure." Then to the visitors, "You're all dressed up."

"Friend's fiftieth birthday," Calvin explained.

"But we're *not* catering it," Keith added. "Thank God."

"Come sit," Julie said, kissing them, cradling a spacey, just-awakened Jake in her arms. She led the way into a living room with too little furniture and too many boxes. Ed pulled some off the sofa and chairs and piled them atop other boxes in a corner.

Keith looked around. "It's huge."

"And you weren't kidding about it needing work," Calvin observed.

"Here we go again," Ed groaned, then smiled.

"We'll be asking your advice," Julie added.

Calvin laughed and executed a mock curtsey. "Faggot decorators, at your service." They all laughed, then Calvin pressed his hands to his heart. "We miss you guys."

"We miss you, too," Julie replied. "But it's only a few blocks."

"And now that the fires are over," Keith said, "we're not going anywhere."

The police had caught the arsonist who'd been torching the condo buildings. It wasn't Latino gangs, but rather an ex-foreman for one of the developers. He'd been fired and decided to try his hand at extortion.

"Have the new people moved in?" Julie asked.

"Yes. A nice couple with a baby. He works for Yahoo; she's a nurse at UC."

"Soon as we climb out from under all this," Julie said, "we'll have you over for a barbecue in our big back yard."

"Our big wasteland," Ed added.

"Not for long, I'm sure," Keith said.

"Could be dangerous living next to the bakery," Calvin said.

"Tell me about it," Julie said. "The Lopezes have already adopted the kids."

"Cal." Keith tapped his watch.

"Oh, God. We have to run."

The house trade had been Beth's idea. She recalled Ed mentioning that his wife wanted a bigger place but they couldn't afford anything. With Ryan gone, Kevin Duffy had hired Billy Jameson to fix up the house to sell, but none of the Duffys wanted to part with it. Ryan had died to keep it in the family.

Beth led her siblings, along with Sheila, Billy, and a realtor, through Fair Oaks. The realtor declared that the modest, newly renovated Victorian on the quiet side street was worth about as much as the larger dilapidated Edwardian on the busier street. They traded. Then the trust Duffy had established for his sons put Fair Oaks up for sale—and in San Francisco's crazy market, it sold in five days for over asking.

Ed and Julie had sworn off renovating. Once was enough. Not to mention that they'd just emerged from fire repairs. But here was the family home of their dreams—at least, it would be someday. They swallowed hard and decided they could live in a construction site one more time.

"*When*, Daddy?" Sonya called from the top of the wide staircase.

"Real soon, honey," Ed called back. "Is your mother ready? Is Jake?"

"Almost!" Julie yelled.

She sounded far away. She was probably in Jake's room down

the hall in the back. They weren't used to such distances. They needed an intercom. Ed added it to his lengthening list.

The ringing of an old bicycle bell reached Ed's ears. It took a moment for him to realize that someone had turned the key on the antique front door bell. Only they weren't expecting anyone.

Ed saw three silhouettes through the dark wavy glass. He opened the door to find a smiling Sheila Duffy offering a bouquet of flowers, and behind her Billy and Aunt Clara. Sheila said, "I hope you don't mind us barging in. Aunt Clara—"

"What a surprise," Ed said. "Come in, come in. The place is a mess. We're still unpacking. Boxes everywhere."

"Who is it?" Julie called from upstairs.

"Sheila Duffy! Come say hello."

"I want to apologize again for slapping you," Sheila said. "I don't know what got into me."

"Water under the bridge." Ed took the flowers and led them into the kitchen.

"No, you helped find Ryan's killer, and I want you to know how much I appreciate that."

"I'm just glad McCain's behind bars. Can I offer you anything? Beer? Wine? Calistoga? Soy milk? Grape juice?"

"No, thanks," Sheila said. "We can only stay a minute."

Ed unwrapped the flowers and cast about for a vase. Among half-unpacked boxes, he couldn't find one. He grabbed a pitcher and ran water into it.

"You like the living room?" Jameson asked.

In addition to new windows, he'd redone the floor, re-sheet-rocked the walls and ceiling, and installed recessed lighting.

"Love it," Ed said. "It's the only room in the house that doesn't need work. You do kitchens and baths?"

"My middle name."

"We're totally overwhelmed at the moment and not sure what we want. But as soon as we do, you'll be the first to know. And Clara," Ed asked a little louder, "how are *you*?" He took her hand.

The Duffy matriarch had been uncharacteristically silent. She wiped her eyes and sighed. "First time I've been in this house since I don't remember when. Brings back memories, this old place does."

"Aunt Clara is the reason we're here," Sheila said. "She has something to tell you."

"Really," Ed said, ushering everyone into the living room. Clara settled herself in a chair and folded her hands as if in church.

"I just pray you boys aren't as stubborn as Pat and Mike. Gives you cancer, stubbornness does."

"I'm trying, Auntie," Billy said.

"Me, too," Ed chimed in.

"I like the way you told the story of my brother and Michael," Clara began. "Lord, I hadn't seen some of those pictures in fifty years. Do you remember me saying that Pat didn't burn Mike out?"

"I do." The loyal little sister.

"Well, he didn't." She bowed her head and gazed into her lap.

Ed leaned forward. "You know this for a fact? Pat didn't set the fire?"

"I do. He didn't."

Ed had a dozen questions, but held his tongue. Clara had clearly made this pilgrimage to get something off her chest.

"Mike was a fine lad," she began, "and I loved him dearly. Everybody did. But he had a wee touch of the Irish melancholy."

Ed said, "I'm not sure I—"

Jameson interjected, "He was an alcoholic."

"He liked his drink," Clara said. "With the strike, with what he had to do to keep his job, and his best friend cursing him, shunning him—those were terrible days for Michael. So, yes, he took his refuge where he could find it. He also smoked. In those days, everybody did. The night of the fire, Mike was drinking. He passed out on the sofa and dropped his cigarette. Thank the Lord, Liza was having a bath. She smelled smoke and got everyone out."

Ed's eyes widened. "So he burned himself out?"

"It was an accident," Clara said.

"Amazing."

"You're probably wondering why I didn't tell you before."

Ed started to speak, but stopped.

Clara looked him in the eye. "Because it was private. Family business. You were a stranger. Now you're not anymore."

Ed smiled. Sheila took Clara's hand and squeezed.

"Mike knew what he done, but couldn't face it. He was so mad at Pat. And he was all liquored up. So he accused Pat. Liza was furious, but Mike was so stubborn! Him a cop, and Pat a striker, one word from Mike and they arrested Pat. But Liza told Mike that if he didn't do right, she'd go to the papers and tell what really happened."

"And that's why they dropped the charge."

"Yes."

"I'm curious how you know all this."

"We all knew—Susie, Pat, everyone in the family. But we all kept it hushed."

"Why? To spare Mike embarrassment?"

"Because Pat asked us to."

"*Pat* asked you?" This was the last thing Ed expected.

"Pat always thought he was destined for greatness. But with the Depression, he had a very hard time. He was reduced to odd jobs at St. Paul's. When the house burned and he was arrested, on the docks he was a hero. Everyone wanted to shake the hand of the man who avenged Harry's beating. People noticed him. He liked that—he wanted them to think he did it. After the strike, he became a crew boss and eventually vice president of the union. Of course, by then, Liza and Mike were long gone."

"And Pat never set the record straight?"

"No."

"What about Susie and Liza? It must have been hard for them to wind up so far apart."

"Oh, it was. It truly was. When Liza left, Susie wept bitter tears. She was very low for a long time. But she and Liza stayed close. They wrote back and forth, and sometimes called long distance—even visited a few times."

"But not the men," Ed said.

"No, never. Each of those boys was more stubborn than the other."

"I'm surprised. As the years passed and they got older, you'd think they'd patch things up."

"When Pat was dying, Mike tried, but Pat wouldn't budge. Stubborn as a mule, that one."

"Sad," Ed said. "What about Bloody Thursday? The beating of Harry Bridges? In the photograph, Mike has his club raised—"

"Pat always swore that Mike hit Harry. Mike always swore he was going after—Lord, what was his name?"

"Sean Callahan?"

"Yes, horrid man. Mike said he was going after *him* to *protect* Harry."

"What do you think?"

"I don't know," Clara said. "I just don't know."

"It lasted only a few seconds," Billy said. "Who knows what really happened?"

"According to the diary, Mike said he couldn't quit the force, that there was 'a gun to his head.' But after the fire, he left town, which suggests otherwise. Was he threatened?"

"Mike always said he was. But after the fire, when the charges were dropped, when the police learned what really happened, they were afraid of a scandal. The general strike was on. The police were in the middle of it and didn't want Mike's—" She groped for the word.

"Lie?" Billy offered.

"His *version*," Clara said. "They didn't want his version to cause more trouble than they already had. So they sent him packing."

"I spoke with Molly McCain," Ed said

"Did you now?" Clara's lips curled into a crooked smile.

"She said Mike and Pat were both after her."

"I'll bet."

"That their falling out wasn't only about the strike."

"Let me guess. It was about Juliet and her two Romeos." Clara snorted. "Let me tell you about Molly McCain. She's read too many fairy tales. If you ask her, every man who ever laid eyes on her fell madly in love with her, including the Archbishop."

"So you don't believe her."

"Not for a minute."

"All right. But I'm still surprised about Pat. As the years passed, as he was dying, it's hard to believe he wouldn't bury the hatchet with Mike."

Sheila laid a hand on Ed's arm. "Have you ever heard of Irish Alzheimer's?"

"No."

"Grandpa Pat had it. You forget everything except the grudges."

Clara smiled.

Ed smiled back. "I see."

Sonya burst into the living room.

"Daddy! Time to go! Now!"

Sheila rose. Billy helped Clara up and guided her down the stairs.

"Thank you," Ed called down from the porch. "It means a lot to me, knowing."

Clara looked up at him. "It means a lot to *me* telling you."

Ed shut the door and closed his eyes. His thoughts flew back to the 1930s, to the back yard, to the fence that had been removed, to the post holes Pat dug and refused to refill. There was a new fence on the property line now, across a yard inhabited by ghosts.

"What was that about?" Julie asked, descending the stairs with Jake balanced on her hip.

"I'll tell you later. Right now," he turned to Sonya, "it's time to go to *Carnaval*!"

"Yay!" Sonya jumped up and down.

Carnaval was the Latin Mardi Gras, traditionally celebrated in March before Lent. But at that time of year, San Francisco is too raw and rainy for a street party. So the event was transposed to warmer weather, a summer celebration of pan-Hispanic culture featuring mariachi bands, flamenco dancers, Brazilian drum troupes, and hundreds of half-naked samba dancers gyrating in body paint and feather headdresses. *Carnaval* was the largest of San Francisco's dozen summer street fairs. The whole Mission turned out.

Ed popped a smiling Jake into the backpack. "Now, Sonya, what did you say you wanted?"

"Chicken stick, *lumpia*, ices, and a *churro*."

"Tell you what: Let's start with ices and *churros*. Dessert first. How does that sound?

"Yay, Daddy!"

Historical Notes

The San Francisco history is true—with these exceptions:

Patrick Duffy's diary is fictitious, but the events it describes are true.

The photo of Sean Callahan clubbing Harry Bridges is fictitious.

The Morrissey Mattress Company is fictitious. However, after more than a century, the McRoskey Mattress Company is still in business on Market Street, a vestige of old Irishtown.

James Stetson refused to evacuate in 1906, saved his home, and saw Claus Spreckels' mansion burn. However, his diary and his observations concerning the Spreckels fire are fictitious. There is no proof that agents of Abe Reuf torched the wrong Spreckels mansion to destroy evidence of political corruption, but many historians have speculated about the possibility.

The Poets tavern is fictitious. However, for decades, an Irish bar South of Market was a favorite haunt of San Francisco newspaper people.

Tenants United for Fairness (TUF) and the Association of Property Owners and Developers (APOD) are fictitious, but the rancor between San Francisco landlords and tenants is, if anything, understated.

Finally, after thirty years as a vacant eyesore, the San Francisco Armory was sold in 2007—to a company that produces BDSM videos for X-rated Web sites.

ACKNOWLEDGMENTS

HEARTFELT THANKS TO:

Sang Ick Chang for help with Korean names.

Dennis Church for insights into the politics of land use and urban planning.

Judi Cohen and Syvia Magid for their knowledge of LLCs.

Charles Fracchia, dean of San Francisco historians.

David Hankin and Ruby Tondu for their appreciation of Harry Bridges.

David Steinberg and the San Francisco sexuality community for insights into BDSM.

My indefatigable agent, editor, rabbi, and friend, Amy Rennert of the Amy Rennert Literary Agency, Tiburon, California.

My esteemed editors: Randy Alfred, Charles Fracchia, Jeffrey Klein, Clyde Leland, Andrew Moss, Pat Morin, Larry Morin, Anne Simons, and especially Ed Stackler and my brother, the hawk-eyed Deke Castleman.

And everyone at MacAdam/Cage: Pat Walsh, Dave Poindexter, Guy Intoci, Dorothy Smith, and Michelle Dotter.

Finally, a tip of the hat to Montecito-Sequoia Family Resort in Kings Canyon, California. Some of the book was written and edited there.

About the Author

Michael Castleman grew up in Lynbrook, a Long Island suburb of New York City. He graduated Phi Beta Kappa from the University of Michigan with a degree in English and earned a Masters in journalism from UC Berkeley. He has lived in San Francisco since 1975. He has written twelve consumer health books and two previous Ed Rosenberg novels, *Death Caps* and *The Lost Gold of San Francisco*. Visit mcastleman.com.